AWAKEN

L.C. SON

Reader's Favorite

"Author L.C. Son has crafted a stunning second-in-series novel which is positively dripping with atmosphere. Fans of light horror mixed with dark fantasy will have their fill of the exciting world that surrounds Damina as she continues her journey of discovery, both for her own skills and the affairs of her heart. One of the best features of the work is how much story it packs into the novel, never letting up on surprises, emotive scenes, action, and sudden twists to the plot. I really enjoyed all of the characters, and the dialogue shaped their personalities well, also making the romance elements sizzle all the more. Overall, I would highly recommend Awaken to readers of Beautiful Nightmare (Book One), but also for anyone looking to discover a new author and series with accomplished worldbuilding and intense atmosphere."

Awaken

BEAUTIFUL NIGHTMARE

BOOK TWO

a novel by

L.C. SON

ISBN: 978-1-7336503-5-9

Dedication

To my rock, confidant, best friend, and living dream catcher, thank you for being all that you are in my life. This writing journey has been no small feat, but you have been with me every step of the way. When my own nightmares became too fierce for me, you helped drive away my fears and doubts, constantly reminding me of who I am. It is because of you I can create peacefully and always *Dream Well.* Thank you, husband. I love you.

Awaken
BEAUTIFUL NIGHTMARE

Chapter 1

With a tear-worn face and a bruised heart, I summon enough strength to propel me out of my room in the blink of an eye. Only Dalcour's movements slightly parry my own, and I am surprised even he can't fully match my pace. While I can't see him, I know that Jackson isn't far behind as his brash scent of cinnamon trails Dalcour's ever powerful fragrance of jasmine and lavender. Aunt Delia's sobbing rings aloud in my ears as she cries my name, but even her pleas do little to calm the hurling fury within.

As my force leads me through the halls of the mansion, I can't help but notice something feels different. My motion is more fluid than I recall. The energy within me doesn't feel as chaotic as it once did. There is a symmetry to my movements unlike anything I've felt before. Not only do my feet not touch the ground, but there is now a weightlessness to my body reminiscent of a flower blowing in Spring's breeze. Yet, despite my newfound buoyancy, I still feel tethered to the ground.

All my thoughts are of my precious cousin Dacari. Awakening to the news that she is gone has invoked an anguish to my soul

I have never known. I long for the times when my heart only dropped to the pit of my stomach—because at least I was still in control. Or at least so I thought. But now it's as though a cobra has coiled its body around my heart and is squeezing the very life from me.

My tunnel vision-like motion leads me through the kitchen, where the French doors swing open with the brush of wind I emit at my will. While I am surprised to uncover this recent addition to my supernatural repertoire, I don't linger or try to understand its meaning or the how of it all. It doesn't matter. The only question that plagues my heart is one thing: Where is Dacari?

Darkness fills the morning sky as thick dark clouds cover what was once the making of a bright, sun shining day. Sounds of the chirping birds I heard at my awakening are now replaced with the rush of howling winds and a thunderous sky. Thickly coated tears shield the circumference of my eyes, blocking my view from anything other than my pain.

I want to scream, but I cannot. My vocal cords are still frothy from my unconscious respite; another issue I want to explore, but not as expedient as the whereabouts of my cousin. Knots form in the pit of my stomach like a forge of rocks encasing a dam, draining me of strength and vitality all at once.

I grab the iron bars along the deck to steady my motion and keep myself from falling as I take a deep breath and close my eyelids shut tight, hopeful to allow the standing tears their escape. Although, I immediately regret that decision once the diamond-like stream hits my cheek, tearing into my flesh like tiny paper cuts at its freefall. Grinding my teeth, I squeeze the railing tighter as the pain of my own tears aids no comfort to my plight.

"Damina," I hear Dalcour call my name softly from behind. His alluring fragrance hits my nose just as he says my name, yet I am saddened to find it does little to quiet the raging storm within me. Oh, how I long for the times when just his aroma was enough to calm my storm, but it is not this day.

Once more, I hear my name called through the whipping and whistling sounds of the wind. But this time the wind carries with it the spicy and sweet aroma only found in Jackson Nash. I am surprised when the cool call of Jackson's voice aids to recharge the faint pulse of my heart, all while loosening the hardness forming within the pit of my being. And with that, I exhale and release the toxic fumes rummaging inside me.

Even now, I am yet amazed of the effect of Jackson Nash.

Turning slowly, I see Jackson and Dalcour standing just beyond the French doors while Aunt Delia remains postured between them but still at the threshold of the kitchen. Both men stare at me with longing eyes and endearing smiles that would melt my heart if it were not decaying from within. But I am strangely thankful for the pause this anguish has given me from the tug-of-war between these two stallions that inevitably awaits me.

"Darling, I'm so sorry to drop that on you so fast. I—I just didn't know how—" Aunt Delia's pained voice rips through me and I feel the knots reshape in my gut once more. Jackson turns as if he wants to comfort my aunt but is hesitant to leave my view. He gestures his hand toward me, parting his lips to speak, but Dalcour's tone rings loudest, beating Jackson to the punch.

"Beautiful, we all wish there were a better way to tell you the news. But in these types of situations, there's just no good way to say it." While Dalcour's broad attempt to speak over Jackson is clear, there is no condescension in his voice only a gentle care in his eyes.

"But know Damina, all is not lost." Jackson's words slice through the would-be enticing pull of Dalcour as we lock eyes with one another. Whether it was the thickening of Dalcour's aromatic presence or the syrupy and sultry sound of his voice, Jackson's clipped tone ensured he would not allow Dalcour's allure to take over on his watch.

"What do you mean?" I quickly question as the reality of Jackson's confession rips me from the enchanted eyes of Dalcour Marchand.

"He means she's not dead," Dalcour pointedly responds, aware of Jackson's intent. He shoots a wary glance in Jackson's direction, but Jackson's eyes remain fixed on me.

I exhale once more as relief takes over and belt out a loud sigh, yet still keeping a tight hold on the railing with one hand.

"Explain," I mutter, gazing at the watchful eyes of Aunt Delia. She shakes her head in reply as a waterfall of tears pours down her face. Jackson looks between Dalcour and I with a tight and grim glare but resolves to pull my tearful aunt to his side, allowing her to cry on his shoulder.

"Beautiful," Dalcour begins, recapturing my attention. "Your aunt wasn't here when everything happened. You must understand this news is just as alarming to her as it is to you." Although I know he is trying to redirect my rage away from my aunt, I can't help the burning antipathy I feel toward her.

"Explain," I whisper my words once more through the whipping winds and crackling sky.

"Perhaps we could all talk about it if you can just temper your storm a bit," Dalcour shouts over the sounds of the thunderous skies and thick gray clouds hovering over the mansion with his eyes locked on the decorated darkness behind me.

For the first time, Dalcour's words do nothing but irritate me further. I release my grip from the railing and allow the fervor of my fury to carry me high above the garden maze of the mansion as the sky rumbles in response. My head writhes with both pain and frustration. All I want to do is scream, but the frothiness of my throat prevents me from lifting my voice above a whisper.

Dalcour jumps to the side of the railing, balancing himself perfectly against the wind while lifting a cautionary wave in my direction. "Beautiful, come back to me. Let's go in the house and talk about this. Together," Dalcour says with a trembling echo in his voice I've never heard before. He gazes at me carefully, looking over my shoulder at the small beam of sunlight piercing through the clouds aimed just an inch from his shadow. He sides steps, so he is in front of me and away from the sun. I can't help wondering whether he has lost his ability to walk in the sun.

His trepidation does little to quiet my storm. With every sniffle and shriek from Aunt Delia, I am repeatedly reminded of her treachery. How could she keep the truth of our heritage hidden all these years? What good did she think would come of her actions? Did she ever consider what news like this would do? And now with Dacari gone, I have only one person to place blame. Aunt Delia.

"Damina, baby, Dalcour is right, let's talk about this—inside." Jackson leaves my aunt's side and stands tall against the direct sunlight. Although I can tell he is trying to be gentle, Jackson's commanding tone is as pronounced as ever. Yet, I am surprised that I am not immediately irritated at his rebuke; rather, his voice is more calming than I would expect. His eyes plead with me to settle my rage, but it is the way his warm and perfect smile follows his words that ease the suffering of my heart.

At least a little.

Jackson's eyes lock with mine and I now see in him what I hadn't before. I see him. His wolf. His protection. His love. Everything that is Jackson Nash is carried in the tide of his sea-like emerald eyes. If it weren't for the calamity of my heart, I would give anything to dive in and immerse myself in his embrace.

The knots in my stomach uncoil, and I feel the heat of the sun at my back. I watch as Jackson steps further into the sunlight, smiling at me as I drift down toward him. Yet, despite his draw, it is Dalcour's warm and sturdy hand that grabs my forearm, steadying my descent.

"I've got you, Beautiful," Dalcour says as his aromatic scent implodes in the tight space between us while he grips me in his arms, placing me gently on the deck floor. Although his hands are firmly at my waist, his body remains a few inches apart. Just enough to let me know he's near, but not enough that our bodies touch. "Are you okay?" Dalcour questions taking my chin in his hand ensuring our eyes connect. He smiles and my body rivets as my eyes trail the alluring curl of his mustache against his supple raspberry-coated lips. In that instant I am reminded of the intoxicating enchantment of Dalcour Marchand, and I gently pull his hands from my waist before I lose myself in him.

My body shakes as he releases his hold, and I recall just how painful it is to be apart from him once we touch. A wave of nausea comes over me as I regret pulling away from Dalcour, but Aunt Delia's quiet sobbing echoes loud in my ear, drawing me back to the core of my grief. Dacari.

"Let's talk." My tone is sharper than I intend as I keep my gaze fixed on my aunt, fearful of being entranced by the watchful gaze of either man at my side.

Aunt Delia nods her head in reply, wiping her cheek and squaring her shoulder, unwilling to appear weak for too long, she turns and walks toward the great room.

Jackson and Dalcour mirror my steps closely as I follow behind Aunt Delia. She paces back and forth in front of the fireplace before taking a seat in a wooden chivari chair near the tall glass candelabras to her left. Her constant pacing makes me anxious, so I plop into a large leather chaise opposite the fireplace.

Gazing around the room, I notice something feels different. There are more chivari chairs here than I recall, with small black wooden dinette tables to match. I look behind me into the kitchen and see framed menus hung on the wall and pub height stools perched at the counter side of the island. Unlike the home-like state of the mansion before my slumber, it now feels more commercial and boutique-like.

I don't have time to ponder the new aesthetics now arrayed before me when Aunt Delia offers a faux cough, turning my direction back to her.

"I suppose I don't know where to begin, darling. But I suppose you have a lot of questions to ask of me," Aunt Delia begins in an unusually distilled tone. As I watch her grief-stricken face while she speaks, my heart immediately aches for her. I know I am not the only one hurting. I can only imagine the painful state churning within her. Yet, her pain does little to squelch my churning rage. I am still mad at her.

"What happened?" I whisper, taking my attention away from Aunt Delia's pain-staked face and shooting fleeting glances to both Dalcour and Jackson. "Well, don't you all speak at once!" I demand as I stare at their downcast faces. It's apparent that neither want to be the bearers of bad news as they exchange grimaces with one another.

"You saved me, that's what happened," Jackson blurts. He saunters in front of the fireplace and leans against the shelving along its edge. I don't think I'd noticed how handsome he looked since I had awakened. I'm surprised he's not adorned in his typical suit and tie. He's wearing jeans! This is a shocker! The dark denim jeans and fitted silver tee accentuate his form in all the right places. Dalcour forcibly clears his throat behind me and I quickly trail my eyes past Jackson's chiseled biceps back up to his perfect smile that awaits me.

"How do you mean?" I reply rubbing my eyes trying to regain my focus.

"When I came to, there was a blinding, bright golden light covering us and shining throughout the room and there you were laying in my arms. You were so still and cold, but there was also an intense heat radiating from the light you were emitting like I'd never felt before. It was like the sun. Every injury I had completely healed, and though I wasn't sure how, I knew it was all because of you."

As Jackson speaks, jolting memories of that night flicker through my mind. I remember more about that night than I care to recall. Fighting both Scourges and Skull throughout the mansion. Dauphine's death. Kieron's treachery. But it is the memory of Mikkel plunging a sword through Jackson's abdomen that shreds my heart in two. I know it was the thought of a world without Jackson Nash that unleashed a power inside me I never thought capable. More than that, I know it was the love I have for him that made such a power permissible. And in that I have no regret.

Jackson smiles at me as our eyes meet as though he could see into my soul. I wonder whether he, too, can read my thoughts like Dalcour. But it doesn't matter. If he never knew how I felt for him, I would hope that night gave him every assurance.

Though it still does little to bring me total relief. As the true matter at hand, the means of Dacari's disappearance have yet to come forward.

"And what about Dacari?" I answer quickly, forcing thoughts of my love for Jackson aside.

"Well, I guess that's where I come in," Dalcour interjects pushing through the budding thick space between Jackson and me. He strolls in front of my view, ensuring not to block my sights of Jackson yet brushing past me just enough that I capture his jasmine and lavender scent. As my eyes drift up to meet his, I can't help but be dazzled by his charming and almost giddy smile and the way it instantly lifts my mood.

How does he do that?

"When Mark, Braelyn and I reached the parlor, the brightness of your light was too much for even us to bear. Scorching heat instantly rose from both me and Braelyn at the threshold. I could only withstand just a step across the door before my skin simmered. Thankfully, Mark pushed us away from the door—"

"If I recall, Gregory was there with his aid," Jackson snips in a coy tone to which Dalcour only shrugs his shoulders and huffs.

"Why yes, I suppose the mutt offered some help," Dalcour replies over his shoulders without taking his eyes off me. "As I was saying, once the wolves, that is Gregory *and* Mark, came to our aid, they could get you and Lord Nashoba out of the parlor. But by the time they got you to your room, your light diminished. And to be honest, we were afraid we were too late. You were so— so cold. Still."

Dalcour stares at me with a haunting gaze as I watch him in awe while his memories of my eerily laid body lay still before him and Jackson flash through my mind. A pounding thud jolts through my head, more intense than any headache I've ever had when I suddenly realize somehow, I have glimpsed Dalcour's mind.

"Damina, darling, are you okay?" Aunt Delia asks as the coolness of her tone tears me from the replay of Dalcour's memory.

"Yes," I reply quickly, brushing Dalcour's intrusive thoughts aside. He gazes at me, narrowing his eyes, likely knowing I just read his thoughts. He parts his lips to speak, but I break through the silence before he can form his words. I don't want to discuss me right now. "Okay, but what happened next? What happened to Dacari?"

"Well baby, once Vonnie checked your pulse and vibed you, she let us know that you were just in a deep sleep," Jackson begins. I can't help but be distracted by the fact Vonnie *vibed* me and I softly repeat the word. Still, I refuse to linger on any issue of me and return my attention back to Jackson. "But when Dacari saw you laying so still she went into a panic. She screamed at all of us, throwing each of us out of the room. She only allowed Brian and Brae to stay with her for a little while before she eventually kicked them out too."

"To be honest, I was shocked such a small person could throw two guys out at once. I have to say I was impressed. My pride was slightly injured, but I was impressed just the same," Dalcour jokingly mutters.

"Do you mean she actually threw you out?"

"Yep, baby, she did. You two are definitely related. It felt like my backyard all over again," Jackson answers. Though I know he's trying to play it down, I find no joy in knowing how I flung him across his own yard as I yielded to my rage.

"For two days Vonnie and Brian took turns standing guard at the door," Dalcour's tone is dark as he speaks, and his voice drops an octave while his gaze darkens as he recounts the events of that night. Tiny sparks tear once more into my mind, but I work hard to steady my breathing. I can't allow even this writhing pain to distract me now. Jackson forcibly clears his throat to get my attention, giving me just the distraction to look at him and break from the intense energy I feel from Dalcour. Jackson shoots me a warm, soft smile that meets his eyes. "Dacari refused food. She even refused to speak with anyone. She only demanded that we get your aunt here, stat. That's why we found it strange that on the morning your aunt arrived, Dacari disappeared. No one saw her leave and all her things were gone."

"Was she taken?"

"No, darling, it doesn't appear so. You know more than anyone your cousin would've put up quite a fuss and fight. No, I think she left on her own. I'm sure the thought of seeing me after everything was too much to bear." Aunt Delia allows a half-smile to drape her face, but it is unconvincing. Typical of my aunt, she is trying to stay strong, but I know better.

"Then I don't understand. If no one took her how could she possibly escape? Under your noses? On your watch? How is any of this possible?" I shout through the cringing crackle of my hoarse throat. I jump from my seat as I feel heat rise from my body and blue embers of light radiate through me.

"Beautiful, that's what we're all trying to figure out!" Dalcour shouts back. I'm surprised at the defensive stance he's taken, but I know he's not backing down.

"Look, we all need to stay level-headed here. Baby, now that you're awake, you can help us make some sense of everything. Mark and Brian have used every resource to track her down. Braelyn has done everything from keeping this place together to playing a bit of CSI to locate her. And Lord Marchand has every legion of his Guard on watch."

"And you?" I mutter hardly above a whisper as the truth of Jackson's words whip me back to my seat. Jackson only smiles in reply, but it is the gentleness of his eyes that reins in my rage.

"I'm afraid Lord Nashoba is too modest to confess that he's hardly had a goodnight's rest himself since he's been perched at your bedside and consoling your aunt all while training up the next young Alpha to lead the city," Dalcour says in a soft voice as he steps to Jackson's side, gripping his shoulder.

Although I'm comforted that the two have bartered a truce since my respite, it does little to bring me comfort.

"Well, do you have any leads? I mean, it's been over a month. Dal, doesn't this place have a security system or something?" I hate that I'm barking my words, but my irritation is growing with every minute.

"That's just it," Dalcour begins as he steps aside from the shards of light beaming through the cracks of the wooden blinds. "All my systems went offline for a few hours the night she left. We don't have any viable footage of her departure—at least not yet."

"What do you mean, not yet?"

"Braelyn has been looking into it. She even snagged a few forgotten favors from the police to get street cameras from the night in question. It's been a slow push, but she's been diligent," Dalcour answers with a hint of pride.

A smile escapes from behind my otherwise gloomy disposition as I think of Brae's unrelenting prowess. I know she'll never give up her quest.

"So you see, darling, everyone here is doing everything possible to locate Dacari. But I know you probably blame me for all of this—and I suppose I would understand why," Aunt Delia bluntly confesses, cutting through my brief musing of Brae's relentless spirit.

"Now, there's enough blame to go around, Delia, but right now our focus must be on Dacari. Isn't that right, Damina?" Jackson replies in his typical overstepping and slightly rebuking tone.

"Well, since you bring it up," I abruptly snap, turning my attention away from Jackson. I refuse to let him dictate my feelings, even if he's only playing the broker of peace. "Tell me, Aunt Delia, why didn't you tell Dacari and I the truth all this time? You had to know you couldn't keep this up forever. I mean, when I woke up today, I had no thought of drudging this up now—"

"Then it can surely wait—" Jackson interrupts.

"No, it can't! It's been long enough! Even when I saw father in my dreams, he was never clear about why you all kept this a secret for so long. And who knows, perhaps Dacari figured out something that even I still don't know. What do you think, auntie? Care to elaborate? Care to add something of worth to the story?"

Both Dalcour and Jackson shout my name, protesting in unison to my now testy tone. Yet, I pay neither of them any mind. It's time my aunt owned her part in all this.

"Let her speak. My niece has every right to be upset with me. I am so deeply sorry, Damina. Truly, I am. Your grandmother and I had planned to tell you the day she died. And well, after her death it just got harder and harder to get enough courage to tell you. We never committed to a pack in Washington, so we were alone mostly, until you met Jackson. And well, things were just going so well for you, and for once you were finally happy. Once we came under the protection of his pack and he received the blessing from the Duacin elders I had hoped everything would be okay."

"Right because now you had Jackson to lie for you. Isn't that right, auntie? Jackson told you he wanted to tell me the truth, and you begged him not to go through with it. Why? You are my family! I trusted you with everything—and now look at the mess we've all made. Yes, I say we because I include myself. Dacari begged me to stay, not to run—but I just couldn't help myself. I just had to go because I couldn't live in a world where either of you two were harmed or worse. Now she's gone and we're all to blame!"

"Well as much as I'd like to cave and take the blame for you loving me the way you do, Beautiful, I won't. Because as much as I know it pains you to accept it, it must be said: Dacari left on her own accord."

How dare you? The thought immediately springs into my mind at Dalcour's words, but only my expression echoes in reply and I am sure Dalcour is keenly aware.

"It's the truth and you know it. She left for one reason or another. Even though it is clear you all are used to treating her as if she were a porcelain doll, she is not. She's a woman. A grown woman who decided on her twenty-fifth birthday to leave. Perhaps she is trying to teach you both a lesson, I don't know. But one thing is clear: I will go to whatever end to help you find her and bring her to safety."

While I am thankful for the softened tone near the conclusion of Dalcour's rant, I remain irritated that he is holding my cousin solely responsible for her disappearance. More so because I know of everyone in this room, he alone can read my thoughts and knows I fault my endearing love for both he and Jackson as the cause of it all.

"Blame me, Damina," Aunt Delia begins as she rises from her seat, once again squaring her shoulders, refusing to shrink even in the face of her own shame. "After all his gracious hospitality, please do not blame Lord Marchand and certainly not Jackson! I and I alone held the key to the secrets of our family. I could have told you. I should have told you both the truth. I didn't. For that I am sorry."

"There will be ample time for apologies and truth bearing once we find Dacari," Jackson asserts before I can counter my aunt once more. Although a part of me wants to challenge her with one more dig, the calmness of Jackson's tone simmers my growing rage. He smiles at me softly, lowering his eyes and bowing his head slightly so that our eyes meet.

Now, more than ever, I am convinced that Jackson alone is capable of not only weathering my storm but controlling it wholly.

"Ah-hem!" The loud belting of Dalcour's faux cough serves its purpose, breaking the growing lure between Jackson and me.

A small, bashful smile crosses Jackson's face. I'm sure he's quite pleased with himself. He knows he still has a jarring effect on my heart. Dalcour saunters in front of the fireplace and stands between Jackson and Aunt Delia, no doubt a ploy to recapture my attention. *Oh, how I wish he knew he never lost it.*

"Then might I suggest we take Damina to the one person who has the answers we seek," Dalcour says in a low throaty tone.

"No, it's too soon!" Aunt Delia exclaims.

The softness of Jackson's face gives way to a rebuking glare in Dalcour's direction, and the pace of my heart quickens. Both my aunt and Jackson appear appalled at Dalcour's suggestion, allowing my impulsive rage to rekindle within me once more.

"Absolutely not!" Jackson shouts.

"Wait, who has the answers? Tell me, Dalcour!" I answer, rising to my feet.

"Jackson's treacherous brother. Let's go see Keiron."

Chapter 2

Keiron. His name is not one I expected to hear again. At least not so soon after my awakening. Even a hundred years from now would be too soon. Yet, despite the gnawing and rattling sound in my ears at the mention of his name, I can't help but allow curiosity to assuage my rage. Dalcour is right. Keiron was the first to mention Dacari when he brought Mikkel, the Scourges and Skull aiding to his threats. It was Keiron who alone slit Dauphine's throat, offering only a callous rebuke and slithering grin when I denied his demand of my cousin. And through it all we never learned the true motivation behind his heinous betrayal, nor his devious schemes.

"You can't possibly be considering this ridiculous suggestion, Damina! Tell me you're not!" Jackson barks as a dim look of intrigue crosses my face as I think on Dalcour's recommendation. But it is the sound of Jackson's typical rebuke that sends my thoughts from mere interest to defiance. Despite everything, Jackson doesn't understand, *I'm not that woman anymore*.

"What other recourse would you offer, Jackson? That is

anything other than your condemnation!" I shout back at Jackson, allowing a low snarl to bellow through me. A quivering jolt of energy rivets through me, sending my body hurling in his direction, squaring him toe-to-toe. He jumps back, likely more out of disbelief than fear. He's still not accustomed to this side of me, nor does he like it.

I don't care.

"Look, Beautiful, I don't want to make you do anything too hasty. Maybe Lord Nashoba is right. Maybe it is too soon," Dalcour says softly coming to my side, resting his large palm on my shoulder. At his touch, I feel the unnerving energy within me settle. I am equally comforted by his fragrance. Closing my eyes, I inhale enough to fill my lungs, exhaling slowly as I reach my arm across my chest to squeeze his hand. Dalcour closes the gap between us slightly, allowing our bodies to touch as his belt buckle grazes my abdomen. He squeezes my hand and takes a step back while his fingers lightly trail down my shoulder as he pulls away.

I am thankful that Dalcour can still quiet the chaotic force surging through me. Looking over my shoulder I smile at Dalcour and he returns the gesture until his eyes meet Jackson's watchful glare.

"Damina, I want answers too!" Jackson begins in a more subdued tone. "I'm just worried about you is all. I mean, it hasn't even been an hour since you awoke. Besides, my brother hasn't said one word since he's been in captivity."

"Well, he did say one thing," Dalcour replies in an equally calm voice.

"What? What did he say?" I ask.

"He asked for you," Jackson answers.

"As a matter of fact the only thing he said when he came to is, 'Where is Damina?'" Once more, as Dalcour replies, his memories flicker sharply through my mind. Images of Keiron screaming my name in a panic as he came to after I fell cold in Jackson's arms rip through my core. Now, more than ever, I realize Keiron may in fact have the answers I seek.

"Damina, darling, before you speak to Keiron there is more we should discuss," Aunt Delia exclaims in an almost brutish manner.

"Aunt Delia, what else needs to be said? If Keiron has any inkling of where Dacari might be then I need to speak to him now," I snap in a tone brasher than I intend. Aunt Delia's eyes well with tears once more, and it is evident my harsh mood is more upsetting to her than I realize. Although I'm still upset with her, I need her to know the love between us is untarnished. "Listen, Aunt Delia, I know there is much we need to cover. But we've lost too much time already. If I'm the only person Keiron is willing to speak to, then I must confront him. Perhaps we can finally get some answers. Know this, I love you and I always will!" I tug her arm and pull her in for a brief embrace and immediately turn to follow Dalcour down the hall. Jackson shares a quaint nod with Aunt Delia before rushing to my side, taking my hand in his as we head to the Civility Center.

"Here take this," Dalcour says in an unusually commanding tone with his arm extended toward me, holding a long beige trench coat.

"What's this for?" I question.

"Well you can't go storming through the Civility Center in nothing but your jammies. It's enough I've had to ask Mark to close the mansion today. I haven't been able to give Titan and the others a heads up to clear the CC. I'm sure neither Lord Nashoba nor I are in the mood to knock the lights out of the first person who sees you in that cute little ensemble." Dalcour regards me with a familiar and hauntingly seductive glare reminiscent of the night we met at Razors. I can't help feeling weak in the knees as my mind recalls that night. Quickly, I turn to face Jackson and put on the coat, hopefully to douse my want for Dalcour.

Just when I thought I had enough strength to resist him, I now know that is impossible.

Jackson regards me with narrowed eyes and a stern stare as he helps me into the coat, but he presses his lips tight, likely reining in his disapproval. He's working hard not to upset me. I can tell neither he nor Dalcour want to break whatever truce they bartered, but one thing is sure: it won't last long. I only hope it holds long enough for us to find Dacari.

Despite the obvious changes I noticed during my brief time in the mansion, I am comforted the path to the Civility Center remains untouched. Dalcour continues leading the way as Jackson and I follow close behind. Jackson's hand in mine is firm, and I spy him gazing at me periodically from my periphery. As much as I want to turn my attention to him, I am fearful of what would happen if I did. My gut tells me he would toss me against the wall and kiss me. Although that would be uncharacteristic of Jackson Nash, something tells me that like me, he's not quite the same as I remember. Perhaps it's my desire playing tricks with my mind, but I'm not opposed to the idea of him taking a little liberty.

At least a little.

Nonetheless, I wouldn't want to do anything to hurt Dalcour. I'm sure all of this is hard enough on him as it is. To be fair, I don't want to hurt either of them. Thankfully, my pursuit of Dacari and seeing Keiron will douse the vacillation of my heart long enough for me to weigh my options.

The oval wooden door of the Civility Center makes a rattled and squeaking sound as it opens just as Dalcour lifts his fists to knock. But it is the look of a familiar yet beautifully stunning woman holding the door open that makes the pace of my heart quicken while bringing the first sincere smile to my face since my awakening.

How happy I am to see my beloved Brae on the other side of the threshold! Although, I did not expect to see her so soon, I am thrilled to see her!

"Well, well chica! Aren't you a sight for sore eyes!" Brae shouts as she immediately yanks me over the threshold for a tight embrace. I equally surrender to her hold on me and squeeze her tight. For the first time, I detect the sage smell of juniper berry and lemon exude from her pores. Her scent is akin to the essential oil diffuser I keep near my bed at home. Just as I feel her letting go, I maintain my hold enough to take in one more whiff, thankful to see my friend again.

"I missed you too, Damina!" Brae exclaims as she pulls herself from my grasp, smiling up at me brightly. "But if all you wanted was a pajama party, you could've just told me, girl!" Just as she speaks a sweeping wind wafts through the hall of the Civility Center, blowing my trenchcoat open as the door slams shut behind us. We both chuckle as Brae tugs on both ends of the belt, motioning me to wrap up.

"Yes, it is wonderful to see you again, Damina—and I mean all of you," I hear a rumbling and husky voice call from the narrowed darkened corridor. Titan steps from beyond the shadow of the hall with his hands in his pockets in a more casual manner than I expect from him. Wearing a muscle-sculpting black tee, dark navy trousers and with his hand rested on his holster, he paces toward me in his usual confident stride and broad smile. He keeps his eyes locked on me, ignoring all others in the corridor as if it were just us two.

Attempting to break his gaze, I peer around his shoulder for his sisters, Ketu and Keitai and am surprised not to find the playful twins ambling behind him. I pull the belt of the trench tight and hold my hand at the top of the coat hoping to conceal as much of myself as possible but as I catch Titan's eyes trail downward, I notice the top of my legs forcing through the unbuttoned coat. He stretches his arm toward me offering a hug but Dalcour jumps between us with Jackson marking his place dutifully at my side.

"Well, I see not much has changed in the last forty-or-something days, huh Damina? Still got these fellas in a tizzy I see," Titan says in a lighter tone looking just over Dalcour's shoulder until our eyes meet.

"She's come to see the prisoner, not you Titan," Dalcour snaps.

"What a shame. I was only hoping to thank Lady Damina for protecting my sisters," Titan answers while never taking his eyes off me. Though I am not remotely attracted to Titan, I can't help but blush in the presence of these gorgeous stallions surrounding me. From where I stand, there isn't an imperfect blemish on Titan. Yet, despite his deified physique, marble-gray eyes, and enigmatic smile, not a jolt of electricity moves me at the thought of him.

"Where are your sisters?" I reply over Dalcour's hulking shoulders. I know Titan can read my thoughts and I want him to know they are my only concern.

His eyes fall slightly at my response, but he quickly shakes off my dismissal and his smile brightens once more.

"My sisters are with Trieu. There are celebrations here today and I didn't think it wise to bring them to the CC."

"Celebrations?" I question. I've never thought of the Civility Center as a place for celebration.

"Why yes. Today Ms. Grenoble is celebrating the anniversary of her making. She became a vampire right here in New Orleans. She always comes back here to commemorate the day. I am sure Lord Marchand will attend the celebrations as he always does. Isn't that right, Lord Marchand? He is her sire," Titan coyly replies with a dark glare.

While I detest the sneering smirk etched across Titan's face as he speaks, it's the familiar sound of the name, Grenoble, that causes an unknown stir within me. I feel as if I should know this name, but I can't place it.

"Well, there's a first time for everything," Brae abruptly replies, yanking me from my pondering between Dalcour and Titan, but

Jackson remains firmly at my side. "Look, are you sure you want to do this now? You're just waking up!" Brae stands squarely in front of me, attempting to keep me from spying the intense stand-off between Dalcour and Titan.

I can't help but be curious for their indifference. The two seemed like allies the last time I saw them together, but something has changed. But they are not the only ones who have changed. Brae looks noticeably different from what I recall. There's little evidence of the goth girl I once knew save her purple lipstick and trademark gloves with leather bracelets to match. Instead of her usually overly gelled hair, she lets her bouncy auburn ringlets hang free with only a light smear of blush framing her pear-shaped face, all while wearing a salmon-colored tee and torn black jeans.

"Chartreuse Grenoble!" I blurt, turning back toward Dalcour as I finally recall why that name churns like butter in my memory. She's the one Jerrica referred to as her rival. "You sired her?" I can't help but feel threatened by the mentioning of her name.

Dalcour opens his mouth to speak, but Brae yanks my hand once more, pulling my attention back towards her. "Hun, no worries. That was a long time ago! Eons before you two became little love magnets!" Brae says, nudging my shoulder. Jackson forces a faux cough and Brae lowers her head and pulls me away from the men.

"You have absolutely nothing to worry about," Brae whispers in my ear before turning back toward our company. "Look guys, I hate to break up whatever you have going on, but Titan is right, there's a bunch of my kind on their way to the CC today. So if Damina is going to talk to Keiron, now is the time. Mark's got all the Loup-Garou Guard ready to protect the Quarter and Garden District. The last thing we need is any distractions. Besides, Big D, I need you to check out the footage we just got back from some of my contacts."

"*Loup-Garou* Braelyn? Really? Is Mark really sticking with that?" Jackson laughs darkly over his shoulder.

"Excuse me, but what does that mean?" I asked confused as all the men chuckle in unison. Brae pouts her lips and folds her arms, turning her head away from us with childish petulance.

"Stop teasing guys! Look, Mark's building something different here! He's the resident NOLA alpha so, if he wants to call it Loup-Garou instead of Wolf Guard, then so be it!" Brae counters.

"You are right about one thing, Braelyn, he is the resident alpha and he can lead his charge as he sees fit," Dalcour replies in a soft tone, still laughing as he walks to Brae's side and pats her shoulder in consolation.

"Well, Brae hopefully when he is professed as the sovereign alpha at the next *Lunae Lumen caeremonia* he won't have to defend his freewill to name his guard as he sees fit. Once we find an elder willing to perform it—"

"What is a Lune Lumen caeremo---whatever you just said?" I ask Jackson, feeling like the only dummy in the hall.

"It's Latin for Moonlight Ceremony," Jackson answers over his shoulder, followed by a warm smile. He forms his mouth to continue but is quickly interrupted by Titan.

"So we're going to just act like the wolves control the city now, huh? I've carried the weight of guarding not only New Orleans, but overseeing the Guard operations for this entire continent, and you act like this little mutt can just take over? I'd die first before I see the Guard led by a sniffling mongrel!"

"Watch your next words carefully," Jackson snarls, squaring himself in Titan's face.

"Make me, Nashoba. I dare you to try," Titan taunts, his eyes gleaming bright red and fangs protruding.

"Titan!" Dalcour shouts in a commanding tone. "Calm yourself, old friend, lest you forget your place and to whom the entire Guard belongs!"

Quan as-tu perdu ton chemin? Titan mutters his response in French, almost too quiet for human ears to comprehend.

"No, my friend. It is not I that lost their way. Besides, this is not why we're here," Dalcour gruffly responds with a low snarl escaping his curled lips.

"Well, now that we've defined pecking order, can we get moving? Really, Big D, I need you to come with me to the security room. I'm sure Jackson can take Damina to see Keiron. Dranoel is at the gate with Lux and all other entrances are secure." Brae tugs on Dalcour's arm, but he remains unmovable as his face-off with Titan remains.

"Dal," I say softly, pulling away from Jackson, moving toward Dalcour's view, hopeful to avert his gaze away from Titan to me. "Brae's right. I need answers. I need to find Dacari."

The hard lines in Dalcour's face soften as I speak and he turns toward me, cracking a reluctant smile. Titan walks back to the dark corridor from where he first appeared but stops briefly and looks at me over his shoulder with a coarse smile. Something about Titan still feels off to me, but I do my best to shrug it off. Dacari, not Titan, is my number one concern.

"Damina," Brae's loud and brash tone snaps me from the gloom-ridden gazes of Dalcour and Jackson. "Like I said, if you want to see wolf boy, you're gonna have to do it now! I'm sure Mr. Nashoba can keep you company in the lair. Big D, you're with me. We need to view this footage pronto." In a flash, Brae rips Dalcour from my view, leaving only Jackson and I in the hall. I'm surprised Brae could pull Dalcour from his frozen-like state, but I can only reckon the mood was a bit too awkward even for him.

"Well, I guess that's our cue." Though I expected Jackson's tone to be stiff, it's surprisingly light. He cracks a half-mouthed smile while his eyes search my face as he tries to discern my mood. I place my hand in his extended palm and momentarily relish in the warm and peaceful comfort of his touch. "Are you ready?"

Jackson asks, pulling me closer so that our bodies are touching.

I inhale his spicy and sweet aroma only to meet his longing eyes staring back at me. I'm not sure if it's my intuition or not, but everything in my being says that Jackson wants to plant his lips onto mine. Oh, how I wish he would. Instead, he takes a deep breath and steps back and continues leading us through the corridor with my hand securely placed in his.

We reach a tall steel door and Jackson pulls a rope to his right and a loud bell chimes on the other side. Almost immediately the door opens, and I see Dranoel standing just beyond the threshold. He's wearing a long black leather trench with leather pants to match and a deep purple colored tee. Although I can tell Dranoel is old enough to be my father, the youthful bright smile gleaming through his bearded cocoa skin makes me think otherwise. His golden eyes shimmer as he and Jackson nod at one another before returning to its normal hazel hue.

"Lord Nashoba, it's good to see you," Dranoel says in a tone more husky than his frame suggests.

"Always a pleasure, Dranoel. Though I wish it were under better circumstances. Let me introduce you to—"

"Ah yes, the lovely Lady Damina Nicaud. Yes, she needs no introduction. I know we didn't get a proper meet-cute when you were here last, but I'd never forget a face. At least not a face quite as beautiful," Dranoel responds, cupping my hand while offering a slight bow.

"It's nice to meet you, *officially* Dranoel."

Dranoel bows with a broad smile before looking back up to me and Jackson. "Well, I know our time is limited so I've taken the liberty to secure your brother, my lord. Of course he still hasn't spoken, so I'm not sure that he'll be up to holding conversation."

"He will talk to me," I quickly answer just as Jackson parts his lips to respond. As much as I want to linger in the pleasantries with Dranoel, I need answers and I intend to get them from Keiron.

"Yes, my lady," Dranoel answers while waving his hand for us to follow him through a large gated door. He opens the door with a long metal key, and we go down a small flight of stairs to the prison area.

Just as we walk down the staircase, the stench of urine, blood, and what I detect to be the smell of rotting flesh sours my stomach and I instantly cover my nose and mouth. Jackson's nose squinches as well, but he keeps a protective glance on me while keeping my armed draped tight through his.

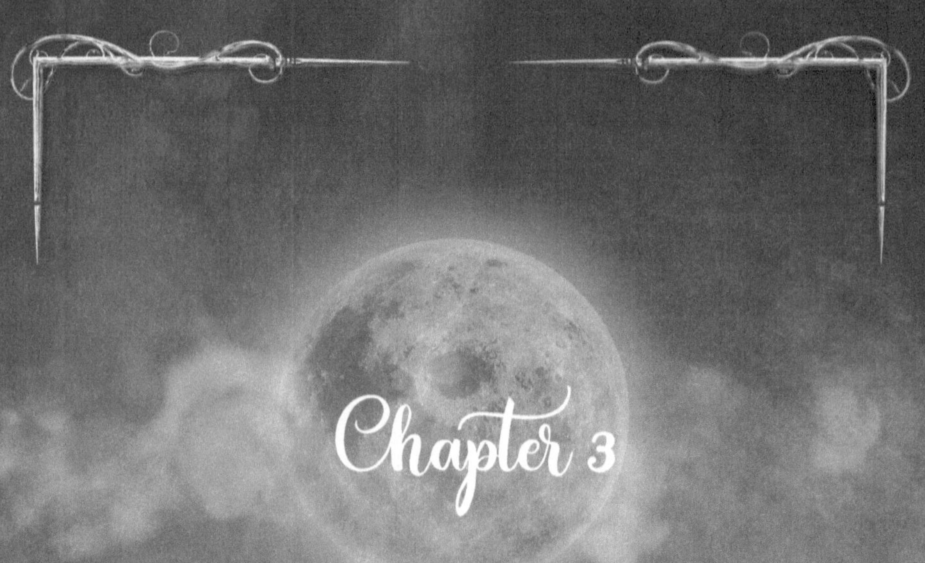

Chapter 3

"Are you sure you're still up for this?" Jackson questions me with a strong squeeze of my hand as his eyes scan a dark corner. He gazes back down at me and I see sweat forming at his brow as his jawbone tightens while he searches my face.

Exhaling the rank odor invading my nostrils, I affirm with a quick nod and strengthen my hold in his grip. We both turn to our left when we hear Dranoel pound on a thick glass wall.

"Get up. You have company," Dranoel shouts.

Jackson firms his grasp on my hand, locking them together and wedging mine beneath his thumb. A tiny current of electricity rivets between us and a shocking sensation jolts my attention squarely aligned with Jackson's eyes. The greenish-golden hue of his irises glow at me in the darkened corridor and a sweet gasp of his sweet and spicy aroma escapes his mouth. Inhaling it wholly, I can't resist the alluring sweetness of his scent as I press my face up toward him, taking in every molecule of his fragrance. A small smile forms beneath his thick brunette goatee, and I feel myself giving in to the all-too familiar and slightly sensual gaze of

Jackson Nash.

It's the same look he had the night he lifted his paddle in the auction hall on the day we met. I've never been able to withstand *that look.*

"Should I wait until you two are finished your eye-cavorting or should I just stand here in the shadows and play third spoke to your wheel? Four, if you count how uncomfortable you've made Sir Dranoel for the last ninety seconds," Keiron scoffs just after a faux cough as he wanders out of the shadows toward the glass wall.

An uncomfortable silence rests between us as Jackson and I share awkward glances. Although I know we need to deal with the matter at hand, I can't help marvel at the revelation that what Jackson and I once shared is alive and well. *But different.* Of course I never stopped loving him, but I am somewhat surprised to find just how much he still affects me.

Even more, a deeper part of me believes he's just as shocked as I am.

"Come into the light, brother." Jackson forces his words through the void as he calls to Keiron, lightly loosening his grip on my hand.

Dranoel lights a small oil lamp and hangs it against the stone wall as Keiron walks further into the light.

I'm not sure what I thought Keiron would look like since last I saw him, but I know one thing. He looks hideous! Gone is his typical dapper but casual attire. Locked in thick chained cuffs and wearing a beige prison suit, his matted, chestnut hair drifts past his jawline, blending in with his bushy beard. Only a tint of gold rings through his grayish eyes as he locks eyes with both me and Jackson.

"Not quite what you were expecting, huh, my lady?" Keiron mutters, looking through the crevices of hair dangling against his forehead. A small smirk cowers beneath his grunge bearding and a familiar ire kindles within me in response.

"I have no expectations of you!" I snap back as thoughts of Keiron's atrocities flash forward in my mind.

"And yet here you are—*expecting something*," Keiron sneers with his smirk growing into a callous grin.

"She's only here for answers, Keiron. We both are. We know you have answers about Dacari. Now tell Damina what you know!" Jackson barks, pressing his face against the glass.

Keiron's eyes shimmer with defiance as he glares at Jackson. Tugging on Jackson's shoulder, I pull him back and away from the glass wall, back to my side. Keiron grunts, shaking his head in annoyance before pulling a small round stool from the back corner. Jackson's muscles tense as Keiron scrapes the chair along the cement floor and I hear a low rumbling snarl bellow from him as he carefully watches his brother's movements.

Plopping down onto the stool and crossing his legs, Keiron brushes his hair away from his face and exhales loudly. He glances down at his fingernails for a moment before staring back up at us and over to Dranoel.

"Fine. I'll talk. But only to you, Damina. I have nothing to say to the impotent troll who I once considered my kin, nor is there anything I wish to say in the presence of one who's resigned his royal status to be nothing but a gatekeeper to these vile vermin," Keiron lashes while peering over his shoulder toward Dranoel and nodding toward Jackson.

Both Jackson and Dranoel growl at Keiron's defamation and Jackson leans toward the glass wall, but I place my arm over his chest. Dranoel's defensive posture is almost surprising, but I'm quickly reminded he's the sole trainer of all wolves in the Guardian. If I know anything about my limited time with both Dalcour and Titan, Dranoel must be worth his keep despite his seemingly demure posture.

"Then speak with me, Keiron," I say quickly putting myself

between Jackson and the glass wall.

"No, Damina! I will not leave you here alone with him!" Jackson shouts back, his face still aimed at Keiron.

"He's right, my lady. We can't allow you to be alone with this traitorous feign!" Dranoel protests.

"*Allow me*?" I bite back. Boiling heat rises inside me and streaming electricity blankets my skin.

"Damina, please he's just looking out for your safety," Jackson pleads, grabbing my shoulder to keep my attention on him and away from Dranoel.

"I don't need him or anyone to *allow* me to do anything, Jackson!" I counter.

"I know, Damina. I know," Jackson calmly replies as the coolness of his breath prickles my pores, dousing my growing frenzy. Watching me intently, Jackson catches my eyes, locking us in place. "I know more than anyone you are capable of taking care of yourself, Damina."

While I know it shouldn't, Jackson's words disturb me. Not only am I surprised by his sentiment, I am taken aback that *he's not* trying to control the situation.

Who is this man?

Jackson parts his lips before squeezing them tight and blows out an air of frustration. Keiron huffs behind us as Dranoel growls back, shining the oil lamp directly in Keiron's face. Ignoring their posturing, Jackson keeps his sights squarely on me, gripping my shoulders to return my focus to him.

"Listen Damina, Dranoel and I will be just at the top of the stairwell. If even for a moment he causes you even an ounce of distress—"

"I'll call for you, Jackson. I promise," I softly reply, lightly twining my fingers through Jackson's thick, long mane. I'm still a tad shocked at how much his hair has grown while I slept. Looking at him, I know more than his hair has grown. There's maturity in his manner to me that is both unfamiliar and reassuring. *I could get used to this Jackson.*

Jackson smiles back at me warmly as he takes my hand from twirling his hair and kisses my knuckles. "The top of the stairwell. Just say the word," he affirms once more before turning back to Keiron as he issues a faux cough.

"I mean, I have nothing except time on my side. But I thought you wanted to know the whereabouts of your precious cousin, Damina," Keiron adds.

"Make it quick." Jackson keeps his attention on his brother and waves Dranoel to his side without turning away from Keiron.

"I'll be fine, Jack. And don't worry, I have no intention of spending any longer with him than is necessary."

As Jackson and Dranoel make their way toward the stairwell, I lean against a tall pillar adjacent to the glass wall and raise my hand, gesturing Keiron to begin. I need to get this over quickly.

"Tell me what you know, Keiron. Speak fast."

"Well, before I tell you what I know it would help if I knew what you knew. I mean, it's apparent you're just coming out of your month-long slumber. And seeing as though you are traipsing through the mansion with nothing save your nightwear, it would appear you rushed down here as soon as you learned of her disappearance."

"You are correct," I answer, clenching my trenchcoat tight by the belt.

"But if all you know is that Dacari has disappeared you barely know half the story."

"What does that even mean?"

"Well, my lady, aren't you remotely interested in my reason for coming to the mansion? Or even my involvement in breaking up your engagement with my brother—though from the looks of things I barely sullied your affection for one another—seeing as though you nearly died to save his wretched life and you two still can't keep your sights off one another," Keiron scoffs, annoyed.

"I know all I need to know. You are jealous of Jackson. You want to be the alpha and conspired to end our marriage. Oh, and you tried to have your own brother killed! Did I cover all the high points, Keiron?"

"Quite the contrary. You've barely grazed the surface of the truth."

"What truth is there?"

"The truth is, I've actually been trying to *save your life*—and my brothers for what it's worth."

"How dare you even presume to make yourself some hero in this, Keiron! I saw you with my own eyes! You tried to kill your brother! You sent that wench as a changeling to end my engagement! What hero does that?" I snap. Just the sight of him raises my fury to new heights.

"Let us be clear," Keiron shouts back, pressing his hand and forehead against the glass wall. "Mikkel tried to kill my brother. I only wanted to fight and take his rank. Just because I don't put on an ill-fitted onesie, wrap myself in a cape with an insignia etched across my chest, doesn't make me any less of a hero. Sure, my tactics may seem vicious, but I alone did what needed to be done to protect this world from the carnage you will inevitably inflict!"

"*Me?* What carnage could I possibly inflict on anyone?"

Keiron glares at me, gently pulling his forehead from the glass wall, his face softening as he rests his palm against the wall. "Yes you, Lady Damina can cause more harm than any of those two lovesick fools care to admit. And while they insist on parading about with their noses wide open, too smitten with thoughts of you and too fearful to learn which one of them you'll choose. I have done the hard and dirty work to keep us and all the world protected from the lot of you!"

"I thought you had something worth sharing, but now you're just wasting my time. Putting the blame on Jackson, Dalcour or even me does not absolve your treachery, Keiron. Now, if you have nothing to add about my cousin, you serve no purpose. God knows it took everything in me not to end your life that night. You live as you do now out of courtesy for Jackson. However, I would not test the bounds of that courtesy."

"Then, I'll speak plainly," Keiron responds in a grubby tone, folding his arms at his chest and narrowing his eyes.

"Finally."

"You are Fated."

"*What?* What does that even mean?"

"As I'm sure you now know you are of the Duacin Elders—in the Order of the Altrinion."

"Yes, I know my lineage."

"Ah, I see. Well, did you also know who is the sole progenitor of the Duacin? Have you heard of Anuel? Nuhtlus?"

"Of course. They were the first blood drinkers. The first vampires."

"And do you know how—or rather why they became so?"

"*They feared death above all things,*" I whisper, recalling Dalcour's account of the legend. Once more the foreboding dread locks me in place, like a snake coiling around my throat.

Keeping his gaze on me, he loops his leg behind him and drags a small stool beneath him and plops down. He sighs loudly and continues. "Not only did they fear death, but they feared the death of their one and only true loves. You see, Damina when the Changeling Order was cast aside to only the darkest depths of the world by your lineage, the Altrinions, they cursed every house of elders. The Fated Ones are remnants of that very curse."

"What curse?"

"A curse of inconsolable insanity. Almost akin to a magnetic melancholia, the Fated Ones are destined to love so deeply that the separation of that very love drives them past the brink of madness!"

"You're lying!"

"Oh, how I wish I were! But just like Anuel and Nuhtlus, Fated Ones sink to such a depraved state not only will they turn to the drinking of blood to endure their lives, but they become the progenitors of savage predators like the Scourge—vampires! And since you are Fated, you are bound to the same curse!"

"Stop it! I'll hear no more!"

"Don't believe me? Fated Ones are so laced within the fabric of human history you can hardly tell fact from fiction!"

"I've never heard of any stories of Fated Ones!"

"Oh sure you have, my lady, you just didn't know it. Pompei. Elizabeth Bathory. And by far the most infamous of your Altrinion kin, Vlad, or should I call him Drac—"

"What does any of this have to do with me? Or my cousin?"

"It has everything to do with you and those two besotted buffoons who made their home at your bedside these forty-odd days. And your cousin, well, she may just be the only saving grace in this whole matter. That is, if it isn't too late!"

"Quit your riddles and your stalling. Speak plainly, Keiron. Do it fast!"

"Fine, I'll speak plainly, my lady, but you won't like it," Keiron shouts back, rising from his seat, pressing his face once more into the glass. "You bear the sacred crest of the Great Oak and you are Fated to be with one true mate of equal lineage. In this case that would be Lord Marchand. While I didn't know for certain that it was Marchand who was to be your equal, I learned you were Fated when my brother received the approval from your father, Lord Duacin after some digging of my own. Now, while your father didn't reveal that truth to my brother—I knew I had to put a plan in motion before you succumb to your fate."

"How so?"

"For one, my brother is maddingly in love with you. His love toward you is unrelenting. When I discovered you were fated, I knew my brother would never do what needed to be done. His heart—his love toward you would not allow it."

"What needs to be done?" I almost hate to ask.

"This is the part you won't like. But first, a brief history about the Primes. There are three Prime Packs. My brother and I are Alphas. Prime Alphas are the higher, earthbound order, put in place to maintain the balance of every creeping thing and protect the Order of Altrinions. Beta Primes are the foot patrol. Guardians, if you will. That's why Sir Dranoel and the others are so keen to reclaim Guardianship for the Beta Primes through their young alpha, Mark. There's more to that story—but I digress."

"You said there were three Prime Packs?"

"Ah, yes. So you are listening. Well, the third is more complicated. The Omegas are what all primes hope to ascend. You see, as the alpha of the Prime Alphas, my dearest brother can one day rise to Alpha Lord status as an Omega. While it's way more complicated than I can explain the bottom line is that only an Alpha Lord can correct the curse of the Fated Ones."

"Correct?"

"Oh did I say correct? I suppose a better word would be, kill."

My mouth gapes open and Keiron keeps his piercingly grey eyes fixed on me. I can almost feel my heart plummet to the cold floor beneath me, but I do my best to maintain my composure. I refuse to give Keiron the desperate response he so obviously craves.

Slowly his hardened gaze softens as he continues searching my face. He allows a small smile to creep beneath his beard, but I remain guarded.

"Damina," he begins quietly, his voice more delicate than ever. "Listen, I do not say these things to bring you pain."

"How can you say that? You just said that Jackson's sole purpose for living is to one day end my life!" Oh no! I'm giving him more emotion than I wanted.

"No, I said, Alpha Lords are the only ones capable of correcting the curse should it arise. My initial goal was clear. Strip my brother of his status—have him abjured if need be—anything to keep him from doing the one thing I know he'd never have the power to do."

"Kill me."

"I said you wouldn't like it. Now in all fairness it could just as easily be Lord Marchand that would bear the brunt of that charge. Yet and still I know my brother could never even harm Lord Marchand if even the thought of it would bring you pain—or if nothing more than out of respect of his endless affection toward you."

"But you could? Without question—"

"I'm afraid so, my lady. Only because I fear the cost of not doing so much more."

"And so what? You align yourself with the likes of Mikkel to kill me!"

"Mikkel had his own charge with you that is not my own. But his claim was still the same—end the Fated Ones—protect the world."

"Well I melted his bones to ash, so I doubt he'll be protecting anyone."

"I'm afraid he wasn't alone. There are more like him. The Vitreous Altrinions."

"Vitreous?"

"Yes they are an old faction of Altrinion Vampires. They claim to be the first made from the wretched house of Nuhtlus. Their main goal is to ensure they are the only elder house of power. They want to wipe the remaining Fated Ones from the house of Anuel from the earth and purge any Scourge that remain. Most have always considered them the Nazis of the Altrinion-vampire race."

"Fine. You've covered wanting your decision to correct what you feel your brother incapable of doing."

"More like unwilling—"

"Whatever. And now that you've shed some light on the Vitreous, I still don't understand what Dacari has to do with any of this!"

"That's just it! She is the anomaly. The wildcard if you will."

"Wildcard?"

"Damina!" I hear Jackson call to me from behind while Keiron holds my attention between the glass. I've wasted enough time with him.

Ignoring Jackson, I push away from the pillar and move closer to the glass wall. "Explain! Quickly!" I yell.

"Well, I'm afraid there's no expedient path to the truth behind her story, but I'll attempt a simpler path for the more impatient mind," Keiron says over my shoulder, staring at Jackson. Although I feel Jackson inching close behind me, I do not turn around. I need to know more. "As you are aware, it's not just the Duacin who account for your Altrinion lineage, but also the LeClaire. That would make the ever lovely Dacari Altrinion as well."

"Of course, so she's Altrinion. So what?"

"Damina! We really need to go," Jackson says, now resting his hand on my shoulders. I feel the same kinetic energy spike through me at his touch as I did before, but I dig my feet into the cement, hopeful to douse his pull.

"And then there's the Peyroux lineage," Keiron continues, ignoring Jackson's plea. "The Peyroux were Dunes Paw until good old Elias Peyroux paid his penance to Saint Roch and had the Dunes curse lifted from his family's bloodline. The lifting of the curse created a new lupine strain not captive to the Order of the Primes nor marred by a doomed state. Something different entirely." Once more the foreboding fear within me looms about as Keiron's mysterious and dark tone matches the new darkness covering his face as he steps back from the light.

"Okay so she's a hybrid. There are other hybrids. Right?" I ask over my shoulder to Jackson.

"Just what are you implying, brother?" Jackson questions, pushing his voice through Keiron's calculating silence. Our angst is making this too fun for him.

"I guess you could say she's a hybrid—on her mother's side. But then there's her father side of the family," Keiron replies, keeping his attention aimed at me, ignoring Jackson.

"*Her father's side?* But Dacari has never met her father." The words whisper from my mouth, meeting Keiron's shadowy scowl.

He offers a broad and wickedly cagey half-smile in response before he answers.

"*Hasn't she*?"

My heart sinks at his words, but I have no time to dig further as Jackson lifts me in his arms and carries me away.

Chapter 4

"Jackson!" I shout, banging against his back while I hang over his shoulder as he races to the top of the staircase. Jackson's motion is so fast I only caught a dim view of Keiron's ominous frame watching us as we exited. I am still in awe at how fast Jackson is able to move. I didn't realize he was so swift.

Jackson lifts me over his shoulder, allowing me to slide past his chest as he maintains his hold on me, keeping me just shy of his waist. Once more, the rippling current pulsates between us as it has before, and I fear I'm slipping back into his lure. With our bodies so close, it takes all my strength to fight the tempting hold of Jackson Nash.

Thankfully, my thoughts of Dacari are slightly stronger than the budding draw growing between Jackson and me.

Only slightly.

"Jack," I begin, slowly pulling our bodies apart. His expression is warm, but his deepened gaze seems to peer through me, and I wonder if he can see just how much he's affecting me. What's more is I can distinctly tell I'm affecting him just as much. *If not more*.

"Yes, Damina," he answers quietly, his eyes locked with mine.

"Dacari. I didn't get to hear what Keiron had to say about her. We need to go back."

"No, babe," Jackson replies, his hands slowly trailing my face. "I needed to get you back up here."

"But Jack—"

"But nothing, Damina. There's something you need to see," he adds with a firm hold on my chin while gazing deep into my eyes. There's an intent longing in his glare that is hard to miss.

"What do you want me to see, Jackson? What could be so important?" I now know his only wish has ever been for me to see him. Now I do. *I do see you, Jack*, is what I want to say, but I can't. Not yet.

My words hang between us as Jackson's thumb strums my jawline, and I almost wonder if he just wanted to get me alone with him. Once more, his sweet and spicy scent petals past my nose and I instantly feel even my angst for Dacari dissipate. As his lips part, I am unsure if it's in response to my inquiry or if he'll plunge his mouth to mine.

At this moment, I almost hope it is the latter.

However, a faux cough interrupts our passionate exchange. "Oh, I'm sure you'll find this important, Beautiful," Dalcour's throaty reply halts the shared kindling fire between me and Jackson. And with the way Dalcour is staring at us, my nervousness rings through my being.

Taking a deep breath, I turn to face Dalcour and distance myself from Jackson. Jackson's stance instantly mirrors my own as he squares his shoulders in a slightly defensive posture.

"What did you find?" I quickly answer back, doing my best to shake off my longing for Jackson and concentrate on Dacari.

The strained glare on Dalcour's face doesn't go unnoticed by either of us. While I can tell he's upset with us, there's something more behind his eyes I didn't think I'd see. Fear. Something has him spooked. I only wish I knew what was causing his distress.

Stepping forward and away from Jackson, I try to keep Dalcour's sights on me as a grimace mars his otherwise perfectly sculpted face.

"Dal?" I question, softening my gaze, hoping to keep his attention and relieve the tension I sense building within him. Jackson shifts behind me and a low rumbling echoes through his chest, but I keep my focus on Dalcour.

"Hey what's the hold up? Get up here!" Brae shouts to us from a long corridor adjacent to the stairway.

"Right behind you! Come on guys, let's go!" I yell back, gesturing for both Jackson and Dalcour to follow my lead.

"Damina, wait!" Dalcour calls from behind me as I follow Brae down the long dark hallway.

"What is it, Dal?" I question as we arrive in a room with small monitors along the wall. Each screen has real-time footage of the mansion, the CC and even Razors nightclub. While I'm surprised to see Razors on the screen, I'm more in awe by the sophistication of the security suite nestled in the hub of the Civility Center.

Dalcour grabs my arm and looks around the room as if he wants to tell me something, but his eyes continue scanning the suite. Again, I can tell he's bothered. I just wish I knew how to help him.

"So Braelyn, tell us what you found," Jackson says, walking around Dalcour and me as another small grumble rumbles through him. Jackson's eyes scan Dalcour's grip of my arm and a small scowl grows beneath his goatee.

Whatever truce the two men bartered seems to fade.

"Okay, then! Damina, you might want to grab a chair," Brae sharply announces, breaking through our awkwardness as she grabs a remote and quickly slides a chair in front of me. "I almost wish I knew where to begin, but let's start with this. Thankfully, I was able to cash in a few law enforcement favors to get this footage. Apparently, the night of the *big ordeal* we lost all our security footage. Somebody was playing with our blind spots. Maybe even from the inside. Anyway, we were able to get this traffic cam footage near the Riverfront Expressway. Check it out."

"Damina," Dalcour calls my name again, tightening his hold on my arm. Looking over my shoulder at him, I see the same worried expression as before. A part of me knows that seeing Jackson and me at a near kiss was probably painful to watch, but I can't help wondering if there's something more.

"Quiet, D, Damina needs to see this," Brae says in a hurried tone.

Dalcour sighs but reluctantly gestures toward the screen. I know I've spent too much time ogling both Dalcour and Jackson. I need to remain resolute so we can find Dacari.

In this moment, she is all that matters.

Watching the screen, a large black SUV pulls into the frame and stops just shy of the underpass. The time on the video shows it's 2:38am. My heart races as I wonder why my cousin would be out at this hour. The footage also reveals a heavy downpour and with the rapid motion of the wiper blades it's obvious the weather is horrid.

"Whose car is this?" Jackson questions, his tone hard and steady as he keeps his attention on the screen.

"It's Dorine's car," Brae says quietly, gazing back at Dalcour who remains pensive with one arm folded at his chest and his other holding his chin.

"Dorine's car? I don't understand," I reply.

"Keep watching," Brae mutters.

The SUV remains at the underpass for a full two minutes before a car door opens and Dorine and Padma get out of the passenger and driver's side doors. Dorine enters the tunnel for a few seconds and shortly comes out on the other side while Padma opens the backseat door.

Then I see her.

Dacari!

A part of me almost expected to see her bound in chains with a bag over her head, but that is not the case. Dacari gives a small smile to Padma when she gets out and Padma gently rubs her back, extending her hand toward Dorine. Draping her coat over her head, Dacari quickly makes her way toward Dorine and they both stand still at the entrance of the tunnel.

"I don't understand what's going on! What are they doing with my cousin? Is she under some spell?"

"Damina, I think you and I should talk first in the hall," Dalcour begins with his hand now resting on my shoulder.

"Talk about what? What do you know? Do you know where she is? Have you known all this time?" I shout back. Inquiry and rage both fuel me, and every ounce of the Altrinion force within me is buckling at the bit.

"Damina, really we should—"

"Stop the tape!" Jackson orders Brae. "Damina, look!" Jackson commands, yanking my arm and turning my attention back at the screen.

The racing of my heart slows to an almost deadly rhythm as my eyes lock to the monitor. With the footage paused, I trail my forefinger along Dacari's frame, but my sights are now set to another person who now stands opposite Dorine and Dacari.

His face looks familiar but doesn't. All I can see is a thin goatee and plump raspberry colored lips that almost resemble Dalcour. He smiles at Dacari, but while his smile isn't as enchanting as Dalcour it is almost just as hypnotic. But it is when I see the haunting deep crimson ring encasing his irises my mind flashes back to the morning, I ran down Dalcour's hallway when Dacari arrived.

Images of Dalcour with a man in Spanish regent attire and other antediluvian portraits score through my memory in one painful pulse. A sharp current of energy rings through me and panic overrides my intellect as I work to disavow the truth before me.

Decaux Marchand.

Dalcour's wretched brother.

The one who Jerrica once said wanted to set the world ablaze by unleashing broods of Scourge and Skull upon the earth. The one who gave a deadline to Dalcour to restore the supernatural balance. The one who created a timebomb so deadly even Dalcour Marchand himself chooses to comply.

Why is this man with my cousin?

Why would Dorine and Padma take her to him?

What possible reason would he need or want to see her?

Or she him?

What is the meaning of it all?

A loud shrieking cry echoes through me and a bursting wave of the Altrinion force blows through the room like a violent windstorm.

"Damina!" Jackson shouts my name, making me aware of the effect I'm having on everyone. Even Jackson shields Brae, likely fearful I'll emit a light too powerful for her to bare as she hides beneath his broad frame. Looking behind me, I notice Dranoel clutching the frame of the door as the gale growing from me pulls him slightly off his feet.

Only Dalcour remains firm. As he gazes at me, his truth becomes plain. He knew this would be my reaction, and he wanted to prepare me. He just didn't know how. Still, as I search his mind, I now know he is just as surprised as I am to uncover this revelation.

While it does little to appease my angst, it does assuage my rage. At least a little.

As I work hard to pull back my growing storm, I stifle my ire just enough to turn my attention back to the screen. Brae crawls from beneath Jackson's grip and a part of me is thankful to see him shield her. If I wasn't furious right now, I'd be impressed.

"Press play," I command, my eyes once more locked on the screen.

Brae does as I instruct, and I see Decaux extend his hand to Dacari and she places her hand in his. I almost want to stop the tape again. I know if I see an inkling of romantic overtures, I know I'll blow the roof off this mansion. Blazing heat rises from my skin and Dalcour calls my name from behind, but I don't turn around. I can't look at him right now.

Then something happens I did not expect.

Decaux smiles. Wide and big. And while it's hard to see through my flame-filled eyes or past my anger, I notice his expression is soft and his smile meets his eyes.

Now it hits me. *He is happy to see her!*

Why?

Dacari lifts to the balls of her feet and squeezes his hands tight and he nods his head down toward her and they both laugh.

What is going on here?

Do they know each other? If so, how?

"Brae, is there any sound?" I snap, snatching the remote from her hand, punching the volume button.

"No, there's no sound, Damina. Just raw footage, I'm afraid," Brae answers quietly.

Dalcour grunts from behind me, dragging his feet to pull himself to my side. I sense his aromatic scent waft over me, but this time it does nothing to douse the erratic energy buzzing through me. Jackson also makes his way to my side, yet still keeping his attention on the screen.

Dacari turns to both Dorine and Padma and offers both women a warm smile. Surprise fills me as I watch her smile brighten through the pouring rain. Another truck comes through the opposite side of the tunnel and a man comes from the driver's side and opens an umbrella to both Decaux and Dacari. Dacari waves farewell to Dorine and Padma and then turns to hug Decaux.

His hold on her is tight and they both linger in the embrace. Taking her face in his hands he plants a small kiss on her forehead, and she throws her head on his shoulder and he smiles broadly, but this time his expression has changed.

Yet, once more, it is not what I would expect.

Keeping his eyes shut as she nestles deeper in the cavity of his hold, he takes in a deep breath and exhales before gazing up at the sky. Then it becomes clear. I know what he's doing. I know because as of late I've done it a thousand times.

He's trying to fight back tears.

Batting his eyes a few seconds before wiping the corner of his eye, I spy one lone tear drift past his cheekbone. The shimmering gem falling past his face gives it all away. Those are tears of joy! And while I've had little experience with it in my life, I know what his tears mean. Although I almost hate to admit the truth.

There's only been one man to which I've had the effect Dacari now has on Decaux. My father. Only a father holds a daughter with such complete love, care, and ardent protection.

This can't be!

"No!" I breathe out as the revelation becomes clear. Panic and dread fill me once more, but I hardly have air to breathe. While I don't quite understand how any of this is possible, this wouldn't be the first time where the impossible laid before me bare.

"Yes, Damina," I hear my aunt's small, still voice behind me announce. "It's true. Decaux is Dacari's father."

Chapter 5

Turning to see Delia's tear-worn face is harder now than it was before. At least when I awoke, she was just as disillusioned as me with Dacari's sudden departure. Now, I can't help wondering if she knew of Dacari's whereabouts the entire time.

"How could you?" I whisper through steam-wrought words. "All this time! You've lied about this! You've lied about everything, Delia! Tell me, did you know where she's been this entire time?"

"No, Damina! Please, you have to understand!" Delia sobs. Her tears do nothing but enrage me further.

Without a blink, my movements quickly carry me squarely before her. Only Dranoel pulls her back just enough to evade the force of wind that blows through me at my landing. Dranoel keeps his hands locked on her shoulders and she turns her head slightly to relish in his comfort. A part of me questions just how close the two have grown since my slumber, but right now it is of no interest to me.

"Answer me!" I snap back.

"Yes, I've always known Decaux was her father—but I didn't

know she knew. I had no idea she would try to contact him—or even that she found him at all," Delia pleads.

"Damina, let's all calm down and talk about this," Dalcour interjects, but his words do nothing but infuriate me.

"Talk about what?" I shout, turning quickly to meet his fear-laden eyes. Once more, I marvel that someone as powerful as Dalcour Marchand could fear me. But I know the truth. It's not me he fears. It is Decaux. The one he's always feared. His truth invades my conscience and I know he is just as worried as I am. Terrified even.

But I will not share this pain with anyone. Not Delia. Not even Dalcour.

Betrayal is all I feel in this moment. Everything I've known to be true has been a lie! Over and over the veil of deceit keeps me from the hidden secrets that not only sneak up on me but haunt me. For all I know, everyone in this room has yet another secret that can send my life crumbling in one blow.

Gazing around the room, the air feels thin and I gasp. Figures of Brae, Jackson and Dalcour distort before my view and a dizzying motion rides me hard. Gripping the door post, I try to keep my footing, but I feel as though I'll be sick. Or worse. Faint.

Darkness swathes my vision and a clear case of vertigo sets in. The walls seem to invert, and I can't stand straight as the room spins around me. Dalcour grabs my arm, attempting to steady my motion, but his touch is unwanted. Yanking my hand away from him, I hold myself at my knees and try to get my bearing. Brae's tiny hands rest on my shoulders and it's the only comfort I can accept.

"Just breathe, Mina," I hear Delia call out to me, but it only rekindles my mania, resetting my panic.

It's too much! Everything is too much.

Dacari's disappearance. My eclipsed heart. Me being Fated. And now this.

Decaux is Dacari's father.

I can't take it!

What's wrong with me? Why do I feel like this?

A rippling current topples me to my knees, and I buckle as a swathing sense of gloom pools over me. Hearing Delia's continual cries wreaks havoc on my heart. I want to comfort her, and I don't. This is all too much!

I can't breathe.

Before the suffocation grips me further, I see a sliver of light at the end of the hall and I know what I must do. I must make my escape.

"Damina, no baby," I hear Jackson's calming voice echo behind me. Looking over my shoulder, I look up and see him as I hold myself steady at the knees. He shakes his head, pleading with me not to do what he knows too well I will do next.

Run.

I can't be here any longer.

Not now.

Whatever explanation Delia has will have to wait.

Closing my eyes, I exhale and punch my fist to the ground and inhale the freeing fragrance of the wind I emit at my will flowing around me. Lunging forward, I use every ounce of the Altrinion force to propel myself past Dalcour, Delia and Dranoel. Faintly, I hear Brae and Jackson call to me from behind as Delia's cries bellow loudly in my ear.

Surprisingly, Dalcour is silent. I don't even detect an ounce of his effervescence at my clearing, which is a first. Still, I don't allow his despondency to halt my motion. With tears flushing my face, I can barely see my way clear, but I press forward, allowing the slither of light at the end of the hall to guide my motion.

I am shocked when the light drives my movements through two large doors that lead to the DJ platform at Razors. It only takes a moment for my mind to replay memories of my first dance with

Dalcour on the very dancefloor before me.

Now, more puzzle pieces come together. It makes sense the CC would have security footage of Razors—Dalcour probably owns the club! How could I be so foolish? Of course he does. Everything is connected to him somehow. Even more, I get the strange feeling it wasn't a coincidence we came together on the dance floor that night.

Crap!

Have I been a fool this entire time?

"Can I help you?" I hear a dark, froggy voice call to me from a shadowed corner near the bar. "Club's not open yet. We open tonight at six."

"Sorry, I was just leaving," I mutter under my breath. A chill wraps around my body and I realize that somehow, along the way, I lost the trench Dalcour gave me.

"Lady Damina?" The Voice says as if we were familiar. Just then, a huge, hulking figure of a man stalks from behind the shadows, peering with golden eyes just beyond the sun's light. "You're awake!" The Voice exclaims as though he were happy for my uprising.

"Yes," I say, shyly gazing around the darkened club floor.

"My apologies. I know we've never met. But Lord Marchand has ensured all his staff are aware of you. The name is Crawley. Is there anything I can do for you?"

"No, Crawley," I answer tepidly. "I—I just need to go!" I cry, just as I spot the exit, lunging forward once more and make my escape. The door swings open behind me and a part of me hopes Crawley kept back from the door. Something tells me he's not a candidate for sunlight just yet.

Bursting outside, the sun rays are too much for me and my eyes burn as the blinding light envelops me. Shuttering, I scream and cover my face, trying to shield myself from the brightest known star of the cosmos. I'm not sure how early or late it is, but the sun seems brighter than ever.

I want to return inside the club and attempt to make my way back to the Civility Center, but my strength feels depleted. Weak. Anguish and fear grip me once more and I sense the Altrinion force forsake me as my legs give way to the weight of my heart.

Just before I topple to the ground, I feel strong arms wrap around me and a cool, nutty scent tickles my nose. Peering through the blinding light, a slender young face and crooked smile are all I can make out before exhaustion takes over and I leave myself in the strength of the stranger's arms.

This time, opening my eyes is starkly different yet familiar. The smell has changed. Gone is the crisp, clean smell of the mansion. Now the aroma of fresh baked goods, seafood and all manner of delightfulness fills the air as the melodic sounds of jazz play in the distance. This bed is also familiar but not. The silky satin sheets I've become accustomed to sliding around on are now replaced with a high-count cotton that is cool to the touch.

"I was so hoping you would wake up soon! I mean, I really don't like being out and about at this time of night and such. But tonight I thought I'd make a special exception. Only for you sugar," I hear Melvina's distinct deep southern voice say just beyond the terrace doors.

"Melvina? Is that you?"

"Well, of course it's me, chile! Who'd you expect? I didn't think you and my Bésame were on good speaking terms. I figured when Lorien got you here, it'd be best for my face to be the first you saw," Melvina replies through a hearty laugh. She saunters toward me, hands on hips as usual, and laughs once more, this time only her shoulders move in response.

"Lorien? Lorien brought me?"

"Why yes! He found you almost laid out in the streets in nothing but your unmentionables. Good thing he was out getting his art supplies and such. Could 'a been somebody else—someone uncaring to find you and such the way you were," Melvina replies in a motherly tone. She plops down on a chair adjacent to me and smiles as she takes my hand in hers. She glances at me for a moment before asking, "Are you all right, honey?"

"No, I'm not. I am so not all right, Melvina. Everything is so messed up!"

"Well, every time I've seen you everything is messed up and such. When you gon' git it right?"

"Me? I'm sorry, but it's not me who needs to get it right. I'm not the one messing up everything, Melvina. That would be everybody else!" I snap back, pulling my hand from beneath hers, pushing myself up against the headboard.

"I suppose there may be some truth to that. But honey, you the only one I keep seeing run. You were running from somebody when I first met you and now every time in between. You gon' have folk think a bounty hunter was chasing you the way you about on the run and such," Melvina answers with a sly laugh as she pulls a crochet net out of her hip pocket.

"*But it is everyone else*, Miss Melvina. Every time I think I can breathe, the walls of deceit all around me come closing in. Every time I think I know the truth, I find out everything is a lie!"

"Oh, really?" Melvina says as she begins her cross stitch.

"Yes, really! I mean, at first there was Jackson! I didn't know he was a wolf-now I do. I thought he cheated on me before our wedding and then he didn't! Oh, and don't get me started on my family! First, I think I'm just a regular, ordinary human being. Now I find out I'm Altrinion!"

"I see," Melvina mutters quietly, only lifting up one eye over in my direction. I hate feeling like she's not taking me seriously! I need to drive my point home!

Popping up to my knees, I near the edge of the bed, hoping to get her attention. She needs to understand the gravity of the situation. "And then there's your boy—Dalcour! He knew I was an

Altrinion, but he waited to tell me until I fell for him. Then he says, 'oh yeah, by the way, I'm an Altrinion Vampire, and Braelyn, well she's a vampire and that one over there he's a wolf, and this one is a pra—' what do you call it?"

"A praesidium."

"Yeah that!"

"So, I see it's everybody else's fault that you're in the mess you're in?"

"That's what I've been trying to tell you!"

"Then why are you telling me that, child? Shouldn't you be telling them?"

"Well, I suppose so. But I just couldn't be in the same room with any of them. I needed some space. Some room to deal. To breathe. I have to try to wrap my head around this myself first."

"Ah! I see, so you just needed a little time to come to grips with everything that's happening now?"

"Exactly!" Great, now she's understanding my point.

"So, I should also guess that is why you didn't tell your cousin right when you found out you were Altrinion. Right?"

"Well..."

"And that's probably why you didn't call your aunt or Jackson the moment you found out you were Altrinion, right?"

"Well—I—I."

"That stands to reason that's why you ran to Perry's friend to get you here, and after you got here and found out what you were, you ran away from here with Dalcour only to run back now. Right?"

Slowly, Melvina's words both infuriate me and disturb me all at once. Mostly, it hits me square in the heart. A deep rumble pulses through me and the sky darkens at my dismay. I know as of late I've had a bad habit of running away from things I don't like or that are unsettling. But this is different.

Isn't it?

"You can tell your little storm to settle, missy. You won't be scaring me away with that. I got some storms of my own, you know." Melvina's words are sharp, daggering my heart, but it's her surprisingly cool hands on my shoulder that send a tidal force of calmness to my otherwise erratic state.

Looking up at her, tears pool in my eyes and the eminence of my situation boils within me. I don't like this bratty person I'm becoming. How can I save my cousin from Decaux like this?

"Listen, honey, I know all of this is enough to send anyone, yourself included, hurling about like a windstorm and such. But how do you think the supernatural community has survived all these years? It's certainly not because we're traipsing through the French Quarter in our underroos and ballgowns leaving cyclones and hurricanes in our wake."

As she speaks, I think on my actions as of late. I'm not doing too well controlling my emotions. Dalcour has told me more than once I needed to get my abilities in check. If I keep at this rate, I'll inflict more damage than the Altrinion of Pompei ever did. In fact, even Mikkel and Keiron said it's been all my Altrinion activities that alerted them of my arrival.

Get it together, Damina.

"Now, look, don't be so hard on yourself, honey," Melvina softly says, lifting my chin. "No one is saying all of this is easy for you. It's gotta be difficult. To be honest, it's within your rights to be mad about the truth being kept from you all these years. But your family only did what they thought was best for you. Even Jackson. And even my boy, Dalcour. Your auntie is a nice woman. A bit more sophisticated than this ol' bag of bones, but a good woman, nonetheless. I'm sure she wanted to tell you and your cousin the truth all these years, but put yourself in her shoes. There she was, a single woman, single-handedly taking care of an aging parent, her orphaned niece, and no other family support. And since she was a hybrid, she didn't really have a pack to lean on. She's a strong woman that one. Made sure you had a roof over your head, clothes on your back, and kept your light cloaked on her own until you got with that good looker of yours—your Jackson. I would say she did a darn good job."

"I would say so too. She's amazing," I quietly acknowledge, as tears stream down my face. She's right.

Melvina pats my head and stands up, pushing her crochet kit back in her hip pocket and walks to the terrace door.

"Now, then there's that Jackson. Well, he's just a bowl of good soup as I like to say. Just all hearty and healthy. A nice bowl of everything that's good for you. I know he's got his own story to tell, but let me just say, the way that man sat at your bedside these forty or so odd days—that man loves himself some you, child! He really and truly does. I've known a lot of wolves in my day—some good—some not so good—but that one is good through and through. Not perfect. But good. If I was a betting woman, I'd put money on my word and swear. That man is gonna do right by you until his dying breath. You can hold me to that, fo' sho!"

I can't help chuckle and blush hearing Miss Melvina speak of Jackson with such admiration. Then again, I've never met anyone who didn't think well of him. I can see why.

Melvina bends over and checks the terrace door border as if she's inspecting the work Lorien did when all the water came into the suite from before. For some reason, however, her quietness is disturbing.

"And what about Dalcour?" I question delicately, almost afraid of her response.

"Oh, my boy?" she answers brightly as she lifts up and leans against the walls adjacent to the terrace. "Now I know why you and my baby are Fated. You're so much alike. Stubborn as a mule but always on the run like a bull. I swear you two see red everywhere!"

"I've never seen Dal run."

"Ha! Lucky for you then! Because when he runs, it never turns out for no good," she replies darkly. Turning to peer out the terrace, she exhales and then folds her arms at her waist and looks back at me, searching my face. "Well, I guess you can handle it now, so I'll tell you. First, let me ask, did Dal, as you call him, ever tell you why he can't come into the Tavern?"

"Well, no as a matter of fact he hasn't. But Javier did mention something about him bringing those women through the Tavern. Is that why?"

"Please, child! I hate to be the one to tell you, but Dalcour's been bringing women in and out all his life. And that's a mighty long time, let me tell you. But no, it wasn't them women. It's what he did before he brought the women. You see, the night before you two became star-crossed infatuations with each other, Dalcour went on a rip and binge as I call it after dealing with some of his calamities with his brother. Things got pretty bad. A lot of people died. His inner beast was in full swing. It took everything for the Guard to clean up behind him. So when he came into the Tavern, we weren't sure if he was on another binge or what."

As she speaks, memories of his beast coming toward me the night after the ball haunt me. I have no doubt had I been anyone else, I'd be a dead woman right now.

"I've seen it. His beast, I mean."

"Then you know what I'm talking about. See, when you run, you disturb the balance of nature. When he runs, if you will, he not only disturbs nature, but life itself. To be honest, I don't know if the world can handle you two!"

"I guess we're quite a pair, aren't we?"

"Well, only you can answer that, Damina. *Are you and Dalcour a pair?* Or is it Jackson? That's your choice for sure. And I am certainly not biased. I'm sure you'll be fine either way. Frankly, I'd hate to be you. It's like choosing between better and best. You can't go wrong."

"Whatever I choose, somebody will get hurt."

"I suppose there's some truth to that. But even you can admit there's some freedom in the truth. Right? So why don't you do for them what you wish was done for you. Give them your truth. How they handle it is on them. You're not responsible for their response."

"You're right. The only thing is, right now, all I care about is Dacari. I need to get her back from Decaux."

"Ha! Ha! Good luck with that!"

"What do you know of it?"

"I know enough to know whatever Decaux wants, it's best for everybody to let him have it."

"I'll never let that monster have my cousin. Father or not!"

Melvina stares at me for a moment before pushing herself from the wall and walks toward the door as I hop off the bed to my feet. Twisting her mouth as if she's trying to bite back her words, she turns away from me and then turns back again. "Listen, Damina, I know you want to get your cousin and I can understand your reasons. Sure, Decaux is a monster, but before he became a monster, he had a heart. Don't just go running in, guns a blazing to get your cousin. Try to understand what he wants and if it makes for your good and the good of the world, then so be it. Because I can tell you this, it was his broken heart, and the broken hearts of those before him that got us all in the mess we are in. Nowadays, nobody is looking to fix the monster's heart—maybe that's where we've all gone wrong. Just my two cents."

Her sentiment puzzles me. How can she even think I'd allow my cousin to remain with someone so vicious and cruel? Dacari doesn't know what she's gotten herself into. I may not understand everything, but I do know I need to get myself together so I can save my precious cousin Dacari.

"Thanks for the talk, Miss Melvina. I appreciate it. I should probably get going," I reply with a forced smile.

As if she sees straight through my bull, a sly smile forms at the corner of her mouth and she grabs my hand. "Well, I don't think you need to parade through the Quarter in your nightwear. Your aunt came and took most of your things, but you left a few things in the drawers and such I think you can use. There're some toiletries and such in the bathroom so you can freshen up too. Once you're out, I'll send some dinner up for you. You can't go on being nobody's hero if you can barely stand. After that—by all means go and save the day!" Melvina says with a dismissive laugh as she walks toward the door.

"But I—I."

"I won't take no for an answer, missy. Besides, I told your men folk and aunt you were here and safe. They'll be along to come get you after a while. Now, go and wash yourself. You were sleeping for over forty days, you know. You ain't gonna have no man left to choose if keep walking about stanking and such!"

Chapter 6

The cool breeze of the meadow lingers upon my skin as the glistening shimmer of the golden leaves of the Great Oak radiates all around me. Leaning on the bark of the tree, I run my hands through its wooden ridges, delighting in each brush of timber tickling my fingers. Although not quite an eclipse, the sun and moon combine, creating obscure rays of both light and dark, forming the most beautiful refraction of light and shadow I've ever seen.

A strong wind blows, funneling golden leaves around me in a cyclone of lights as it pulls me from the reach of the Great Oak. My heart falters at the loss of the peace I felt under the shade of the tree and I drag my feet, hopefully to tow even the slightest root with me. Only a golden path of the fallen leaves follows me, and I marvel at the meticulous adornment of each leaf on the earth beneath me.

Once more, a powerful gale force pulls me at its will, lifting me from the ground as the windstorm of golden leaves encase around me, heating my body like a furnace. Looking down, I am high and suspended at the equal height of the Great Oak and I peer through the leafy funnel and see the maze garden and waterfall just beyond my reach. Despite my present entanglement, I find solace in the sight of the labyrinth and my budding dismay dims.

Turning to counter the rotation of my leaf-bound funnel, I cause enough force to press my way through its bluster, plunging me forward toward the maze. Lunging against the strength of the wind, I feel small droplets of dew spraying from the waterfall, landing delicately upon my face. There is a comfort to each drop as it attaches itself to me, and I feel both resilience and strength return to me.

Another comfort I did not expect hits my face as well.

Cinnamon.

He smells of cinnamon.

The inviting spicy and sweet scent fills my nostrils and a wave of peace reinforces my growing defiance as the rustling leaves trail my flight. Nearing the clearing of the maze, I hear the fluttering of what seems to be a hundred butterfly wings as I see a bright blue ember shield the entrance of the floral labyrinth. With it, the overwhelming and hauntingly distinct aroma of jasmine and lavender envelops me in an iridescent dew of sparks of gold, red and electric blue.

Firecracker like sounds pop and fizzle all around me as powerful jolts of both jasmine and lavender pierce into my every pore, digging deep beneath my flesh and weaves through my veins like shocks of electricity.

Now, even the sweet and spicy aroma of cinnamon is faint as each floral pulse forges its way through my entire being. Once more, I feel my strength depart as I slowly drift to the ground and away from both my view of the waterfall and the maze.

Taking one final whiff, I no longer detect the comforting smell of cinnamon as I freefall toward the earth beneath me. Again, the piercing, flapping sound of butterfly wings grows stronger and I look and see an emerald and turquoise wave of butterflies blanketing me as I drift slowly to the ground.

Knock-knock.

Uh-oh!

When did I fall asleep?

How long have I been sleep?

Crap!

One would think being in a coma for over a month would be more than enough sleep! All I recall is taking a shower after Melvina left. I put on some clothes and laid back on the pillow for a hot second while I listened to the street band play. Now it's dark outside.

Full on nighttime!

The courtyard sounds busier as night life in the Quarter awakens. That can only mean the Tavern is picking up with guests for the evening. I need to get out of here.

Once more, the knocking outside my suite grows louder as I sit up on the bed and try to gather myself. My mind is still foggy with all the cares of the day from when I awoke. So much has happened. Then it hits me. Dacari. I need to find Dacari! I don't have time for this.

The knocking grows incessant and I look toward the terrace and consider my odds at taking flight back to the mansion. But I know the truth. It's not a good idea. I'd likely draw too much attention. Besides, I barely feel as if I have the strength to try. However, I don't feel like being bothered by whoever Melvina has sent up, nor do I care to see either Bessie or Javier.

That would not be a good idea.

Walking toward the terrace, I look over my shoulder and consider my options. I'd hate to fall flat on my face and look like a fool in the courtyard either. I take a whiff toward the door and the strong smell of Cajun cooking hits my nose and my stomach instantly rumbles in response.

Lingering too long in the comfort of the delightful smell of the food, I'm startled when the door opens and my muscles tense. Although I still feel a tad weak, I'd gladly take on anyone with adverse intentions.

"Well, aren't you a sight for sore eyes!" I hear a familiar sweet tone shriek. Only a silhouette frames the doorway and I press my eyes tight, trying to make out the intruder. "Okay, I know the last time you saw me I was a fright, but goodness girl, I'm not the Ghost of Christmas Future!"

"Kate?" I reply in disbelief as her golden tendrils outline her perfectly rosy cheeks. Bright, sea-blue eyes stare back at me as her shiny pink painted lips smile wide. Stepping beyond the shadows of the threshold, I'm in awe at the lovely woman standing before me. Gone are the razor-sharp fangs, beady red eyes, and reptile-like features. The woman before me now is beautiful. Jaw-dropping. Runway model beautiful. Not that she wasn't lovely when I first met her, but now everything that was once perfect has been perfected. If that's even possible.

Wow!

"Yep! It's me! In the flesh, chica! So how'd I turn out? An upgrade, huh?" Kate laughs and spins on her heels and lands in front of the floor-length mirror, sifting her fingers through her bouncy, long, blonde hair. "And look at these," she says, pointing at her boobs. "Mother Nature finally gave me what no push-up bra could ever do for me. Oh, and let's not even talk about this world class a—"

"I get it! I get it, Kate! Can you pull yourself from the mirror for a moment to give me a hug?" I reply, turning Kate toward me, throwing her into my embrace. Even hugging Kate feels different from before. She smells of wildflower honey and her arms are strong at my back. Her skin shimmers with a dew-kissed hue, but her touch is almost as cold as ice.

Holding her face in my hands, her blue eyes flicker with a flash of scarlet and her bright smile fades as she presses her cheeks into the palm of my hand. Closing her eyes, she exhales deep and one lone tear falls to her cheekbone. Kate quickly pulls away, wiping her face, and turns toward the door.

"Well, come on in, Maria! Don't just stand there! I'm sure Damina is starving!" She fakes a laugh and wipes both eyes, escaping into the bathroom. "We weren't sure what you were in the mood for, so Mel just had them send up a little bit of everything," Kate adds peeping her head out of the bathroom door with a wad of tissue stuffed between her tiny fingers.

"Thank you, Maria," I say softly as she nods dutifully and continues arranging the table.

"Sorry, Damina," Kate says as she rounds the corner. "I guess I can't get the thought out of my head."

"What?"

"The thought that I almost hurt you that night. I mean, I tried to—"

"Is there anything more you need, madam?" Maria quickly interjects as she walks back to the doorway.

"No, that will be all, Maria. Thank you," Kate answers and Maria closes the door swift.

"I guess she was in a hurry," I chuckle.

"Yeah, well, I think I give her the creeps. She's not too fond of Scourges like me. Can't say I blame her!"

"Oh, Kate, don't talk like that. Besides, it's not your fault."

"Perhaps. But the fact remains. I'm a wretched monster!"

"You're not a monster, Kate! You're—rehabilitated!" I say with a bright smile, thinking on how Brae once described herself.

"Now you sound like Braelyn!"

"Exactly!"

"Well, I've only been out of the taming wells just shy of two weeks, so Maria has good reason to fear me." Kate slumps onto the bed, propping her knees to her chest while wrapping her arms around her legs. Resting her chin on her knee, she looks up at me and I see more tears pool the corners of her eyes.

"Please, Kate, don't cry. It's okay," I say as I sit next to her on the bed, squeezing her shoulders.

"It's not, Damina! I could've really hurt you that night at Saint Roch's," Kate exclaims.

"But you didn't."

"But I could have. What's worse is I wanted to! And do you want to know what's even worse?" Kate shouts back, pushing up and away from me. She heads toward the door and grabs the knob tight before pressing her head against the door frame. "It's taking everything in me to resist you right now," she mumbles with a low snarl.

"I know, Kate. I know. And since I can hear your thoughts, I have to say I'm very proud of your progress," I softly answer as she turns to face me, surprised by my admission. While I haven't gotten a handle on how to minimize the thoughts of others from rampaging my mind, Kate is unknowingly giving me good practice. From the moment she crossed the threshold, I've heard almost every thought she's had. Whether it's her newly abhorrence of the smell of the crab broil platter, annoyance of Maria's well-placed fear of Kate, or thoughts of me smelling like a vanilla cupcake— Kate's mind has been on speed dial from the moment she stepped in here.

"Sheesh, Damina! Girl, you could've reminded me you could hear my thoughts! That would've saved me a lot of grief! Goodness!" Kate laughs, turning back toward me as she leans against the door.

"Well, you know this is all still pretty new territory for me too."

"I guess we're both gonna have to figure this whole supernatural stuff out, huh?"

"That's right. And no worries. While we're figuring it out, I'll make sure you never find out if I taste like a vanilla cupcake!

Although had you said chocolate—"

"Oh my gosh, you heard that too? I'm so embarrassed. I'm such a monster!"

"It's okay, Kate!" I laugh.

"Look, you better eat something before your ride gets here. Miss Mel said they were coming to get you soon," Kate says sweetly as she sits back on the bed and lifts the silver serving tray, revealing the food.

"So, Kate, how did all this happen? I mean, how did you turn into a vamp—"

"A Scourge, you mean? Well, let's see, missy, I'll tell you my back story if you promise to eat. And just so you know, the stink of crabs and oysters is really muting your otherwise tasty cupcake-like scent, so I'd eat it up—if you know what I mean," Kate teases.

"Fine. I'll eat. Now spill it."

"Okay, okay. You Altrinions sure are pushy! That's probably why Miss Mel can't wait to get you back to Lord Marchand!"

"You know Dalcour?"

"Know him? I wish. I've only seen him from afar. And my what a sight he is! I see why you're stumped! I'd be in a pickle too if I were caught between him and that Jackson! He's quite a looker too!"

"Enough about them! Back to you," I snap as Kate's admiring thoughts of both Jackson and Dalcour flood my mind. Although I can't blame her for having good taste, I certainly don't need images of her swooning over Jackson's chest as he trained Mark in the taming wells or memories of her ogling each step Dalcour took as he walked through the Civility Center.

"Sorry—I guess my thoughts are quite vivid," Kate says, biting her fingernails as her cheeks flush with warm pink. "Anyway, back to my transformation—it was the night of Abahana's second line. After Cal couldn't find you at the cemetery, everyone went out looking for you. We figured in all the confusion of the funeral parade you may have gotten lost. I was deep in the middle of the line when I saw Brian drop you off. I screamed your name, but you didn't hear me. I kept trying to get near you, but with all the festivities I got pushed further away. When you went into the alleyway, I followed you but by the time I got there that Mikkel—that Altrinion—Vitreous—Vamp traitor, as Brae calls him was reeling from the hurting you gave him. He saw me in the middle of the alley and attacked me."

As Kate recalls her encounter with Mikkel, my eating halts as my heart plummets knowing I am the epicenter of the demise of yet another person I care for.

"*This is all my fault*," I gasp.

"No, Damina, don't you dare do that to yourself. This isn't your fault!"

"But it is, Kate! Can't you see? If you weren't out looking for me—if I'd never come here—"

"Honey, please! You are certainly not to blame. Look, I live in the supernatural capital of America! Something like this was bound to happen. Look around here! I live in a B&B run by a hybrid and her wolf hubby and brother. Not to mention the Bulwark who keep watch. And you know what? None of this is nearly half as bad as the battered life I lived with that wretched Alonso before Bessie found me. So guess what—thank you!"

"Kate, please!"

"No, seriously. Thank you. After Mikkel turned me, he dropped me off at a Scourge nest. I was alone. Cold. Afraid. But most of all, I was hungry. It was a hunger like I never felt before. The first night I traveled out with the nest to eat was when I ran into you at Saint Roch's Cemetery. If I hadn't seen you—if you hadn't called my name and reminded me of who I was, I don't think I'd be sitting here with you today. As a matter of fact, I know I wouldn't. Because it was your belief in me that got me through. Brae told me she would've killed me if it weren't for you. So yes, thank you.

It was my gratitude that got me through every grueling trial Titan put me through in the taming well—but here I am!" Kate's eyes beam as she recounts her transformation. I take special note of her lingering thoughts of Titan but opt to chug down the tall glass of iced tea, hopeful to force her abandoned feelings about Titan aside.

I really need to get a handle on this mind invasion!

"I'm glad you were able to make it through, Kate. Really. So you're back working here at the Tavern?" I question Kate. Forcing a few bites of food into my mouth, I'm hopeful the tastiness of the meal would overpower Kate's mental dump.

"Well, not full time. This is only my third time, and Titan only lets me out of his sight for a few hours. Although he'll never admit it, I'm sure having Miss Mel here as Bulwark is the only reason why he tolerates it as he does. He said he normally puts young vamps like me at Razors or one of Lord Marchand's places in Baton Rouge. But since Miss Mel vouches for me, and with the hybrids Bessie and Javier keeping watch, he knows I won't cause any fuss. Still, every night he's here like clockwork to get me. He's such an overlord!"

"I bet," I reply quietly as I sip the remaining tea, giving Kate a knowing glance.

"Okay-okay, you got me! I mean heck, Damina, he's a hunk of a man! Of course I'd think he's hot!"

"I didn't say a thing!" I say with my hands raised in surrender.

"You didn't have to! I'm sure you're mowing around up there," Kate laughs, tapping her forehead. "But not to worry, Brae told me enough about Titan to know I don't stand a chance." Dipping her head, Kate twirls her blonde coils between her fingers, dangling them at her nose as she tries not making eye contact.

"My lips are sealed," I gently reply, tapping her shoulder.

A soft knock at the door breaks through our forming awkwardness and Kate jumps at the chance to answer. I am surprised when Lorien stands at the entrance. He gives Kate a shy smile before leaning over Kate's shoulder and waves at me.

"Hi Lorien!"

"Hey Lady Damina!" He responds with a smile brighter than I thought him capable.

"So I hear I have you to thank for bringing me here safely. Thank you, Lorien."

"Aww, it's nothing really. I—I'm glad I could help."

A sincere smile crosses his face as he watches me, and I see something in his eyes I didn't expect. Admiration. I'm not sure what has changed his once uninterested and unbothered youthful demeanor, but this look is a better fit.

"And well, Lady D," Lorien begins as he moves past Kate, entering the suite. "I just wanted a chance to apologize."

"For what, Lorien?" I ask.

"For being such a louse to you before. I mean, I know I was rude to you. But after everything you've done to help the Dunes and really just the whole community—I just wanna say thanks," Lorien adds as he leans in for a warm hug.

"Wow! That's so sweet!" Kate exclaims.

"Lorien, really, you don't have to thank me for anything. Besides, you really weren't that bad."

"But I could've been better. I mean, I didn't even give you a chance. I just thought you were just another high and mighty Altrinion like some of the others. But that wasn't fair of me. I didn't give you a chance—a real chance to show me—to show us all who you really are."

As he speaks, thoughts of Aunt Delia pain my heart. Like Lorien, I haven't given my aunt a chance to explain. Instead, like Melvina implied, I ran away before giving her an opportunity to share her side of the story. All I thought about was *how I was hurt*—how everything has hurt me. It's not my daughter missing. It's her daughter. *Her Dacari*. And it's my job to help my aunt. Not judge her.

"You know what, Lorien, all of us could take a page out of your book. Sometimes we don't give others the benefit of the doubt as we should. But you've inspired me! Which means I have somewhere I need to be."

"Actually, that's the other reason I came. I wanted to let you know your ride is here," Lorien answers with a broad smile as he extends his hands and helps me off the bed.

Chapter 7

Arriving outside the Tavern, the Quarter is everything I expected. Full of bustling night life from street jazz bands, art on the sidewalk, and the delightful fragrance of the finest French Quarter cuisine wafting through the air. Everything in me wishes I could bask in both the beauty and charm of the City, but alas, I cannot.

Despite my musing, I am all too aware of the fact I need to set things right with my aunt and do whatever I must to recover Dacari from Decaux's dangerous grip.

"Hey, Ms. Nicaud!" Mark's bright and chipper voice breaks through my darkening contemplative state. As he steps out of the black SUV, my mouth drops at the sight of him. He's gained what appears to be twenty plus pounds of pure muscle. He also seems much taller than I recall and now with a thickening goatee and mustache, he no longer resembles the boy I remember.

He is a man.

And a distinctly dapper looking one at that!

As he strolls toward me, heads turn in his direction and no

woman in eye view can stop staring at him. It almost reminds me of how I've seen people ogle Jackson. Almost. More important, I'm thankful Brae isn't here right now. I'm sure she wouldn't take too well to all the attention her beau is attracting.

While a small part of me wonders why neither Jackson nor Dalcour came to pick me up, I'm thankful to have a moment without the eclipse of my heart.

"What's good, Lorien? Hey there, Kate!" Mark says with a dashing smile. Both Kate and Lorien share brief pleasantries with Mark, but he keeps his attention toward me. With his arms outstretched, Mark passes both Kate and Lorien with a wide grin that almost matches his wingspan. Tossing his large biceps around me, Mark's hold on me is strong as he lifts me slightly from the ground as we hug.

"I'm sorry," he begins as he lowers me to the sidewalk. "I guess I'm just so happy to see you—awake! When I heard you were up, I begged them to let me off post so I could come see you! I mean really, Ms. Nicaud, you really had *me* scared. I'm glad you're okay."

"Thanks, Mark! It's good to see you too! And apparently there's so much more of you to see," I tease, tapping his hulking arms.

"Oh, you can thank Lord Nashoba for these pythons! He's got me on his regimen. I can only hope to make it to his insane fitness level. But then again, some of this is just all part of the alpha package!" Mark laughs as he opens the rear passenger car door.

I turn back to Kate and Lorien and quickly wave goodbye before getting in the back of the truck with Mark. As I slide in the backseat, I notice a driver I've never seen at the wheel and shoot Mark an awkward glance.

"Yeah, we'll talk about B, first let's get you buckled in," Mark says in a hushed tone. "Hey Tony, I'm gonna sit in the back with Ms. Nicaud—that is, if you don't mind?"

"Only if you promise to stop calling me Ms. Nicaud," I reply.

"We'll do, Ms.—Damina!" Mark laughs.

Once Mark is in the back with me, he taps the driver on the shoulder and presses a button overhead and a privacy glass raises.

"Tony is one of our newer drivers since—"

"Since what? Is Brian with Dacari?" I quickly ask, knowing I rushed away before I caught the remainder of the footage.

"No, Damina. Brian isn't with Dacari. But after Dacari's disappearance, he has been out with the Guard more regularly to look for her. He even said he had a few contacts from Abahana who were very skilled trackers—wolves—but expert trackers. So I figure with Brae and Brian on the job, we will find your cousin soon enough. Besides, he hasn't wanted to hang around the mansion as of late. Seeing Jerrica the way she is right now is just too much for him. So I guess he's trying to keep busy—"

"What do you mean? What's wrong with Jerrica?"

"Oh, man! I thought they told you!"

"Told me what? What happened?"

"Well, I don't know how much you recall from that night, but Jerrica was attacked. She was stabbed pretty bad with an *Obsidian Blade*. Or what we call a Mercy."

"What is a Mercy, Mark?"

"It's the deadliest blade known to supernaturals. The sole purpose of a Mercy is to end the life of a supernatural. It literally strips the supernatural essence from a person and is the only blade deadly enough to kill an Altrinion."

Grief fills me as haunting images of Jerrica's eerily still body in Claudia's arms replay in my memory. Flickering flashes of Jerrica's torn flesh ripped from her chest down through her waist grip me with dreadful fright. With everything going on, it's no wonder I pushed these thoughts to the far corners of my mind.

"How is she doing?" I mutter.

"Not good, Damina. Not good at all." Mark's grim expression tells me more than I need to know, even though I cannot read his mind. "She can't keep blood down, and without it, regeneration is impossible. She's—dying."

Tears freefall to my cheekbone at Mark's words and I can't help thinking how all of this must be affecting Dalcour. Not only did he have me and my cousin to worry about but also his best friend. Now, more than ever, I know I've got to stay strong.

I'm not the only person hurting.

Taking a deep breath, I force a small smile as I see Mark's posture shift from his earlier and typical cheerful persona to a more staunch reserve, I softly squeeze his shoulder. "It's going to be okay, Mark. I don't know how—or when—but I know we'll all be okay."

"You sound just like Brae," Mark says with a covered grin, as he rests his hand on his chin.

We both laugh as the SUV pulls up to the mansion, and I'm surprised just how fast we've arrived. The driver opens our door within seconds of our arrival, and I sense his urgency. Besides, it doesn't take a genius to know both Jackson and Dalcour are the likely architects of my expedient return. I can almost feel their shared brooding emanating from the steps of the mansion.

"Let's get you inside. I do have my orders," Mark says with a cracked smile and his palm outstretched to assist me out of the truck. Taking his hand, I almost wish I could read his mind. A part of me feels like he wants to say something more, but he's towing the line. While it's clear, he's loyal to Dalcour, I can also see he's grown fond of Jackson.

I guess I am not the only one caught in the middle.

"Take me to Jerrica first," I quickly say, breaking through the awkward silence that has loomed between us as we made our way toward the mansion.

"Um, I was instructed to bring you right back to the guys and your aunt," Mark quivers with an uneasy glare. I knew he felt torn between both Jackson and Dalcour, but this seems like something more.

"I know you have your orders, but I need to see my friend. If it weren't for Jerrica bringing me here in the first place, she would have never gotten hurt. I can't help feeling responsible. And who knows where the road will take me once we begin tracking down my cousin. I need to do this now, Mark."

Mark stares at me, uncertainty dancing in his eyes with lips squeezed tight. "Okay, Lady D! But you've only got a few minutes," Mark says as he lightly pulls my arm and leads me past the parlor toward Jerrica's suite. "Before we go inside, there's a few things I need to tell you."

"Spill it."

"Like I told you in the truck—she's dying. No regeneration. Nothing. She's well over three hundred years old, so her decay is kind of—"

"Oh, I get it," I respond as a rank odor tinged with sage wafts pass my nose.

Mark looks me over once more before his eyes search around us and I can tell he is still unsure about taking me to see Jerrica. Tightly clutching his forearm, I nod toward the door and smile, hoping to reassure him this is the right thing to do.

As the door opens, I see Charlotte sitting in the small chair next to Jerrica's bed. She is patting Jerrica's forehead with a towel and holding a large cup with a straw to Jerrica's mouth. Ms. Zamora is also in the room and she walks around muttering an unknown language with a wad of smoking sage in her hand.

Neither Ms. Zamora or Charlotte acknowledge our entry and I look to Mark wondering if I should say anything to either woman. He hunches his shoulders, likely sensing my unease, but he keeps us moving forward to Jerrica's bedside.

Nearing Jerrica, my stomach coils in knots at the unsightly view before me. Gone is the beautifully breathtaking woman I remember. Decomposed flesh now replaces once shimmering and flawless skin. Sunken and grayed out eyes cover what was once almond shaped pellets of sea-glass emerald. Rotting and chafed lips with long, protruding fangs supplants a once supple rose-tinted mouth.

A low gasp whispers through me at the full revelation of Jerrica's unsightly form as I watch her chest cave in and expand as she works to take deep breaths. Mark firms his grip on my shoulders and pulls a chair to the bedside as I sit next to Jerrica.

Lowering her mummified-looking hand toward me, Jerrica sucks in air as her head turns toward me and she attempts a smile.

"You came," she wheezes as she wraps one finger around my thumb and tugs it.

"Of course I did, my friend," I reply, trying not to wince at the putrid smell emitting from Jerrica.

"I held on for you as long as I could, but you slept a long time," she adds with a weak smile.

"I'm sorry. Felt like a catnap to me. But I'm here now."

"I see you came alone. I'd hoped he'd at least come with you," Jerrica wheezes once more, peering over my shoulder.

"I'm not alone. Mark is with me, Jerrica," I answer, tugging her finger and nodding to Mark behind me.

"She's not talking about me, Lady D," Mark quietly replies.

"There is no need to talk about him either," Ms. Zamora exclaims, halting her motion behind Charlotte.

"Are you talking about Dalcour?" I question Mark.

"He hasn't been to see her in a while," Mark says with his hand over his mouth, lowering his eyes.

"Not since the first night," Charlotte whispers, and I realize it's the first time I've ever heard her speak.

Mark and Ms. Zamora share awkward glances, but I squeeze Jerrica's finger and smile at her, hopeful to regain her attention. Although I plan to confront Dalcour and understand why he hasn't visited his friend, I don't want Jerrica to focus on that right now. Jerrica smiles back at me with a knowing glare, and I am quickly reminded she can likely hear my thoughts as well.

We spend the remainder of the time laughing about my flight through the Quarter in my pajamas and a trench coat as well as sharing news of Kate's new transformation. However, our time is short lived when Ms. Zamora insists we leave so Jerrica can rest. As much as I don't want to go, I know even in her staunch stubbornness, Ms. Zamora is right. Jerrica needs her rest and I need to find Dacari.

Chapter 8

Butterflies swarm my stomach as we walk through the mansion and stirring images of Dacari with Decaux and the truth of it all once more flood my mind. So many questions ravage through me. And while the *why* and *how* of it all perplexes me, it is the *who* which disturbs me most.

Decaux Marchand.

Decaux Marchand is Dacari's father.

Once more, I am reminded that the nightmare which has become my life is not as beautiful as I hoped.

My breathing is raspy as we near my suite and I can almost smell the effervescent and perfumed scent of my Aunt Delia luring me with each step. She's always had a floral and warm smell, but today is the first time I can detect she's something more.

More surprising is that it's only her fragrance and Mark's wolfy aroma permeating my pathway. I can't smell Jackson or Dalcour nearby. Only faint traces of their scent remain. Odd.

Rounding the corner of the hall as we near my suite, I am shocked to find Vonnie seated in front of my door.

"Lady Damina!" Vonnie exclaims in a tone brighter and more pronounced than her usual timid manner. Pushing the chair back toward the wall, she speeds toward me faster than I can blink. "You have no idea how worried I was for you. I am just so thankful to see you doing well—and awake!" She professes, bringing me into a tight embrace.

"Well, I guess that's my cue!" Mark adds. "I better get back to the CC and make sure things are secured for tonight or both Jackson and Big D will have my head. Besides, I think you're in capable hands now."

"Thanks, Mark!" I answer as I try to wiggle out from under Vonnie's tight hold.

"My pleasure, Lady D! Oh, and by the way, don't worry about tonight."

"Tonight?"

"Yeah, Big D has me running routes with Jackson tonight to keep us Dunes wolves occupied and away from all the—um festivities. But I think Brae will be back to the mansion by then to keep you company. Just be sure to stay close to the mansion tonight with Brae, Vonnie and your aunt. No more—PJ flights, please!" Mark shouts and chuckles over his shoulder as he hurries down the hallway.

He's out of eyesight before I have a chance to get more information. Turning to Vonnie, her tight-lip expression tells me there's more to the story. Just as I part my mouth to inquire further, the botanical scent of peonies in bloom fills the atmosphere and I look over Vonnie's shoulder to see Aunt Delia's tall frame shadowing the doorway.

"Damina," Aunt Delia begins softly, "It's time." Her words are short, but her tone delicate. I don't have to read her mind to know she's dreading this moment more than I can imagine.

Vonnie steps away from the door and pulls her wooden chair closer to the entrance. "I'll be right here should you need anything,

Lady Damina." She says in her typical dutiful pitch.

Nodding briefly, I smile as she takes one more squeeze of my hand just as I cross the threshold. A warm and vibrant golden ray of light shines between our clasped palms as a pulsating current runs up my arms. Everything in me wishes I knew what Vonnie just did, or at least what it meant. And as painful as it is, I almost wish I could read her mind, but it appears Bulwarks are just as immune to Altrinion telepathy as wolves.

Despite my budding interest in my newly supernatural state, seeing my aunt once again reminds me all my effort and attention should be on finding my cousin.

"So I suppose you have many questions," Delia begins as she gestures toward the bench at the edge of my bed. I am almost irritated that my aunt has returned to her more commanding manner, but I opt to ignore it for now.

"And I presume you have the answers," I quietly reply. Although I try to stifle my newly dominant stance, the twitch of my aunt's nose lets me know my tone isn't quite what she expected. I suppose even my aunt will have to learn, I'm not the same woman who left D.C.

I have changed. In fact, everything has changed.

Aunt Delia remains standing near the door. She looks out into the hallway before slowly closing the door shut as she lets out a loud sigh. If I didn't know better, I'd think she was holding herself back from racing out of the room just to avoid this conversation. Not that I wouldn't understand if she decided to bolt. It's been my go-to as of late. Still, this is Aunt Delia we're talking about. I can't imagine her running from anything or anyone.

Especially not me.

Pressing herself against the wooden doorframe, she tilts her head back and gulps a heap of air, exhaling once more as she brings her eyes locked with mine.

"Then we should start with the elephant in the room," she starts.

"You mean Decaux?"

"Yes. Dacari's father."

There's a long pause as we both stare at one another while my aunt locks her hands together, grasping at her wrist and twirling her fingers through the charm bracelet Dacari and I gave her this past Mother's Day.

"How, Aunt Delia? How is Decaux even a part of the discussion? I mean, did you know who Dalcour was all this time too? And if everything I've heard about Decaux is true, how could he be her father? Even more, how could you be with someone like him?"

"You mean like you and Dalcour?"

"That's not the same! Not even remotely!"

"But isn't it?"

"Hardly."

"Well, that's not what I thought back then. In fact, I wasn't so different from the woman you are now. Although, I was much younger when I met Decaux. Only eighteen. But I was quite a mess. Still grieving over the loss of my father, I guess you can say I was in a bit of a rebellious state."

"You? Rebellious? I can't even imagine."

"Ha! Ha! You would think I've been sprayed with a starch-iron spine from birth, but that's the furthest from the truth. Now, your mother on the other hand was born perfect. At least everyone thought so. Even me. And especially your grandparents."

"But Papa Roux wasn't her father—right?"

"Ah! That's right, Dalcour told me you discovered that part so far. Well, for all intents and purposes, Papa Roux was your mother's father. *Our father*. He raised her and loved her as his own. Sometimes in my envy it felt like he loved her more than me. Now, don't get me wrong, I loved your mother—how could I not? She was a wonderful sister. Just a wonderful woman through and through. But I loved my dad and longed for the attention he gave to her so freely. As a parent myself, I can now say that I think he went out of his way to ensure she never felt abandoned or alone since she wasn't his."

"How can you be so sure?"

"Because I've had to do the same for you. At least I've always hoped you've felt a parental love from me. Although I know I could never replace your parents."

"Of course, Aunt Delia! Of course! There's never been any doubt."

"I am glad to hear it. Even though I know I must regain your trust." Aunt Delia pauses once more and bites her lip as she looks up at the ceiling, blinking her eyes rapidly and forcing her tears aside. Everything inside me wants to embrace her, but she clears her throat, pushes away from the door, and walks toward the window, opening the blinds as she settles into the adjacent wingback chair.

"I'm more interested to hear of this wild and rebellious side of you that I never knew existed," I interject through the awkward silence.

"Ah, yes! My rebellion. Well, a few years after Papa's death I became eligible for my alpha valuation and I longed to finally have the one thing that made me feel close to him. But due to the state of the New Orleans wolves there was no one of rank or available for my valuation. The thought that I'd be just another rankless Dunes wolf infuriated me. It angered me more than anything! So much so, I looked high and low—mainly low for anyone who could help me achieve my alpha status. That's when I met him."

"Decaux." My croaky tone almost chokes me as the wretched frog makes his return in my throat.

"Yes," Aunt Delia lowly responds with her eyes fixed on me. Twirling her fingers through the blinds above her head, I realize this is the first time I've ever seen my aunt fidget.

She's nervous.

Clearing her throat once more, she blinks rapidly again and

turns her attention back toward me, but this time averting her eyes from me.

"Well in the beginning it was all about helping me find someone of rank for my valuation."

"I don't understand. Why would Decaux even be interested in helping a wolf?"

"Oh, well I'm sure he had reasons even I still don't understand but mostly it was because I was a Dunes wolf. You see, Damina, the Dunes wolves—the Beta Primes—were largely responsible for the guardianship and protection of Altrinions."

"I thought that was the job of Alpha Primes like Jackson?"

"I suppose technically all wolves are to protect the sacred Order of Altrinion, but the weight primarily fell to the Dunes. After the Dunes were cursed, Altrinions were hunted to almost near extinction. Decaux always said he wanted to realign the Dunes to their places of prominence. I suppose he saw me as a steppingstone to that end."

"And he obviously saw you as much more," I add softly.

"That he did. But his affection was not lost on me. I know I should've known better, but I allowed my rebellion to override my intellect. For the time I spent with him, he was dutiful, kind— loving."

"How can you say that, Aunt Delia? Everything I've learned of Decaux Marchand is that of a monster!"

"Yes and a monster he was. But never to me. At least that's what I told myself. I was so blinded by my need to be something special—an alpha—that I was willing to overlook everything I knew to be true. You see, Damina, we were raised with stories of the vicious Marchand brothers. The Altrinion-Vampire lords."

"You mean stories of Decaux?"

"No, she said it right. The Marchand brothers." The tenor of Dalcour's voice is more pronounced than usual. Just as he speaks, a powerful whiff of his jasmine and lavender scent implodes the space between us as he watches me from across the threshold. His jaws are tight as he searches my face, likely trying to discern my mood. His eyes are glassy and his posture rigid. Everything in me wants to wrap myself in his embrace, but only a half-cracked smile is all I have to offer. Seeing him still stirs me in ways I never thought capable. Relaxing his mouth slightly, his eyes alone tell me he wants to hold me just as much as I desire to be held.

"What do you mean, Dalcour?" I quietly reply, tightly squeezing the wooden bars of the bench, desperate to calm the frenzy brewing within me at the sight of him.

Dalcour's smile widens and I know he's pleased to know he's affecting me. "Well, my brother, as wretched as he may be, is not the sole progenitor of all things evil. And whatever villainous acts he's committed could equally be laid at my feet!"

"Please, Dalcour! You're nothing like him! You're not a monster!"

"Oh how I wish that were true, Beautiful. Although being with you surely keeps the beast at bay," Dalcour answers with a broad smile and chuckle as he saunters into the room.

"There was a time I thought I could keep Decaux's beast at bay, but I wasn't enough. You see, the day I discovered I was pregnant with Dacari was the day I saw the beast in full bloom," Aunt Delia interjects.

"So I take that to mean, you left before ever telling him you were pregnant," Dalcour asks.

Delia nods with her eyes only and bites her lip once more, terror filling her countenance.

"What did you see, Aunt Delia? What made you leave him?"

"It was the most vicious thing I'd ever seen in my life. He and some of *his disciples* were tearing through the flesh of young children. There was no way I could raise a child with such a monster! I left that day and never looked back!"

Aunt Delia's eyes are vacant yet filled with horror as she

recounts her last moments with Decaux. I want to know more, but I'm afraid of forcing her to relive such torment.

"This actually makes a lot of sense!" Dalcour exclaims, breaking both me and Aunt Delia from our speechless state.

"What do you mean, Dal?" I question.

"Outside of his first love, Calida, there was only one other time where I can recall my brother being in love. Only one other time I can remember him forsaking his savagery."

"How can you say that, Dalcour? Didn't you just hear my aunt? He was killing—feasting on children!" I shout.

"Well, sure, but—"

"But what, Dal? How can there be any reasonable excuse?" I protest, bothered by his apathetic appeal.

"Because it is clear his heart was beating." Dalcour gazes at me, hopeful I comprehend his intent.

"What? I don't see what difference," I answer confused.

"Oh, my!" Delia loudly gasps. "I can't believe I hadn't thought of that!"

"Of what? What am I missing here?" I yell, rising up from my seat.

"Damina, remember when I told you how you settled the—um—beast within me? How only you were able to assuage the wickedness within me? Now do you also recall how only my love for you reignited the beating of my heart?"

"Yes, I remember," I mumble as I watch the wary glances both Dalcour and Aunt Delia exchange. While faint to most mere ears, I hear the pace of Dalcour's heart quicken and I know he's nervous.

Taking a deep sigh, Dalcour swallows the thick air in his throat and turns away from my aunt, keeping his eyes locked on me. "When our hearts beat, it also signals the liveliness of every part of us. Do you understand what I mean?"

"No. I'm certainly missing something."

"I mean every part." Dalcour whispers, shooting a cautious

glance over his shoulder and away from my aunt and then down toward my waistline.

Just before I have the chance to try to force my way into his thoughts, Aunt Delia forces a loud groan and makes her way between us. "What he's trying to say is that their reproductive man parts stop shooting blanks!"

"Aunt Delia!" I gasp at her admission. My aunt has never been crass, and witnessing this outburst of hers is both unnerving and intriguing.

"Hold on, are you saying you can't—unless your heart is beating?" I question Dalcour.

"Oh, no! Believe me, Beautiful, my performance isn't hindered at all beating heart or not—but the only way one such as I can be a father is with a beating heart. We have to be fully free of the curse."

"So, you mean to tell me Decaux's heart was beating when you two were together. Are you trying to say you two were in lo—"

"Don't!" Aunt Delia protests. "Don't even speak it! Now look Dalcour, I've never thought of such since that day. How could I? Seeing him the way I did, it never dawned on me that he—that we—the thought is ridiculous!"

"Delia, as ridiculous as it may seem, it must be true. How else could Dacari be his daughter?" Dalcour counters.

Aunt Delia paces between us, chewing on her nails and fidgeting with her bracelet. I've never seen her so jumpy. This is obviously more upsetting to her than I imagined.

"So I suppose Dacari was conceived in love," I say softly.

"No! It can't be!" Aunt Delia shouts back as she continues her pacing.

"Well, that does put some of the puzzle pieces together. But I guess I'm still confused about one thing," Dalcour states.

"What is it, Dal?" I ask.

"While I recall my brother taking a brief pause from his bloody deadline, I vaguely remember him mentioning a woman that had him in a tizzy. He begged me to get an Altrinion elder to perform an alpha valuation. But if memory serves me correct, it was for someone named Anne."

"Yes, it's my middle name." Aunt Delia tepidly replies just shy of a whisper.

"Right that is your middle name? But I thought you hated that name. You always told us to never use it—" Just as I turn to face my aunt, the puzzle pieces Dalcour mentioned become clearer. "You didn't want him to find you. Is that right, Aunt Delia? You told him your name was Anne?"

Aunt Delia nods, keeping her eyes closed shut as tears race down both sides of her cheekbones. "It's all my fault, Damina! I'm so sorry," she sobs as she plops down onto the ottoman.

"Auntie, it's okay. I know Dacari may be upset right now, but once you tell her everything, I'm sure she'll understand." Sitting down next to her, I try to grab her rigid shoulders to console her, but she pulls away from me, tossing her head to her knees.

"Delia, is there something more?" Dalcour asks in a dark and gritty tone. I gaze up at him and see his posture now just as stiff as my aunt. While I know our telepathy doesn't extend to wolves, a reminiscent eerie feeling makes me wonder if I'm the only one in the room out of the loop.

"Aunt Delia, please it will be okay."

"No, my darling. It is not okay, and it is all my fault. You have me, and me alone to blame."

"Please, there's no one to blame for anything," I reply, reaching for her hand, but she pulls away.

"Let her finish, Beautiful," Dalcour darkly mutters.

"He's right, Damina. There is more. As I've said, I told Decaux my name was Anne."

"Well yes. We've covered that part."

"Anne Nicaud. I told him my name was Anne Nicaud. I used

your mother's married name."

"What? Why? Why would you do that? And what does that have to do with anything?"

"It has everything to do with everything!" Aunt Delia shouts back. "Nicaud, Damina. I told him my name was Nicaud. I knew he was a monster! I knew what I was getting myself into. No one just leaves a Marchand! And no one leaves with something that belongs to him!"

"You mean Dacari? But Aunt Delia, she will understand—"

"No Damina, it's not Dacari! It's you!"

"What? I don't understand. What are you trying to say, Aunt Delia?"

"He came for me, Damina. Decaux. The only name he had to go on was Nicaud."

"No, Aunt Delia. I know you're not trying to say—"

"Damina," Dalcour says in a muted breath as he walks toward me, concern glaring in his eyes once more. I retract from his advance, keeping my gaze set on my aunt.

I need to see her when she says it with my own eyes.

"It was Decaux, Damina! Decaux killed your parents."

Chapter 9

Like a vacuum rammed down my throat, air is sucked from my lungs.

I cannot breathe.

Aunt Delia's words hang over me, suffocating every ounce of oxygen from my being as an unbearable tightness locks my body stiff.

I cannot move.

Disbelief fills my mind as rage floods my soul. How can such a thing be true? When will my torment come to its end? Will there ever be a cessation to my continual grief?

Palpitations fill my chest as my heart strikes relentless blow after blow, likely seeking to escape the nightmare that has become my life. Dread looms inside me, digging like the grim reaper's scythe in my soul, tearing me apart, piece by piece. There is no consolation that will assure my comfort nor any vindication capable of forfeiting my vengeance.

And a great vengeance I will have.

"Explain." My muted words slip through gritted teeth as I lay hold on my chest, working hard to recapture my breath.

"I am so sorry, Damina! I am!" Aunt Delia cries, her face a waterfall of tears.

"Explain!" I shout back as a gale force blows through me, shaking the walnut shutters on the windows while the furniture rattles in response to my fury.

"Damina, calm down!" Dalcour's commanding tone is lost on me. As much as I want to unleash my fury on him for his attempt at controlling me, I refuse to take my eyes off my aunt. I need to know everything she knows, and I need to know now!

"I don't know how he found me, but he must have tracked me down. Using your father's name, Nicaud, must've lured him to our whereabouts. I'm sure his henchmen thought they were pursuing me, but they came in contact with your parents and you instead."

"And so he had my parents killed?" I grumble, my eyes sharply fixed on Aunt Delia.

"I am so sorry, Damina!"

"And you've known all these years that it was your ex—Dacari's father that was the cause of my parent's death and you never told me? I'm almost thirty, Delia! How could you keep this from me?"

Staggering toward me with her hands clasped and pleading, Aunt Delia drops to her knees, wailing in pain. "I—I thought I was protecting you—both of you! I thought keeping the truth from you and Dacari would keep you from this—this supernatural world. I only wanted to keep you both from it and away from Decaux. I never wanted to hurt you, Damina!"

"What's going on here?" I hear Jackson yell from behind me, but I don't turn to face him. Peering over at Dalcour, I see his stance has stiffened as he watches my aunt bowing in tearful agony at my feet. He looks up and over my shoulder at Jackson and back toward me. But something is different.

While I haven't fully grasped the full reach of my powers, I've become skillful in telepathy. Yet, I can no longer read Dalcour. His mind is closed to me. As much as I try to pry I cannot. He's not letting me. Even worse, every attempt I make to break through his iron-clad fortress pains me like a sharp shooting migraine.

What is he keeping from me?

"What do you know of it, Dalcour? Did you know about this?" I shout, taking a step back and away from both Dalcour and my aunt.

"Damina, babe, what's going on? We could feel the tremors all the way down in the training room at the CC," Jackson questions with his hand now rested on my shoulder. And though anger rages through me, I am slightly comforted by the coolness of Jackson's breath at my ear and the warm and inviting fragrance of his sweet and spicy scent seeping through his pores.

Dalcour stoops to the ground, wrapping his arm at Aunt Delia's waist and rubs her shoulders, but he keeps his gaze locked on me and Jackson.

"Answer me, Dalcour! Tell me the truth for once!"

"For once?" Dalcour echoes, disbelief filling his eyes.

"Yes, for once! Now tell me, did you know your brother killed my parents? Is this just some other inconvenient information you've chosen to keep from me until you deemed appropriate?"

"What? Lord Marchand, tell me that's not true!" Jackson pleads. Dalcour only glances at me and Jackson before pulling my aunt's arm over his shoulder, attempting to steady her.

Slowly rising to her feet with Dalcour's help, Aunt Delia wipes her face with her wrists and stammers toward me. Jackson squeezes my shoulders to hold me steady, likely fearful of a repeat of my response earlier today. But this time I have no instinct to run.

That time has passed.

"Damina, darling, please!" Delia begins. "This isn't Dalcour's fault. This is me. It is all me! He was after me."

"And Dacari," I seethe through my teeth.

"I suppose. I don't know how he found out I was pregnant, but I'm sure he was furious when he realized what I'd taken from him," she responds.

"Oh, and so do you also suppose he was so furious that he'd want to kill his own flesh and blood, *Lord Marchand*? Please do tell!" My spiteful rant does not go unnoticed by Dalcour as I spit my words past my aunt. Still, he remains staunch. An immoveable mountain. "What, Dalcour? Cat got your tongue?"

Dalcour's skin reddens beneath his pecan-texture and his eyes ablaze in a fiery hue. A part of me fears the return of the beast I saw on our first night together after the ball. Yet, an equal and unsubdued part of me wishes the beast would make his return.

I wholeheartedly welcome the challenge.

Nonetheless, Dalcour remains an obstacle. The more I try to break through the veneer of his mind, the more painful it becomes for me. There is no ibuprofen powerful enough to evade the crash and burn panging through my head as I attempt to read Dalcour Marchand.

My aunt steps toward me, blocking my view of Dalcour, and lifts a single cautionary hand. "Damina, I know it must be hard for you to understand, but you must believe me when I tell you not a day has gone by that it didn't tear me apart to know the part I played in your parent's death. While yes, it's true I kept this secret also away from Dacari, it's you who lost the most. I know there is nothing I can do to take this pain away from you, but please know with everything in me, I am sorry. Please know I love you truly and I am sorry for everything."

Aunt Delia's voice cracks as she speaks, and I am instantly surprised that somehow, the hard shell forming at the center of my heart collapses. With every stuttering cry, I cannot help recalling vibrant memories of my aunt's love toward me. Flashes of her teaching me to swim, skate, and tucking me in the bed at night flow through my mind. Flickering images of us dancing in the kitchen with Grandma Roux and Dacari puppeteer my heart strings, cracking the hard casing of my emotions.

My aunt has been more than an aunt. *She mothered me.* It is Aunt Delia who helped me become the woman I am today. Her only fault was falling in love with a monster and wanting to protect her child. And it is that child—my cousin Dacari, to whom my thoughts now belong. If nothing more than ripping her from the clutches of the monstrous viper that stole everything from me, I must douse the embers of fire burning within me.

This is about Dacari.

Not me.

And I refuse to let Decaux Marchand take anything else from me!

Fire-wrought tears blast from behind my eyelids as I pull away from Jackson's firm hold, rushing into Aunt Delia's welcoming embrace. Streams of water flow between us as I squeeze her tight with the warmth of our cheekbones meeting as I rest at the nape of her neck.

"It's okay, Aunt Delia," I confess with contrition. "I know how much you love me! You've shown me every day! I love you, auntie!"

Squeezing one another tight, it feels as though we've remained clasped for ten straight minutes. Maybe longer.

"Damina, how can you forgive me?"

"There's nothing to forgive, auntie," I begin, gently pulling away. "Of course, I wish you'd told me sooner. But even that wouldn't change the fact that it was Decaux who took my parents away from me."

"Well, he wasn't alone. His henchmen—and she—"

"They don't matter," I interrupt, trying hard to comfort Aunt Delia. "All of it can be laid at the feet of Decaux Marchand. More importantly, the only thing that matters now is getting Dacari away from him. That's the only thing that matters."

Aunt Delia smiles as she takes hold of my face and kisses my forehead. A few more tears fall from her eyes, but this time she looks different. Lighter. It is as if a thousand tons have been lifted from her shoulders. I can only imagine how difficult it has been to carry around such a burden for so long. With Grandma Roux gone, I am sure the weight of it all became insufferable. But my aunt is the strongest woman I've ever known, and not even the threat of Decaux Marchand could hold her hostage.

Smiling back at her, I exhale with one singular thought: *I come from good stock.*

Looking over Aunt Delia's shoulder, I feel a wispy air blow through the room and I now see Dalcour has disappeared.

"He left," Jackson states in a low and throaty tone. "Are you okay, baby?"

Turning to see Jackson standing just beyond the doorway, I am surprised to find him without a shirt and only jeans. His skin glistens like diamonds with his sweat and his damp hair clings to his shoulders and it's the sexiest image I'd never expect to find before me.

I instantly feel my mood lighten. At least a little.

"Um—where did he go?" I mutter, trying not to gawk at Jackson in front of my aunt.

A small smile etches beneath his thick goatee, reaching his eyes, and once more I feel the presence of Jackson Nash, stir the very core of me.

"I'm not sure, I didn't notice. All my attention was on you," he softly answers in response. His fragrance seems to penetrate every inch of my being so much that I feel it clinging to my skin—if that is even possible. A long pause hangs between us as whatever remained of my fitful rage buckles at his whim.

Exhaling once again, my ire dissipates as my eyes linger upon every inch of Jackson's sculpted form before me and I am instantly lost in the awe of him. Air refills my lungs and the suffocating chokehold which held my state is gone at the sight of my *ex*-fiancé.

Yet, and despite everything, Jackson Nash is more than capable of both calming and weathering my storm. *My, what this man does to me.*

"Ah-hem, if you two will excuse me." Aunt Delia's willful interruption of the shared longing between Jackson and I don't go unnoticed. "I—I um need to go freshen up. I'm sure I look a mess after all of this carrying on! Don't worry, Damina. I know we still have things to flush out so we will finish our discussion," Aunt Delia states as she excuses herself from the suite.

Chuckling at her awkward departure, Jackson and I keep our gaze set on each other for a few more minutes before he takes careful steps toward me. Gesturing to the bench at the foot of my bed, we both sit as he takes my hand in his.

"Are you sure you're okay, baby?"

"Yes, Jack, I'm fine."

Narrowing his eyes and tightening his lips, Jackson searches my face, taking my chin in his hand. "Damina? This is me you're talking to now. I think I know more than anyone when you're not okay."

Lowering my eyes to avert his narrowed gaze, my attention falls to his chiseled chest and glorious abs and warmness erupts all over me. Once more, Jackson takes my chin in his firm grasp, holding me steady until our eyes meet.

"You've—um changed quite a bit since my slumber. You've always been fit and all—but—wait a minute! That brings up a good point. Why are you walking around the mansion half dressed, Jack?" I shoot him a scouring glare, but he doesn't fall for my pretense and only smiles in response.

"Okay, so I see you're avoiding the topic of you. Well, if you must know, I was down in the CC training with Mark. With the uptick in Scourge sightings and his upcoming valuation, he has a lot of learning to do. Besides, we couldn't do much in the Civility

Center tonight with all the Altrinion-Vamps and vampires making their way in for some sort of gathering."

"Oh, that's right. Mark did mention he'd be patrolling with you tonight."

"Now, tell me what's going on in that pretty little head of yours. Seems like you're upset with Dalcour?"

"You know me well, Jack. Still, it's kind of weird to talk about this with you," I mumble, averting my eyes from his intense gaze.

"Baby, I know this is a weird time for us now—but no matter what we've always been able to talk with each other. Always." Jackson smiles once more, and I know his words are sincere.

Knowing Jackson refuses to let up, I take in a deep breath, hopeful I'll have the heart to tell him how I really feel—about another man. "Well it is not that I'm upset with him as much as I am confused and irritated. I mean, he blocked himself from me! He wouldn't let me read him. Now why would he do that unless he had something to hide."

Jackson stares at me for a few seconds, lets out a huge sigh, before patting his knees as he gets up from the bench and walks toward the window. Folding his arms, he narrows his gaze once more, breathing out another sigh as he parts his mouth to reply. "Well let me ask you something, Damina. Can you read my mind?"

"Jackson, you're a wolf. You know telepathy doesn't work on you."

"And if we were all human, you wouldn't be able to read his mind then either, right?"

"What are you getting at Jack? And why does it sound like you're defending him?" I snap, rising to my feet.

"No need to cause an eruption, baby. I'm just stating the facts."

"The facts? Well, the fact is his wretched brother Decaux is responsible for my parent's deaths. All I wanted to know is whether he knew about this or not. He only had to tell me the truth!"

"And what if you didn't like that truth? What then?"

Once more, the bastard frog has returned, and I have no words. I want to reply, but I cannot. Staring at Jackson, I am both perplexed and impressed he's siding with Dalcour. Although I can't imagine why.

"Damina, the truth is, that I'm much like Dalcour. Neither of us are capable of controlling our brother's machinations. I have just about as much control over Keiron as Dalcour has over Decaux. No matter your grievance with Decaux, you can't make it about Dalcour. As much as it pains me to admit this, I know that his affection for you is true. Even more, I know you feel the same."

"Jack, I—"

"It's okay, Damina. I'm by no means stepping aside, but I'm not a simpleton. Somehow in the brief time you two shared, you grew to love him and for that, I take full responsibility."

"Jackson, please. I didn't mean for any of this. I don't want to hurt you—either of you."

"I know, Damina. I know. But the truth is had I not allowed my brother's interference we'd be married by now. And yes, you'd know the truth of your ancestry, but you'd learn it the right way. Not like this. Perhaps even Dacari wouldn't be missing. Even that I lay at my feet."

"No, Jack! You can't take responsibility for all of this. I don't blame you—"

"But you should! I do."

Jackson turns away from me, looking between the window shutters. I can't help admiring his lean torso and taut musculature of his back as he leans along the windowpane. Everything inside me is so torn between him and Dalcour, but nothing has doused the fervor of my feelings for him.

My, how I love this man!

"Jackson," I softly reply, running my hands up the seam of his back. Small electric currents rivet through my fingers as I graze the fabric of his flesh, sending chills up my spine. As Jackson turns back toward me, my hands now rest at his chest and it takes every ounce of strength to contain every lustful impulse swarming through me.

"Yes, Damina." Jackson's gentle response sends a cool breeze of his aromatic scent through my nostrils and I inhale and savor every molecule as it floods the entirety of my being.

"You aren't to blame for any of this. I know we have a lot to work through and we will sort this all out. Together. But all that matters is Dacari. I know that now."

Taking my hand in his, Jackson closes his eyes and takes a deep breath. "You're right, baby. That is precisely what you need to tell Dalcour. He deserves to know that as well. I saw you fight through your emotion and forgive your aunt. Now, you've got to do the same for him. No matter what you think, he's holding back. Just trust he'll tell you when he's ready."

I can hardly believe the man before me. Just when I did not think he could amaze me more than he already has, I sit here before him speechless. One thing is now clear. I am not the only one who has changed in our time apart. I do not know what kind of truce Jackson and Dalcour shared during my slumber, but I now know my choice between the two will be harder than I thought possible.

Chapter 10

"Knock-knock," Mark says standing in the doorway. "I'm sorry, I hate to break up this tender moment, but we really need to get going, Lord Nashoba. Lux has already sent word of Scourge sightings picking up near the edge of the Tremé. Cedric and Abigail have also called in evidence of Skull as well. Probably best we get out in front of it."

"Looks like someone is chomping at the bit!" Jackson laughs over his shoulder. "I've never seen anyone so eager to patrol."

"He's definitely more excited about all of this than me!" I hear a familiar voice call from the hallway.

"Gregory!" I exclaim as I see his hulking form round the corner into my suite. I am strangely delighted to see him. "You're still here?"

"Why, of course! You know, I'd never let this guy out of my sight for too long. He'd never make it without me, you know," Gregory teases.

"Whatever your reason, I'm glad to see you, Gregory," I reply.

"And I am glad you are finally awake. Really, Damina."

Gregory answers with a warm smile that matches his sentiment.

"Boy, you D.C. folks sure are mushy! We don't have much room for that here in the N.O.! Now, Lord Nashoba, I brought you a shirt. I figured you wouldn't want to go around half dressed. Plus, I'm sure Lady D wouldn't think too kindly of that. Am I right, Lady D?" Mark chuckles.

"Good looking out, Mark!" I playfully reply.

"I guess I hate to be the one to tell you, Damina, but Jackson won't be needing that shirt tonight or any clothes for that matter," Gregory announces, snatching the shirt from Mark's hand before he can toss it to Jackson.

"Oh, really?" I question, narrowing my gaze at Jackson.

"Not to worry, baby," Jackson tenderly responds with a tight squeeze of my hand and planting a soft kiss on my cheek. "Tonight we're running on nothing but pure lupine steam!"

"You hear that, little wolf? We are donning fur coats only baby! No full moons needed! You ready for that, Mark?" Gregory jeers.

"Are you serious?" Mark leans into Jackson. "We're wolfing out? Tonight?"

"Only if you think you can handle it," Jackson answers.

"Why wouldn't he be able to handle it? I've seen Mark turn before. You've got this, right Mark?" I add.

"Well, tonight's not a full moon, Damina. Nor is this any type of fight-or-flight response. As an alpha—or better, a Prime—Mark has to learn to harness the moon's power without its apex in full effect. We call it a privilege of the Primes. And tonight it's up to our young Beta Prime to master it."

"It's your first master class, little wolf!" Gregory continues, roughly patting Mark's back.

"Lady D is right, I've got this!" Mark announces, proudly pounding his outstretched chest. While he's grown considerably since my slumber, he still appears small with both Gregory and Jackson in the room.

"Then I suppose that is our cue! Baby, I'll see you tomorrow. Please stay in and close to the mansion tonight. Tomorrow, all roads lead to finding Dacari. You'll need a good night's rest." Jackson says while kissing my forehead before he heads toward the door.

"Don't worry, Lady D, I'll keep him safe!" Mark adds with a glint of self-assurance.

Jackson looks over his shoulder at me and grimaces, raising his brow with apprehension. Gregory pats his shoulders as he exits, mouthing *I got him covered!* behind Mark's back and laughs.

"Bring my baby back in one piece or on all fours!" I hear Brae shout from the hallway. All the men laugh and tease Mark as they make their way through the mansion and Brae rounds the corner into my suite, gleaming with a wide smile.

"Hey Brae!" I say as she walks into the room. I am happy to see her.

"Hey yourself! Looks like someone's chiseled bodice brought back the sunshine into your life. It's okay. I won't tell Dalcour!" Brae scoffs with a snorkeling cackle.

"Yeah, and you didn't do Mark any favors swooning on him in front of the guys either!" I tease.

"Touché!" Brae laughs with a faux curtsy. "Anyway, now that you're no longer in flight mode, I thought we'd catch up. There's been a lot of changes since your days in respite."

"I can only imagine. But we can play catch up later. I'd rather find out what more you know of Dacari's disappearance."

"Of course, Damina. What do you want to know?" Brae questions as she sits down on the ottoman.

"Well, for starters, I'd like to know why Dorine and Padma helped Dacari? I mean, they barely know her."

"I thought it was strange at first too, and then I remembered."

"Remembered what?"

"That Decaux sired both Dorine and Padma," Brae quietly responds.

"You mean he made them vampires?"

"Yes. And with that comes a certain obligatory loyalty."

"So are you saying they took my cousin to that monster out of a sense of obligation?"

"Well not exactly, Damina. I mean, she did seem like a willing participant." Brae stares off and I can sense there is more meaning behind her words.

"What are you *not* saying, Braelyn?"

"Wow! Now you are really starting to sound like Dalcour—calling me Braelyn and everything!" Brae hisses back at me, working hard to stifle another cackling grin.

"I suppose it is a fair question, Ms. Dortches," Aunt Delia replies over my shoulder, now standing in the doorway. "Are you implying my Dacari wanted to see that monster Decaux?"

"I am sorry, Delia. I'm not implying anything, just stating facts."

"What facts, Brae?" I question, gesturing Aunt Delia to sit beside me on the bench.

"Okay, I guess it's not going to be easy to say or hear for either of you, but here it goes. We have reason to believe Dacari has been trying to find her biological father for quite some time."

"What makes you think this?" Aunt Delia questions coolly. She seems more irritated with Brae than bothered by what she said.

"Well, for starters, it appears that more than six months ago Dacari hired a private investigator to look for her father." Both my aunt and I gasp at her admission, and Aunt Delia grabs my shoulder, squeezing it tight. "That should have been the end of it because the investigator hit a wall and she didn't have any more contact with him. But then something changed."

I watch as Brae shifts her focus squarely on me and an eerie tingle moves up my spine.

"It seems the week you came here, Damina, she started a new investigation."

"I wonder what made her restart her search?" I ask, leaning toward my aunt. Aunt Delia only shrugs her shoulder, shaking her head in reply.

"More like who?" Brae adds.

"Who?" Aunt Delia questions and we both look at one another in confusion.

"I believe her name is Allyson. The same Allyson who sent you to Bessie's tavern, Damina."

"My friend Allyson? How can you be so sure?"

"More important, why would my Dacari go to that wretched girl for anything?" Aunt Delia protests.

Both Aunt Delia and I stare at Brae who puffs out her cheeks, blowing her bang away from her eyes while swiping her fishnet gloved hand through her hair. She continues gazing at us with a troubled glare before patting her knees and sitting up in the ottoman, prepping herself on what to say next.

"Just spit it out, Brae," I state. I already know I won't like what she's going to say, but I'd rather get it over with.

"Okay, so your friend Allyson apparently linked Dacari up with an investigator here in New Orleans named Sincade DeLuca."

"CADE!" Aunt Delia shouts in horror, jumping up from the bench. "Please tell me my baby didn't have any dealings with that demon!"

"You know Sincade DeLuca?" Brae replies, surprised by my aunt's reaction.

"Who is Sincade or Cade?" I question, looking between both women.

Once more, Aunt Delia paces the floor, distress filling her face. She looks more worried now than she did when she revealed Decaux had my parents murdered.

"Aunt Delia, tell me what's wrong! Who is this Cade person?"

I demand. Aunt Delia never ceases her pacing but clasps her hands together as if she is praying, muttering incoherent words under her breath.

"Damina," Brae starts, "Sincade DeLuca is an Altrinion-Vampire who serves as an investigator of all things supernatural. You know how we have the Guardians who work to clean up supernatural messes? Well, sometimes there are things that go unexplained and folk call on Sincade to look into the matter further," Brae answers.

"No, Damina! That is not who Cade is! Cade is nothing more than a murderous leech! I don't know what he's posed as these last twenty or so years, but he is no mere investigator."

"How do you know him, Delia?" Brae probes, searching my aunt's face intently.

Aunt Delia remains silent, biting her nails as she now leans against the closet door.

"Aunt Delia?" I say her name once more, hopeful to pull her from her trance.

"I met him in Paris when I was with *him. Decaux.* Cade was one of Decaux's wards. Whenever Decaux needed someone to herald his rallying cry—Cade was more than happy to lead the charge. He was extremely loyal to Decaux back then. I doubt much has changed." Aunt Delia's words are flat and emotionless as she looks straight through me as she speaks. Intuition tells me something more is haunting her, but I choose not to push her.

"Well I've heard his past is sketchy to say the least. But whose past isn't these days? I know I can't claim innocence from my own past," Brae says softly. The hint of remorse in her tone is hard to miss, making my heart sink. "At any rate, Decaux sired Cade, so it's no wonder he's loyal to him!" Brae says, snapping out of her short-lived shame.

"Wow! So who didn't Decaux sire, Brae? So far, you've named at least three progenies," I reply.

"Yes, that's because of his master plan to one day dominate and bend the world to his will," Aunt Delia chides.

Watching my aunt, it is clear she loathes Decaux. But it is also obvious there was a time she cared deeply for him. Seeing her with such a stream of disgust marring her face is new to me.

"Alright, Brae then tell us how this all fits in with Allyson and my cousin. And how would Allyson know Cade? Did she look him up online or something?"

"Damina, a person like Cade wouldn't be found online. Only those either in or close to the supernatural community would know to look for him," Brae answers.

"What are you saying, Brae? Are you saying Allyson is some sort of supernatural too?"

"No, darling," Aunt Delia quickly interjects before Brae can respond. "What I do know is that wretched girl has known what you were for quite some time. Do you recall her anger toward Jackson on your birthday?"

"When he got me the red car? She was mad because he didn't know it—"

"She was mad because he wouldn't reveal that he was a wolf and that you were Altrinion. She promised to tell you that day. That is until I told her we would not be bullied by her and warned her to stay away from you and our family."

"Aunt Delia, you threatened her?"

"It's no more than she deserves. And after Jackson recently told me he suspects she is a Jadeite, I do not regret my decision!"

Brae gulps in a heap of air at my aunt's admission, and now she too paces the floor. "Now it all makes sense!" Brae announces

"I'm glad it does for you because none of this makes sense to me!" I stand, frustrated.

"Damina, Jadeites are extremist," Brae begins. "They are a faction of humans loyal to wicked Altrinions like Mikkel called the Vitreous Order."

"The Vitreous. Keiron mentioned them earlier. He also said something about Dacari being more than a hybrid because of her father." Fear grips me as more puzzling pieces fit together in my mind. The thought of Keiron's sinister smile as he spoke erupts goosebumps all over my body. "He knew. Keiron knew who her father was all this time." I mutter to myself. "But what about Allyson? How does she fit in? Are you saying she was working with Keiron? Is Decaux a part of the Vitreous?"

"Decaux? Of course not! He has long loathed their kind!" Aunt Delia exclaims.

"Delia is right, Damina. I doubt Decaux had any dealings with Mikkel or any other Vitreous. Allyson, on the other hand—it's hard to be sure. I mean if she is truly a Jadeite, she'd want to please her Vitreous overlords and leading Dacari to Decaux wouldn't help their cause." Brae states.

"How so?" I question.

"If Keiron is right about Dacari being more than a hybrid, the Vitreous would want nothing more than to end her."

"I'd never let them get their hands on her!" I shout back.

Brae ignores my outburst but keeps her sights square on Aunt Delia and the two exchange wary glances.

"Damina, if Allyson sent Dacari to Cade, ultimately leading her to Decaux, it is possible she did it to protect her after all."

"Doubtful!" Aunt Delia snaps back. "That girl does nothing for the benefit of others."

"Aunt Delia, please. Jadeite or not—all things aside, I know Allyson. She wouldn't purposely put Dacari in harm's way. Maybe she—"

"Maybe nothing, Damina! I don't trust Allyson, and neither should you!" Aunt Delia's tone is sharp and her stance clear. I don't want to argue with her, so I settle within myself to table the topic of Allyson.

"Look ladies, no matter Allyson's intentions, or Cade's

assistance, it's clear that somehow Dacari found her way to Decaux. Now we must figure out how we get her back," Brae states, looking back and forth at me and my aunt.

Aunt Delia's expression remains tight and her posture stiff as she stands still with arms folded against the closet frame. I don't have to read Brae's mind to see her disappointment in my aunt's response. Even I can tell my aunt appears somewhat ambivalent to both Brae and her position on Dacari. Still, I refuse to let neither my aunt's petulance nor disagreeing stance turn me from our combined efforts to find my cousin.

"You're right, Brae. And we will do just that. Get Dacari back. That is all that matters now," I reply. Brae responds with a slight and sheepish smile, averting her eyes away from my aunt's cold glare.

Brae's phone buzzes in her pocket and she quickly answers. "Hey baby. What's up? Wait... slow down. You did what?" she laughs.

"Aww poor little wolf! Gotta get his woman to carry his gear!" I hear Gregory tease through the phone.

"At least I've got a woman!" Mark lashes back. "Boo are you coming or what?"

"No worries baby. I'll be there shortly. Let me just make sure Vonnie is here with Lady D first," Brae replies, looking up at me with a shy smile.

"Oh I've got a woman. She just doesn't know it yet. But she will when we get her back from that psychopath father of hers!" Gregory shouts. My eyes nearly pop out of their sockets at Gregory's revelation, and I pull Brae's arm in shock.

What about Brian? I mouth to Brae. She shrugs her shoulders in response, still laughing at Mark and Gregory's banter.

"And man the ways I'll finally show her—"

"Gregory!" I hear Jackson caution. *"A little decorum, please!"*

"My apologies, Jack-O! Little wolf! Come on, let's get it moving!

Is your girl coming or what?" Gregory shouts.

"Just ignore that big lug nut, Mark! I'll be there soon! Bye baby," Brae says quickly, ending her call. "Sorry Damina, I've gotta bounce. Mark brought all his gear with him and since they're going full wolf, he can't leave his weapons out in the open. He's leaving them at post, so I'm going to get them for him and then I'll be right back. I'll just make sure Vonnie is around first."

"I'm right here," Vonnie answers softly, now standing at the threshold.

"Great! Okay, I promise I will be right back. Maybe we can finally catch up on the mansion stuff or watch a romcom or something when I return." Brae is out of my eyesight in a flash and both Vonnie and I chuckle at her rushed departure.

Vonnie glances in the room and nods toward my aunt, who remains stiff and obviously annoyed with Brae. Turning back to the hallway, Vonnie points to her chair, mouthing that she's just outside the door while pulling it so that there's only a slight crack.

"So Aunt Delia, are you going to tell me why you chose to be so snappy with Brae? I mean, she's only trying to help. Without it, we wouldn't know Dacari was with Decaux—or where she was, for that matter."

Aunt Delia sighs, plopping down in the wingback chair near the window, resting her elbows on her knees to prop her chin. "Damina, darling, I know it seems out of character for me to be as huffy as I've been of late, but you must know this is all taking a toll on me. I've had to remain as strong and stoic as I could be while you were asleep. Now, I suppose it feels like everything is crashing down on me."

"I can only imagine how you must feel, auntie, but you no longer have to hold it all together on your own. You have me, Jackson, and all the wolves. Plus there's nothing Dalcour and Brae wouldn't do to help us get Dacari back safely," I reply.

Sighing loudly, Aunt Delia sits up straight in the chair, crossing her legs and folding her arms as she shakes her head in apparent disagreement. "Damina, look I know you care for *these people*—"

"*These people*? Really, Aunt Delia? They are no more otherworldly than you and me!"

"Please, Damina! Stop fooling yourself. They are monsters! Nothing more!" Aunt Delia protests.

"Wow! I guess that makes us monsters too!"

Jumping up to her feet, my aunt is square before me faster than I've ever seen her move. This is the first time I've ever seen even a hint of her supernaturality displayed. "We are no monsters, Damina! We are nothing like them!" She lashes back.

"Well those people—those monsters are the ones out there right now doing what they can to find your daughter! It is those monsters who took care of me for over a month. And if we're being honest, it's those very same monsters who not only told me the truth of who I am but fought tooth and nail for me at a time when everyone else lied to me!" I shout, digging my feet into the ground, pleading with my inner force not to overreact.

Aunt Delia's posture retracts, her brows lift with the tightness of her jaws softening and her eyes glass with water. She sighs once more, tilting her head toward the ceiling, working hard to fight back tears.

"I'm so sorry, Damina. I am. I know that Dalcour and Braelyn have been our allies throughout this entire ordeal. Most of all, they have cared for you, my darling. For that, I owe them my very life."

"Aunt Delia, I'm sorry I shouldn't have lashed out at you like that," I confess.

"No, you are right, my darling. They were there for you when I was not. No apology needed. Those facts are an undeniable truth," Aunt Delia begins as she resumes her pacing about the suite. "But there is another truth I want you to consider. I do not say these things to cause you distress, but I only say it out of concern—and

I might add, experience."

"I'm listening," I reply as I watch her saunter back and forth. Watching her expression, I am sure I won't like what she has to say next.

"When I call them monsters, I do so out of not only my experience with their kind, but the reality of who and what they are."

"Dalcour is an Altrinion like me, Aunt Delia! So what are you saying?"

"No, darling, not like you. He is an Altrinion yes, but something sinister—a cursed soul! A vampire!"

"Last time I checked, Aunt Delia, he walks in the sun. He is no longer cursed! The love we share lifted the curse of the sun from him!"

"Well, yes, but did it change his appetite?"

"What? What does that even mean?"

"Well, darling, you heard Dalcour earlier today, in order for his wretched brother to procreate he had to have been in love. Which means his heart was beating when Dacari was conceived?"

"Yeah, so?"

"It also means his heart was beating when he took the lives of those innocents as well! Their ability to walk in the sun changes not their venomous brutality! Legend even has it that Decaux's heart was beating when he burned New Orleans to the ground in 1788!"

"What? I don't believe you! Besides, whatever treachery committed by Decaux cannot be equally laid at Dalcour's feet. They may be brothers, but that does not make their misgivings the same. Either way, you don't know Dalcour like I do, Aunt Delia," I counter.

"Perhaps, Damina. However, let's not forget you only spent a week with Dalcour—I lived and spent two years with Decaux. I witnessed all his highs and lows. Darling, I know of what I speak.

Beating heart or not, their first and only true love will always be their own bloodlust. Of that curse, no woman has ever cured."

Both Aunt Delia and I stare at one another in silence. I have no words to say in reply.

Haunting images of Dalcour's red beast flash forward in my mind, erupting a trembling fear within me. Although I've made no decision between either Dalcour or Jackson, it pains me that my aunt doesn't know the loving soul who made a week at his side feel like paradise.

Still in silence, it is clear we are at an impasse. We are both too stubborn to back down.

A light knock at the door breaks our staring match and we both exhale, thankful for the interruption.

"Good evening ladies," Dranoel says, peering through the cracked door. "My apologies for the intrusion," he starts as he widens the door open.

"You're not interrupting anything," I answer over my aunt's shoulder, giving her a minute to dry her tearful eyes. Aunt Delia takes a deep breath and affixes a bright smile before turning around to Dranoel. I watch his eyes dance as he sees her, and I am even more thankful for the interruption. I can't help wondering if my aunt had a man of her own, she'd have little time to meddle.

"Hello, Dranoel! What brings you by?" She questions, her voice now bright and airy. My aunt sounds like a schoolgirl.

"Well, I have come to see if you wanted to grab a bite to eat? Khalil has the kitchen smelling like Cajun decadence! There's a lovely spot on the patio near the firepit. I thought we could go out there if that's okay with you."

"Oh, well—um—" Aunt Delia stutters and I'm shocked the bastard frog has leapt in her throat as well.

"Of course, Lady Damina, you are more than welcome to join us. You and Vonnie. Khalil has made quite a helping of food," Dranoel says shyly.

"No, I am okay, Dranoel. But thanks for the offer. Besides, I am sure my aunt could use the fresh night air."

Dranoel laughs, pressing one hand in his pocket and extending the other toward my aunt. "Well, shall we, my lady?"

Aunt Delia quickly glances over her shoulder at me with a bashful smile and a hand over her mouth and takes Dranoel's hand. "I'll come check on you later, Damina. Just please, think about what I said. There is a reason your father wanted what he wanted for you. *Because he is what is best.*"

My aunt's words hang in the room long after she leaves. It does not take a genius to know she was referring to my father's desire for me to marry Jackson. No matter how hard I try to push the inevitable aside, I know at some point I'll have to choose.

Overbearing as she might be my aunt is right about one thing. I've only spent a week with Dalcour. Maybe there is something I'm missing. Something I've been blinded to by my affection for him. I don't know. What I do know is today Dalcour Marchand was keeping something from me. If I stand any chance at making an apple to apples comparison of Jackson and Dalcour, all the cards must be on the table. The good and the bad.

Even more, I need to ruffle some tree leaves to see if either of these apples have worms.

Chapter 11

"I am sorry, but I must advise against this, Lady Damina!" Vonnie shouts behind me, pulling my arm. Her grip is strong and there is an unusual and stinging ache at her touch which stops me as I grab tight onto the door leading to the Civility Center. "Please, Lady Damina! It was both Lord Nashoba and Marchand's orders to keep you here and safe behind the walls of the mansion," she pleads.

Pulling away from her hold, I rub my arm, trying to cool the throbbing ache of her grip. Vonnie is much stronger than her small frame suggests

"Then tell me, Vonnie. You are a Bulwark, right? *My Bulwark?*"

"Yes," she whispers in response, her lips barely moving, and her eyes locked on me.

"So how are the words of Dalcour or Jackson stronger than mine?" I counter.

"Please, Lady Damina. Do not do this. Don't put me in this position. Besides, this is only for your safety!" She objects.

"My safety? Well technically, the CC is within the grounds of the mansion, so you aren't breaking any agreement. I just need to talk with Dalcour. It shouldn't take long. I promise I won't stay longer than necessary."

"You don't understand, Lady Damina. There will be others there. Scourge. Altrinion-Vampires. You are a pure-blood Altrinion. It is hard enough for Braelyn and Lord Nashoba to control their impulses and bloodlust around you, but to put you in the company of others is simply dangerous!"

"Well then it is a good thing I have you to protect me."

Vonnie's eyes grow wide in alarm and her bottom lip quivers at my words. Taking a deep breath, she bows her head and sucks her teeth. Gazing back up at me, her sky-blue eyes sparkle like diamonds in an almost blinding hue. Shimmering rays of light beam through her pores and she grabs both my arms, locking her eyes with mine once more.

Her hold is tight, but the stinging ache from earlier is now replaced with a warm glow of light that hovers over me like a forcefield.

"What is this, Vonnie? What are you doing?" I question, watching the glittering aura cover me like a blanket.

"It's a barrier light. As long as you are close to me, no Scourge or Altrinion-Vampire can touch you without enduring the pain of the sun."

"But what about Dalcour, Vonnie? Are you saying even he can't touch me?" I snap.

"Look, Damina, it's either this or nothing. I will not risk your safety. Not even for Lord Marchand. You said you wanted to talk to him. Talking doesn't require touching. Not unless you want to see him scorch and burn. Besides, it won't be the first time this barrier made you untouchable to Lord Marchand," Vonnie states with a stubbornness I thought was incapable of her.

"What do you mean I've been untouchable to Dalcour before?"

"That night during the fight with Mikkel and the others here at the mansion. When you saved Jackson, the Altrinion force within you created a barrier such as this to protect you. Only Jackson and I were able to care for you initially. Neither Braelyn nor Lord Nashoba could come in inches of you without feeling the lingering light of the sun upon your skin."

"I had no idea," I quietly reply as painful memories of that night echo through my mind. I still don't feel I have a true handle on everything since my awakening.

Vonnie squeezes my forearms, hoping to regain my attention. "Damina, if you still want to go to the Civility Center, these are the terms." Her voice is resolute, as Vonnie's gleaming eyes search my face for agreement. She is not backing down.

I am impressed.

"Well I suppose we have a deal, Vonnie. After you," I answer, extending my hand for her to lead us down the steps toward the Civility Center.

We make our way to the arched wooden door of the CC in no time and my heart flutters. Tinges of trepidation erupt goosebumps all over me as I fear what I'll see when the door opens. Thoughts of Titan clearing the room at Trieu's arrival my first night here send tremors through my soul. Like me, Trieu is an Altrinion and both Dalcour and Titan took precautions to ensure her safety. Even my aunt's words about the savagery of Decaux and her implication of Dalcour sharing such a trait grip me with fear.

No matter. I can't turn around now.

Taking a deep breath, I sigh, forcing down my remaining angst. The last thing I need is for Vonnie to sense the turmoil brewing within me.

"Are you sure about this, Damina?" Vonnie questions. Her luminescent eyes sparkle in the dark corridor, giving me a modicum of comfort.

"Let's do this," I quickly reply, hoping to the moon I sound confident. Even though Aunt Delia's words hang over me like a dark cloud, I push every thought aside. *Dalcour is not Decaux.* Like a mantra, I inwardly chant to myself as the doors open.

The doors open instantly at Vonnie's first knock, and a man I've never seen here before greets us both with a cagey grin. His bloodred gaze is chilling, but it's Vonnie's bright and diamond-like stare that keeps him at bay.

Everything about the Civility Center seems different to me than before. It's darker. Murkiness shrouds my vision, leaving all my other senses heightened. Headiness is ripe in the air, as is the thick and putrid smell of blood permeating the atmosphere. Rihanna's song, *Disturbia,* plays through the sounds system, fully mirroring the vibe of the CC.

As I've seen before, the bar is once again filled with vampires, both Altrinion and Scourge, delighting in the fountains of blood that pool at their whim. Yet, this time is different. Their bloodlust is more exaggerated than before. Not only do some lick the trails of blood from the floor, but now their lust is on full display. Pouring streams of blood into each other's mouth and kissing to delight in its shared taste sickens my entire being.

In the open lounge area, others are feeding on humans. Some seem somewhat coherent as they gaze off distantly while their wrists linger in the venomous snare of the vampire's mouths. Other humans lay still in the lap of their emptor as two or more take pleasure in the outpouring of blood from their necks, wrists, and ankles.

My heart sinks at the revelation: this is Dalcour's world.

Grabbing my forearm, Vonnie stops our pacing as she peers through the foggy view of the CC, likely looking for Dalcour. But he is nowhere to be found.

As strange as it sounds, even that is a glimmer of hope. Perhaps

Dalcour chooses not to indulge in such depravity. I can only hope.

"My, my, my, twice in one day, Lady Damina. Tell me you're not stalking me," Titan says with a haughty smile as he rounds a dark corner. His luminous gray eyes shine through the murkiness, as does his lustrous Cheshire smile.

"Hello, Titan," I answer flatly. I can't tell if he's flirting or joking, and that bothers me.

"Aww don't sound so glum, Damina," he says, his brow lowered with disappointment. "I'm quite aware you didn't come here to find me. However, I am surprised to see you here. Your praesidium must know it's a Bulwark's duty to protect an Altrinion. Even a young one such as you, Vonnie, should know better."

Vonnie steps forward, away from me, squaring her shoulders and eyes blazing. A low grumble rumbles through her, and I see she takes no pleasure in Titan's admonishment.

Pulling her arm to keep her at my side, I smile, hopefully to douse some of her irritations with Titan. "Titan, please. I am a grown woman. I come and go as I please. And if you must know, Vonnie was not happy about me coming here either. I see you have some interesting company."

"Interesting company indeed. Why do you think you don't see my sisters here? It is not an ideal spot for you tonight. Besides, I do not feel like getting into it tonight with Dalcour if anything were to happen to you. And if your junior praesidium here thinks her little barrier shield will be enough to keep you safe in this place, then you've certainly miscalculated your odds," Titan scorns, shaking his head in annoyance.

"Titan, look, I'm only here for Dalcour. Have you seen him? Or could you get him for me?" I ask.

"And who shall I say is looking for my sire?" A slithering, sultry voice calls to us from beyond the shadows, echoing through the veiled hallway.

Vonnie quickly moves in front of me and Titan even parries

her motion, blocking us both.

"Hey you!" Titan begins with a lilt of pretense in his tone. "It is your party, isn't it? Why don't you continue entertaining your guests? I'll take care of this little intrusion." With his broad back to us, Titan sways side to side, keeping us out of sight of the woman.

"Why yes, Lord Titan, it is my party. That is why I wanted to know who is seeking my sire. Who better than me to protect his interests?" She replies.

The budding inferno within me grows noxious at the sound of her presumptuous stance. I feel the force within me quicken and I am jolted to Titan's side in an instant, coming face to face with the most hauntingly beautiful woman I have ever encountered.

"*Damina, stay calm*," Titan's rebuke implodes my mind as his gray eyes darken while deepening into my own, and I realize his mouth never parted.

Uh-oh! This means he too can break into my thoughts. I have got to get a handle on this!

As I turn from Titan, my eyes nearly pop out from my sockets at the sight of the hauntingly gorgeous woman before me. Her thick, long fire-singed ginger curls hang to one side of her strapless shoulders as her piercing Timothy green eyes stare at me with a strange and disturbing familiarity. Her skin is dew-kissed like Jerrica, but her milky textured skin is void of any presence of the sun. The silhouette of her frame is too perfect! Not even a cola bottle could rival her enviable shape. But it is the evocativeness of her presence which sends a rippling current throughout my entire being.

Much like my night in the alleyway with Mikkel, this woman sets off a sinister alarm within me.

Likely sensing my apprehension, Titan throws his hulking arms around me, pulling me closer to his side.

"Well aren't you lovely?" The woman says in a low and sly tone as she spies my obvious irritation in Titan's tight hold. "And she smells delightful, Titan! Tell me, is she dinner or dessert?" She adds, biting her long pointy red nails through her cherry-stained red lips.

"She's neither! Keep your distance leech!" Vonnie yelps, coming to my side. A bright shimmering aura hangs over Vonnie, and both Titan and the woman turn slightly.

"Ha! How cute!" The woman mocks. "A little light-bright! No need to warm the room, dear. We like it cold and dark. Besides, we're just getting to know one another."

Grabbing Vonnie's wrist, I nod at her and she douses her light. I notice Titan's arm sizzles as the shield Vonnie placed around me starts to wear on him, yet he only bites his lip, grimacing slightly. Loosening myself from his hold, I step forward and the woman's eyes widen with surprise.

"Where are my manners?" I begin with a flat tone, faux smile, and a deathly gaze to match. While everything in me says I should fear this woman, I refuse to give her the satisfaction. "My name is Damina N—"

"Yes, yes. This lovely woman is Damina. She was—um—hired by Jerrica to manage the revitalization project," Titan quickly interjects, forcing himself back to my side. "As you know Dalcour is the benefactor, and she had a few questions about next steps. You know, business stuff. But we shouldn't really discuss this with you since you are the contending bidder, now should we, Chartreuse?"

Both Titan and the woman exchange laughs that are as pretentious as they are cringeworthy. Titan looks over his shoulder at me, narrowing his eyes and once more invades my mind. *"Tread carefully with this one, Damina. Chartreuse Grenoble is no mere foe. She's the most dangerous woman in this place."*

Before I can nod in understanding, the resonance of her name hits me. Chartreuse Grenoble! She is the woman Jerrica described as her rival. It was clear to me then as it is now. She and Jerrica were not friends. A low snarl rumbles through me at the thought of why she and Jerrica are at odds. The fact she names Dalcour as her sire isn't lost on me either.

"Ah, Ms. Grenoble, I think Jerrica may have mentioned you before," I say coolly. Titan's nose scrunches at my admission, and it doesn't take telepathy to know he wants me to back down.

"Oh, well, how is Jerrica doing? I hear she isn't doing well as of late. Please do send her my regards," she answers with a grubby tremor in her voice as her eyes search my face. "Well, now let me mind my manners as hostess. Can I fetch you something to drink? Do you take it from the vein as does Lord Marchand, or is your preference a goblet or sorts? I know you Altrinions have your predilections as it were." Snapping her fingers as she speaks, two men bring a young man with fang markings on his neck and wrist to her side. "My treat!" Chartreuse jovially announces, tipping the young man's head to the side, offering him to me and Titan.

Titan's eyes darken, and a low churning growl rivets through him and I grab his forearm, allowing the scorching heat from my skin to distract his growing bloodlust. He shakes himself free from my grasp and backs away from Chartreuse, raising his hands in protest. "I'm good, Chartreuse. I had something at the bar earlier," he adds.

"Oh now, Titan when did you become such a bore? I recall the days when your barbarity knew no end! Those were the glory days! Why shouldn't you partake in my merriment? This is the day of my making, is it not?" Chartreuse smiles wide, revealing long razor-sharp fangs. Her eyes fade to black as she sinks her teeth into the young man's flesh, draining the remaining life from him.

I work hard to steady my breathing as I witness his lifeless body fall at my feet. Chartreuse lets out a loud screeching cry and a chorus of menacing snarls and growls echo through the corridor. With her blackened eyes staring at me and a small pool of blood lingering in her open mouth, she smiles once more and snaps her fingers. This time, two more men bring another near-lifeless young man to us with similar bite marks etched on his body.

"Damina, what about you? Will you have a drink with me?" She questions in a dark tone, her voice reverberating through the hall.

"Back away from her, Chartreuse! Now!" I hear Dalcour's thunderous voice shout from behind me.

Chartreuse trembles at his call and the two men drop the sacrificial young man to the floor, quickly disappearing into the smoke-filled hallway. Her eyes return to their green hue and her fangs retract as she looks behind me, shaken by Dalcour's arrival.

"Lord Marchand, I—I" she begins, her teeth chattering as she bows slightly at her waist.

"No words, Chartreuse! I'll hear no words from you! How dare you break the rules of sanctity in the Civility Center? Here in my very presence! You know all too well I will not tolerate any loss of life beyond these walls. Yet you dare make this comparable to a bordello of blood!"

"My lord, I—I was only entertaining my guests. I only wish to commemorate the annual of my second birth. The only birth that has ever meant anything to me—your dark gift to me, my lord!" She says, her stance shutters in response.

"Yet you make me regret the day I granted you such a gift! Your savagery is beyond repair, Chartreuse and your wiles know no end! But your brutish barbarism will pale in comparison to my own should I ever find you within an inch of the Lady Damina Nicaud ever again!" Dalcour roars.

Chartreuse stammers back at his words, slowly lifting her face up to meet my eyes, her expression darkening. "Nicaud?" She repeats. "Is this Lady Damina Nicaud?" Chartreuse inquires, malevolence marring her perfect face.

"My lady!" Dalcour shouts back.

Straightening her posture, she resumes a sly smile as she continues staring between me and Dalcour. "Yes, my lord. I do regret however I may have sullied the sanctity of the Civility Center. You know I can be fairly impetuous. For that, I offer my deepest apology," Chartreuse offers with another nod and bow.

"You have an hour to finalize your festivities here, Chartreuse," Dalcour demands.

"Yes, sire. We will make our departure expedient."

"You'd do well to do so. Keep those at your charge away from the Quarter and its borders."

Chartreuse smiles, nodding this time with her eyes only, yet keeping them fixed on me for the duration.

"Until we meet again, Lady Nicaud. *Perhaps in Paris?*" She adds with a mischievous sneer before disappearing beyond the corridor.

"Perhaps in Paris? What the heck is that supposed to mean, Dalcour?" I ask, turning to meet his unwanted scowl.

"Damina," he begins with his eyes closed and skin glowing red. "What in the world possessed you to come here tonight? Weren't you instructed to stay close to the mansion?"

"Well, yes, Dal, but I—"

"But nothing, Damina! Do you not understand you can't just go flying about New Orleans at your whim or wherever your emotions take you?"

"My emotions?"

"Yes, your emotions, Damina! At what juncture will you put this flying by the seat of your pants behind you? I will not always be here to protect you! Titan! Vonnie! What good do either of you have to offer if you cannot protect what is mine?"

"What is yours? Well, Lord Marchand, far be it from me to remind your grace that I am not and never have or will be anyone's mere commodity!"

"Oh please, Damina, you know damn well what I mean! Is it not enough I have to keep peace between Jerrica and Chartreuse that I must now do so with you?"

"How dare you? But since you mention Jerrica, perhaps you would like to explain why it is you haven't been to see your best friend. She is dying, for goodness' sake!"

"Damina do not speak to me of things you can barely comprehend! And so it is for the sake of goodness that I do what I do now!" Dalcour shouts back as he grabs me at my waist and takes flight through the CC and back up to the mansion.

I am sure Vonnie thought her sunlit barrier upon my skin would prevent Dalcour from touching me. She was wrong. We both were. Neither my kicking, twisting, nor pounding at Dalcour's back does anything to thwart his motion as he reprimands me in an unknown tongue with smoke simmering from his skin. Vonnie trails Dalcour's movements while Titan remains at the Civility Center, watching our departure with fear-laden eyes.

Carrying me over his shoulder, Dalcour tosses me down on my bed and rushes back to the threshold. Without turning back to face me, he leans his head over his shoulder, taking a deep breath. "Damina, you still cannot fathom the ferocity of my affection for you. Someday I hope you will come to understand it. But I cannot—will not allow any harm to come to you." Dalcour takes in one more gulp of air as he takes hold of the doorframe. "Vonnie, I want you to place a barrier on this door. I don't want her leaving this room until daybreak."

"Dalcour! You wouldn't!" I protest, jumping up from the bed and racing to the doorway.

"Yes, Damina for your protection I would. I can't have you taking another flight away from safety."

Vonnie looks at me and back at Dalcour before guiding her hand along the door frame, as she mutters an unknown language, yielding a bright white light around the threshold of my suite. Yet,

I do not blame her. I know she is only doing what is commanded of her.

"Dalcour!" I shout, hoping to regain his attention. Once more he looks over his shoulder before opting to turn to lock eyes with me. "You should know one thing. I did not take flight as you may think when I went to the Civility Center. I want you to know that. You need to know how I got there."

Dalcour's eyebrows raise with interest and his face softens. Hopeful, I try to peer into his mind, but I cannot. Still, he is blocking his thoughts from me, infuriating me further.

"How, Damina? How did you get to the CC?" Dalcour inquires.

"With my two feet. I walked, Dalcour. I walked. And now you can do the same."

Dalcour flinches, with his mouth slightly parted. I know a part of him regrets his actions tonight, but he maintains his stubborn stance. His eyes narrow as we stare at one another, and he steps an inch closer to the door. Yet, I dare him to cross the threshold as my now reddened skins warms all over. Watching me closely, he retracts once more, keeping his distance.

"Damina," he whispers my name past the doorpost. Dalcour's tone is both pleading and placating.

I know one thing. I am not interested in anything he has to say beyond the mention of my name. And with that thought, the door slams shut at the wind I emit at my will.

Standing with my face to the door, I sense a new and more fiery inferno kindle within me, and I know with all certainty the events of tonight have changed things between me and Dalcour.

Perhaps forever.

Chapter 12

The blanketing comfort of electric blue butterflies keeps me afloat from the ground. Although I can sense the coolness of the breeze blowing in the air, I find solace in the strumming sound of the butterfly wings as they hover around me. Tingling bright currents of electricity swarm through me, awakening my senses with each touch.

Like a newly discovered sixth sense, everything is heightened.

For the first time, I can detect the juniper and honey aroma of the golden leaves as well as the brown sugar glazed dust of the earth beneath me. Never before have I known the world to be so tantalizing!

Even my skin has a silkier texture than before. There is a blend of softness and strength to my touch I have never known. Warming rays of light protrude through my pores, mimicking the brightness of the butterflies, and I feel my muscles contract and strengthen within me.

The wind blows once more and my flickering companions douse their light, gently guiding me to the ground below. Golden leaves *swirl at my backside, pushing me upright as the butterfly wings hold me steady at each wrist. A bright and iridescent light shimmer overhead and a dewy film covers my face, invading my pores, filling my lungs with a fresh wind, causing my chest to expand.*

I exhale and a golden mist excretes through my mouth and nose, pushing the golden leaves back and away from me. My feet dig deep into the earth beneath me and vigor rises through me. The smell of fresh water from afar invades the atmosphere and the rushing symphonic sound of waterfalls strum through my hearing.

The sound is enchanting, leading me away from the comfort of the butterflies and even further from the Great White Oak and its golden leaves. Howling stirrings and menacing snarls grow stronger in the distance, but the cadence of the waterfalls carries me beyond the consolation of my winged cohorts.

Entranced, my leaf-like motion leads me farther from the meadow than I've ever been. Still one thing remains. I smell him. Cinnamon. He smells of cinnamon. His spicy and sweet aroma greets me before I spy his crystalline eyes gazing at me through the newfound darkness surrounding us. His comforting smell gives me relief, and the warmth of his presence fills me with peace.

Extending his hand toward me, he smiles, speaking my name so softly it tickles like feathers along my flesh. Slowly, I reach for him, hopeful once more to be in his embrace. But a strong wind blows between us and the wild floral scent of jasmine and lavender overtakes the spicy and sweet aroma filling the air.

Darkness again swathes my sight and coldness stirs within me. I can no longer see or smell him, nor can I hear the buzzing of butterfly wings or the rushing waves of waterfalls. In fact, I no longer see or smell anything.

Silence is deafening all around me and an all too familiar sensation overwhelms me.

Fear.

Jumping up from my bed, I land squarely on my feet and am back in front of the door once again. As flashes of Dalcour carting me to my suite, kicking and screaming replay in my mind, fury floods my thoughts.

Not only do I need to find Dacari, but I need to settle the score with Mr. Marchand. I barely care to know what he is keeping from me and why anymore. I am more interested in what makes him thinks his behavior acceptable. Lord and progenitor of vampires or not, he will soon learn *I am not the one*. Nor will I ever be the one to allow such treatment by him or anyone.

Flashes of electricity ripple inside me once more and the current zips me through my suite, washing and dressing with a speed akin to superheroes from Krypton. A small smile escapes me at the thought as I grab the doorknob, watching in both delight and dismay at the luminous white light glowing from my hand as I pull the door open.

Vonnie's face is full of surprise and wonder as the door flies open, ripping from the hinge. "How? Impossible!" She exclaims, her mouth covered in shock.

"Good morning, Vonnie," I reply softly. I want to assure her that I don't hold her responsible for Dalcour's lashing from last night. Slowly crossing the threshold, Vonnie steps back, holding the wall, fear laden in her eyes.

"Ms. Nicaud, you—you're—"

"Yes, I am awake. Now, where is Dalcour?"

"He-he's not here. I—I mean, I haven't seen him. How did you break my barrier? That's impossible!"

"I suppose anything is possible these days, Vonnie."

A loud scream of expletives with the mixing of my name explodes through the hallway and Vonnie jumps in front of me, facing me head on.

"Vonnie, what was that?" I quickly question, peering around her shoulder.

"It's you, my lady. It's your light," Vonnie mutters, with a firm hold now at my shoulders.

"What?"

"Look at yourself! You're shining brighter than the sun, Damina!" Vonnie shouts at me, pushing me back inside my suite.

"What gives, Vonnie! What is going on in here? Brae nearly got scorched coming down the hall!" Mark yells as he rounds the corner.

"I'm sorry, my lord. I—I didn't know she could—well, at least not like this—not so soon." Vonnie stutters, bowing back and away from Mark's pensive stance.

"Damina, are you okay?" Mark questions, shielding his eyes with his forearm. "What's with the sun coming out of you?"

Turning toward my mirror, I now see the brightness emanating from me.

"I'm sorry, Mark! Is Brae okay?" I shout back as thoughts of hurting Brae pain through me.

"She'll be fine. Do you think you can douse your light some?" Mark adds, lowering his arm from his face, trying to smile through my luminous rays of light beaming at him.

"Vonnie! What can I do? I don't know how to turn it off!"

"Maybe I can help," I hear Jackson's calming voice break through my cries.

"She just needs to calm down, my lord," Vonnie says softly.

"Is that all? Now tell me baby, what's got you in such a fluster so early in the morning?" Jackson lifts my chin with one hand while taking my hand with the other. "Just breathe baby. Breathe," he whispers into my ear.

Taking in a deep breath, I exhale, leaning my head into Jackson's shoulders, allowing the warmth of him to calm the shivering frenzy erupting through me. His scent implodes the space between us, comforting my senses with every gulp of air I intake.

"That's it, baby. You've got it," Jackson says with a reassuring kiss on the cheek, wrapping both his arms around me. Jackson's touch is welcoming as my body relaxes in his embrace.

"It's working," Vonnie exclaims, the lilt of relief apparent in her tone.

"Well, I see somebody hasn't lost their touch!" I hear Gregory's voice croon from afar. A slight air of angst gnaws within me at the thought of my growing list of onlookers.

"Looks like we've got an audience," I whisper in Jackson's ear.

"Does it bother you? Because it doesn't bother me in the least," Jackson answers with a wide smile.

"My, how things have changed, Mr. Nash," I reply softly.

"Not everything, Damina. Not everything." Jackson counters, his gaze deepening into mine. Though I cannot read his mind, I know that's his not-so-subtle reminder of his love for me.

"I'm glad to hear it," I answer as he kisses my forehead.

"Ugh! Get a room people!" Mark shouts at us and he, Gregory and Vonnie laugh.

"Um—I'm in my room!" I tease, pointing around the suite.

"Fair point!" Mark exclaims.

"Okay that's enough people watching for one day folks!" Jackson states, taking my hand in his. "Besides, now that we've got my lightning bug under control, I'd like her to enjoy a nice breakfast."

"Breakfast?" I question. The thought of eating has not entered my mind. I want to find my cousin and follow up with Dalcour.

"Yes, breakfast, Damina. Look, you are still getting used to all of this newfound power, and being supernatural doesn't mean you don't need to eat. So before we get going for the day, I thought I'd whip up something for you. You know something like my famous three-layer spinach quiche!" Jackson says with a bright smile.

Before I can respond, my stomach growls loud and Jackson looks at me with assurance. "Okay, fine. I guess I can stand to eat a little something. But then all roads lead to Dacari!"

"Of course!" Jackson replies with his hands raised in submission.

"Well, I'll go check on Brae. Hopefully, she is recouping," Mark says.

"Please tell her I am sorry, Mark. I will certainly try to get this under wraps!"

"It's fine Lady D. Maybe Big D can help you in that regard. I mean, he has been an Altrinion for almost a millennium!" Mark continues. His eyes shift to Jackson and the two exchange uneasy glances before Mark leaves down the hallway. It is still obvious Mark feels just as caught between Jackson and Dalcour as I am.

Interesting.

My nose scrunches at the thought of Dalcour, but I work hard to push thoughts of him aside, lest I light up like a firefly once more. Jackson's expression turns tight as he stares back at me, but he forces another smile, squeezing my shoulders while bringing me in for a second hug. As he holds me, he takes a deep breath and I feel his chest expand against my face and the soothing rhythm of his steady heartbeat calms my remaining frenzy.

"So, baby, you think you're ready for a little breakfast? Khalil has everything set up in the kitchen," Jackson asks, lifting my face to meet his eyes.

"Well if either of you think I'm waiting for you to kiss again while we stand here starving, you've got it all wrong! Come on little Miss Bulwark, let's go get some grub while these two do whatever it is, they do—or don't do," Gregory says, pulling Vonnie by the arm. She doesn't have time to respond before Jackson walks to the door and closes it, preventing our exit.

"Now, Damina, do you want to tell me what's really going on with you this morning?" Jackson asks sternly, yet his face remains relaxed.

"What do you mean, Jack?" I shrug, turning toward the mirror to ensure my lightning effect is under control. "I'm fine, just trying to keep a lid on all this energy of mine is all."

"Damina, please baby, I know you better than that. Give me a little credit. Did something happen this morning? Last night? Vonnie's stood watch at your doorpost like a gargoyle all night. She wouldn't even let me in to see you when I got back from running post with Mark and the pack. Even when I saw Dalcour in the hall, he seemed jumpy—like something was off."

"You saw him? What did he say?" I snap, curious if Dalcour shed any light on the reason for his behavior last night.

"He didn't say anything, Damina. Why? What's going on with you two?"

"Jack—I—I—it's nothing," I stutter, returning my attention to the mirror and away from his pensive glare.

"The truth please Damina. Please. I'm a big boy I can handle it."

"Handle what, Jackson? There's not much to tell, really."

"Damina, I'm not a simpleton. I know what's at stake here. As much as I hate to admit it, I know you feel caught in between us. And I know—I know I promised Delia I wouldn't put any demands on you, at least until you were ready, and we found Dacari, but if you've made your choice—"

"*My choice?* Jackson, please! I can't even begin to choose anything at this point. How can I?" I reply, frustration filling me up from the inside.

"Well, Damina, we can't keep ignoring the elephant in the room. I am sure you think it changes the way I feel about you, but I can assure you it does not change anything for me. I meant what I said earlier. Nothing has changed for me."

"I'm sorry, Jackson, but yes so much has changed for me—but not my love for you. That hasn't changed one bit. So I don't know what other elephant there could be."

"I know you love me. I have never doubted your love for me

for a minute. But of course things have changed for you—and possibly for us—well, that is since you and him—you know since you two—"

"Oh goodness, Jackson! Is *that* what you're thinking? You think Dalcour and I—you think we--?"

Confusion laced with relief fill Jackson's eyes as he stammers toward me. "What are you saying, Damina? Are you saying that you and Dalcour didn't—sleep together?"

"Jackson! Of course not! That's what I wanted to tell you that first night you came to see me here. What I wanted to tell you since then. Jack—I—I never with Dalcour, or anyone else for that matter."

"You mean to tell me you're still a virgin?"

"Well, of course I am, Jackson! That's exactly what I'm saying."

"But Dalcour—he said that you'd seen his face! How is it possible to have seen his face without—"

"I know what the legends say but I can tell you with all surety we never had sex! Yes, I saw his big red beast. And yes, I was able to assuage the monster within him. But I did so fully dressed!"

"Damina! Do you know how happy this makes me!" Jackson shrieks, lifting me up in the air and twirling me around! "Don't get me wrong, baby. Even if you and Dalcour had been intimate, it would not change the way I feel about you or the way I see you. In fact, for everything I've done and even for what you thought I had done, I wouldn't blame you if you had—"

"Oh, really?"

"No, no—believe me, I'm glad you didn't. And look, I don't need to know the details. I still know you care for him and I still will respect your decision either way, but this makes me happy. At least Marchand hasn't taken everything from me," Jackson says softly, as he twines his fingers through my hair. "Please, Damina, say he hasn't taken you away from me—at least not completely."

Lowering my gaze, I don't want to spoil Jackson's merriment, but I know I am still unsure where life takes us from here.

"It's okay, baby. You don't have to answer me now. Just know that I am here for you. Always, baby."

"I'm gonna hold you to that, Jack."

Jackson's gleeful expression fades as he lowers me to the ground, and he steps back, folding his arms at his waist. Turning away from me, he paces the floor before suddenly ramming his fist through the wall near the armoire, narrowly missing the window. "That son of a—"

"Jack!" I shout, rushing to his side. "What's wrong? I told you we didn't do anything."

"I know and that's the problem!"

"Okay, now I don't follow," I answer confused.

"All this time he could have told me the truth, but he stayed silent. He knew full well that I thought you two slept together, yet he said nothing! Don't you see? Dalcour wanted me to think you'd given yourself to him, knowing that I'd blame myself. And if I felt guilty enough, I would stand by his side, biding my time on pins and needles until you made your choice!"

"Jackson, please! Don't let it get to you!"

"Don't let it get to me? Damina, he's stolen so much from me! All under the guise that we both just wanted what was best for you. He's known the entire time about Kyra—the changeling— everything. But still he kept the truth away from me. Dalcour knew if I'd known the truth—"

"Well then you should know the full truth, Jackson."

"What is that?"

"On that night, when I saw his face, he was the one who refused me, not the other way around. I'm telling you because I don't want you thinking I'm some porcelain doll or something. That's the truth. Now, in hindsight, I'm glad he refused me because even he knew that night my thoughts were of you."

"They were?" Jackson's face softens at my admission and I

watch a glimmer of hopefulness flicker in his eyes.

"When I called you and asked you to bring me home, I wanted to be back in your arms. But when I heard Kyra, I was furious. I suppose a part of me wanted to get back at you because of what I thought you were doing to me with Kyra. Still, Dalcour knew the truth. So he is the one who turned me down. In his words, he didn't want three people in the bed when we—"

"Okay, I get it," Jackson says, raising his hands in protest. "I don't need to hear anymore. Besides, none of it changes my position. I am not erecting any statues of sainthood to the guy for refusing you. That's his loss. But I will never forgive him for letting me and everyone else think otherwise. Never."

Jackson saunters across the room, folding his arms once more and leans on the closet door, keeping his sight set on me.

"Are we good now, Jack? You mentioned there was breakfast," I say softly, inching closer to him.

"Sure, baby. We are good. You and I are just fine." Jackson tries to smile, but I know for sure the bartered veil of truce he and Dalcour once shared is all but gone. "Just one more question," he adds with a raised brow, curiosity filling his face. I nod and he continues, "Are you going to tell me why you were out of sorts earlier? Does it have something to do with him?"

Jackson's expression remains tight, although he's eager for my response. As much as I want to tell him what happened, I know now isn't the time.

"My dreams. They're just getting really vivid is all." It's not a complete lie, but certainly a diversion. "Ever since I started changing into this—it's been one crazy dream after another. I mean, I actually flooded my room at Bessie's Tavern on my first night in New Orleans. I've got to get a handle on this."

Jackson laughs, relieved. "You know, I think Ms. Melvina told me about your first night. Not to worry though, I think it's all part of the supernatural package. Especially for Altrinions. You should talk to your aunt about it if you are concerned. But us wolves dream pretty vividly, too. When you were gone, I dreamt all the time. But if I can give you a little advice, here's what I know. Treat the dreams like one big painting. Each dream is telling one big story. It's like a supernatural road map of sorts," Jackson says with a gentle gaze as he takes my hand in his. "Come on, baby, let's go get something to eat."

While my diversion has thrown Jackson off the true reason behind my earlier frenzy, I am more thankful for his guidance. It's been so long since Jack and I have just talked, I'd forgotten how much I value his input. Just talking with him sets me at ease.

"Jack," I whisper his name, tugging his forearm as he leads us out of my suite.

"Yes, babe. What is it?" He responds softly, his eyes searching my face with a hint of concern.

"Nothing's wrong. I—I just wanted to say thank you."

"For what, baby? You haven't even tasted breakfast yet," he laughs with a slight smirk.

"No, Jack, not for breakfast," I add, resting my hand on his sculpted chest piercing through his black Under Armor tee. I am still not accustomed to seeing him in such relaxed gear, but I more than appreciate how he looks in it. "For you. I just want to thank you for being you. Before everything, you have always been my best friend. And well, despite everything going on, you remain the one person who I can really talk to—who knows me. So yeah, Jackson, I just want to say thanks."

"You are more than welcome, baby. But know this, I'll be whatever you need me to be if it means keeping you in my life. I love you, Damina."

As Jackson pulls me once more into his arms, planting a soft and lingering kiss between my brow, everything in me wants to match his sentiment. While I cannot form the words in reply, I am comforted by the peace I feel in his embrace and I know with all certainty: *this is love.*

Chapter 13

"Hey lightning bug!" Gregory taunts as Jackson and I arrive in the kitchen. The room erupts in laughter as Vonnie, Mark, Khalil, Dilano and Alana all add to Gregory's teasing.

"I don't see what's so funny!" Brae shouts from between their huddle at the kitchen island. "I could've really been hurt or worse!"

"I am so sorry Braelyn! Really, I am! I'm trying to get a handle on this whole Altrinion thing," I say rushing to her side, but she turns away from me with folded arms and pouted lips.

"Brae, baby, stop messing with Damina! You know she didn't mean any harm!" Mark laughs, pushing Brae's shoulder.

Brae turns around slowly, reshaping her pouty lips to a wide grin! "Okay, I just had to mess with you! You should have seen your face! I mean, you got all formal with me, calling me Braelyn like Big D and everything! I should've kept it going!" Brae cackles as she brings me in for a hug.

"Are you sure you're okay?" I question, searching her face.

"Scout's honor!" Brae answers, holding two crossed fingers

in the air. "I'm fine Damina, I promise. I just needed to get a refill, and I was back to normal!"

"A refill?" I question, perplexed.

"You know *my smoothie bottle*," Brae says with air quotes.

"Not at the kitchen counter, baby. We're eating here," Mark says with his nose scrunched as the others mirror his sentiment.

"Okay, I know I'm the only Scourge at the table but—"

"You're not a Scourge, baby," Mark counters, resting his hand on Brae's shoulder.

"Fine—the only vampire then—but the point is still the same! I think everyone here knows I drink blood! How else am I supposed to heal?"

"Okay, that's it!" Gregory shrieks, backing away from the island. "I've officially lost my appetite!"

"Oh please Gregory, like you wolves don't hunt and eat your fill of whatever crosses your path!" Brae shouts back across the island.

"That may be, but at least I'm in full form at the time. I can neither deny nor confirm those claims! I am no monster!" Gregory adds with his hands raised in protest.

"It's quite all right, Braelyn. We're all monsters in somebody's story," Dalcour interjects as he strolls through the kitchen coolly, with one hand in his grey trousers and his eyes locked with mine. "Besides, some folk can never truly appreciate what we have to do in the shadows in order to maintain some semblance of normalcy," Dalcour adds, narrowing his eyes, piercing deeper into my own. He wraps his free arm around Brae and feigns a smile, but his growing spite toward me is hard to miss.

He's still blocking himself from me and I refuse to get another migraine trying to rattle through his mind today. I am not in the mood for his games. A small part of me wishes it was him, not Brae, who felt the brunt of my heat this morning.

"So, did you all leave any food for us?" Jackson questions,

breaking through the awkward silence forming in the kitchen amid the intense stare-off between Dalcour and me.

"I sure hope so, because I am starved!" I hear a loud familiar voice call from the adjacent great room.

"Brian! Man am I glad to see you!" Mark shouts as he rushes to Brian for a pounding fist bump and tackling embrace. Dilano mirrors Mark's sentiment and Alana remains close behind.

"It's good to see you, Brian!" Dilano adds with a hard pat to Brian's back.

"I can honestly say for once it is good to be seen. I've missed you all!" Brian says with a wide smile. Looking at him, I see he has changed. His hair is longer, sporting a five o'clock shadow, and gone is his typical dark suit and tie. There's an unexpected ruggedness to Brian that pushes aside the demure demeanor I had grown accustomed to in such a short time.

Brian gazes through the mini mob of friends and locks eyes with me. "My is it good to see you awake and about, Ms. Nicaud," Brian adds as he pushes through everyone toward me.

Throwing his hulking arms around me and lifting me from the ground, his greeting surprises me. Although he's sweaty, the familiar nutty and spicy scent exuding through his pores is calming.

"I'm glad to see you too, Brian!" I shout over his shoulders. His hold on me is firm, and I know he's genuinely happy to see me. As he lowers me back to the floor, a warm smile crosses his face and his sky-blue eyes stare back at me with the same gentleness I've seen since the first day we met.

"So when did you get back, B?" Mark questions.

"As soon as Lord Marchand told me she was awake, I made my way here. I ran through more Skull in one night than I've seen in my lifetime as I made my way back from Natchez," Brian replies.

"Wow, Brian. You made it all the way to Mississippi?" Brae asks.

"Sure did," Brian answers in a flat tone and I notice he and Jackson share awkward glances.

"Mississippi? You went across state lines, Brian?" Jackson's dark tone is marred in rebuke.

"Yes and I'll cross whatever lines and territories I must to find her!" Brian snaps back.

"Yeah and why do you think you perhaps ran into Skull herds? You know those ancient tribal grounds are breeding grounds for herds. Herds, you idiot—not packs!" Gregory shouts between Brian and Jackson.

"*Idiot*?" Brian seethes, his eyes glowing bright like a flame.

"Both of you stop it!" I yell, posturing myself in front of Brian.

"At least tell me you knew about this?" Jackson asks, turning his attention to Mark.

"Well, I—"

"Well, nothing! Spit it out, little wolf!" Gregory barks. "Did you know or not?"

"Watch your mouth mutt!" Dalcour roars at Gregory. "You're in my house! And you will show courtesy to those of my house. Brian only answers to Mark."

"And Mark answers to me," Jackson growls back, leaning into Gregory's side, squaring his shoulders toward Dalcour. Turning his attention back to Mark, Jackson takes a deep breath, blowing the air through his nostrils. "Now, Mark, you are his alpha, but you know how den rules work. Crossing territories without permission is dangerous. If you are accepting of this behavior, that is your choice. But if not—"

"If not what, Jack?" I interrupt. "Did you not understand he's looking for Dacari? Am I missing something here?"

"Damina, I understand that. More than anything I want to find your cousin, but there are rules. And these rules are in place for a reason. Mark hasn't passed his alpha valuation yet. So as far as others in the wolf community are concerned, Brian is nothing more than a lone wolf. He could have been killed or worse! Other packs not aware of his intentions to find your cousin may have considered his arrival a threat. That's why we have rules. The lone wolf mentality is not acceptable! If it were, we wouldn't have Skull!" Jackson responds to me but keeps his eyes fixed on Brian and Mark.

"He's right, Lady D," Mark answers with his head low. "No, my lord, I was not aware of Brian's location. I do ask that you charge it to me, not to him."

Jackson stares at Mark and a crinkled smile swerves at the corners of his lips and he places his hand on Mark's shoulder. "No charge needed this time, Mark. If nothing more, I know the intentions were pure," Jackson adds while crossing his gaze toward Brian. "Gregory, please reach out to the den leaders in Mississippi and let them know the visit was approved by me. If their alpha has questions, send them my way."

"Consider it done!" Gregory quickly answers, pulling his phone out of his pocket and walking out onto the patio.

"Would anyone care to know what led him to Natchez in the first place?" Dalcour exclaims, looking around the kitchen.

"I mean yeah, Jack. I understand rules are important and everything, but nothing is more important than finding Dacari," I yell.

"Of course I want to know what he found there but if we don't do things right Damina, we could be on the verge of setting things in motion that only compound our problems. That is the last thing we need," Jackson replies.

"Well, perhaps Ms. Nicaud should hear it from me and then you can decide if it was worth it or not," Brian answers.

"Please continue, Brian," Dalcour replies, gesturing his palm for Brian to speak.

"After learning of Mikkel's involvement with the Vitreous, I made my way to King's Tavern," Brian begins.

"You mean the place haunted by that ancient Altrinion-changeling hybrid Madeline! Are you crazy?" Brae scoffs, throwing her crossed arms over her head.

"You got it," Brian replies over his shoulder. "Everyone knows anything hybrid or with too little supernaturality ends up either in Natchez or Biloxi. The epicenter of all rejects. And since it's home to every supernatural cocktail that exists. I even came across a few Wolf-changelings."

"I've never heard of such," Jackson mutters to Mark.

Dalcour forcefully clears his throat, extending his palm once more.

"Well, knowing the Vitreous abhors all things of mixed race and such, I figured if any group was keeping a close watch on their movements, the rejects of Natchez and King's Tavern would be the best place to start. And I'm glad I did. Rumor has it the Vitreous weren't only after Damina—but the entire LeClaire line!"

"What!" Aunt Delia shouts from behind us as she and Dranoel walk into the kitchen. Dranoel smiles sheepishly at me as he slowly releases my aunt's palm and tugs the hem of his shirt nervously. A part of me is happy to see my aunt with someone to care for her, but now isn't the time for gushing.

"Yes, I'm afraid that's what got Father McGloin killed that night at Saint Roch's cemetery," Dalcour adds, walking closer toward me, looking over my shoulder at Aunt Delia. A small smile rounds the corners of his raspberry lips as he notices the closeness of my aunt and Dranoel, and his gaze softens as he stares back at me. "It seems it was the good Father's digging into your family's history that alerted the Vitreous to release Scourge to exact their murderous intent."

"But why the LeClaire line? Why my family?" Aunt Delia questions, coming to my side, looping her arm in mine.

"Because the LeClaire line is all that's left of pure Altrinions who bear the fated mark," Dalcour states.

"What about you?" I ask, hesitant as I see Jackson's posture shift. I know hearing about me and Dalcour being fated to one another isn't his topic of choice.

"Well yes, I do bear the mark, but I am also vampire, Damina. My fate cannot be activated without you," Dalcour answers, his own hesitancy ringing true as his eyes drift between both me and Jackson.

"Darling, I think what Dalcour is trying to say is only a pure line Altrinion like a LeClaire is a threat to the Vitreous cause," Aunt Delia adds.

"And so they want to exterminate us!" I gasp.

"But they will never get the chance!" Jackson protests, grasping my shoulders in his firm grip.

"They have already begun, I'm afraid," Brian interjects in a grim tone, as he scratches his chin. Pausing long enough to get an approving wink from Dalcour to continue, Brian turns his attention squarely on me and Jackson. "Kill orders have been issued for any LeClaire within a three-hundred-mile radius. Word has it in Natchez there is one protected LeClaire; which I assume is you, Ms. Nicaud. Now they are after any of your kin and anyone associated with you—like Father McGloin."

"But there's one thing they didn't know. You are not just a LeClaire. You are also Duacin," Dalcour adds.

Aunt Delia paces the kitchen floor as both Brian and Dalcour talk. Turning to face me, she sighs heavily and pulls a counter stool from the kitchen island and sits down next to me. "The Duacin's kept themselves hidden for centuries. While not vampires, they drank blood to keep others off their scent. But you, darling—you aren't a blood drinker—you are the purest of all Altrinions," Aunt Delia states with tear-filled eyes. "That is why we didn't add your mother's given name in marriage on her tombstone. That is why we buried her in the Peyroux crypt—a wolf's resting place. We hoped no one would learn of her ancestry or find you!" Aunt Delia reveals.

"It's likely the good Father McGloin came too close to the truth, and that's why the Vitreous sent the Scourge at their employ to kill him!" Brae exclaims as dreadful memories of seeing his lifeless body and that of my hitch driver plague my mind.

"It's all my fault!" I blow beneath my breath.

"No, baby. None of this is your fault!" Jackson protests, turning me around to meet his gaze. His eyes are glassy as they stare in my own. "This is all the Vitreous! Nothing else!"

"He's right, Beautiful! There is no way you or Father McGloin could have known what the Vitreous were up to. Frankly, none of us knew. They've orchestrated all of this!" Dalcour shouts across the kitchen. Even though I cannot read his mind, I know his barking tone is intentional. While I'm sure the actions of the Vitreous are to blame, the deliberate way his words cut through the forming pull between Jackson and me is hard to miss.

"What does any of this have to do with Dacari, B?" Mark asks. "I mean what happened to the priest is bad and all, but did you find anything on where she and Decaux might be?"

"Well that is the other reason I went to Natchez. Knowing Decaux is a lover of all the usual rejects, I also figured he may have shown his face at some point. You know many of the mixed-supernaturals consider him a champion of sorts," Brian responds as he pours water into a glass and hands it to Aunt Delia. I see her hands shaking as she holds them folded on the island and I am thankful despite everything going on, Brian is just as attentive as always. "Anyway, while no one had seen Dacari, it had been rumored Decaux had finally found the only supernatural being capable of the *Canticum Incantationum*."

"No!" Dalcour shouts as blood leaves his face, turning his complexion ghastly.

"What, Dal?" I question as watch both fear and terror fill Dalcour's eyes. His mouth remains open, and he continues staring straight through Brian, unable to respond.

"Will someone tell us what a Canticum Incantationum is?" Brae yelps.

"It is Latin," Jackson begins, his voice flat and dark. "In English it means song of enchantment. Some say the words spoken during the Canticum are the very words spoken when the supernatural world was formed. Since the beginning of time, the ancient language has remained hidden. No one supernatural can utter the words unless they carry the essence of every earth bound supernatural in their being," Jackson answers, gazing back at Brian in a disturbingly somber tone.

"I don't get it, B? What does that have to do with Dacari?" Mark asks.

Aunt Delia stands up and away from the kitchen island, locking her posture into a stiff formation. She keeps her eyes fixed on Dalcour, but offers an almost muted response to Mark, "It's not what it has to do with Dacari—*it is about Dacari.*"

"What do you mean, Aunt Delia?"

"I can't believe it hadn't crossed my mind before!" Dalcour yells, striking the adjacent wall with his fist.

"Will someone please tell me what's going on here?" I shout back.

"Damina, your cousin isn't just an Altrinion-Wolf hybrid like your aunt. She is a tribrid! Altrinion. Wolf. Vampire. The only one I've ever heard of! Of all the earthbound supernaturals, she alone has the power to fully utter the song of enchantment—the power of supernatural creation!" Jackson explains.

Aunt Delia's knees buckle at Dalcour's claim and she begins to keel over. Thankfully, Dranoel is immediately at her side and takes her in his arms, holding her firmly against his chest.

"She's what my wretched brother has always wanted!

For as long as I can remember, Decaux has wanted to create a supernatural race of his own—one he could bend to his own will!" Dalcour states.

"Exactly! That is why he spends so much time in Natchez. For decades he's made it his home. Some say he's responsible for the coupling of the species—earthbound or otherwise," Brian says.

"What do you mean—earthbound or otherwise?" I question.

"He means like me," Vonnie interjects. "I am a Bulwark. I am not earthbound. We are here as messengers, helpers—protectors of the boundary lines, if you will. Other non-earthbound supernaturals are Changelings. They were the first of our kind, but they are void of form. Changelings must have a mortal or supernatural host to inhabit."

"Vonnie is correct," Dalcour begins. "And if Brian saw Wolf-Changelings in Natchez, that only means my brother has been long at work in coupling the species."

"Why would he want to do that? And is that really a problem?" I reply.

"Well, on the surface it's not a problem. But my brother's only goal is subjugation. Having a world of supernaturals indebted to Decaux only fuels his delusions of superiority. Unlike the Vitreous who only want Altrinion-Vampires to rule in the likeness of Nuhtlus, Decaux desires humans to submit to a world of supernaturals with himself at the helm!" Dalcour explains.

"The worst part is if he can convince Dacari to utter the song of enchantment, she could make not only the power of the Great Oak ineffectual but also bring an end to the power of the eldership of supernaturals once and for all." Jackson says.

Once more, the bastard frog suffocates me, and I am unable to speak. Thoughts of Dacari playing marionette to Decaux sickens me to my core. If that wasn't enough, watching my aunt sob on Dranoel's chest burns a hole through my continually aching heart. I want to console her, but my feet are cemented to the floor.

Just as I part my mouth to speak, Gregory shouts from outside and I know whatever is coming next will haunt me more than any nightmare.

Chapter 14

"Hey, Jack-O! ~~Get over here~~ quick! He's hurt pretty bad!" Gregory screams from the patio. Jackson rushes out the door with Mark and Brae on his tail and Dilano and Alana close behind.

Brian and Dranoel help Aunt Delia to her feet before following the others, leaving just Dalcour and me in the kitchen as Khalil takes his exit through the parlor.

"I guess we should get outside," I say, needing to end the awkward silence brewing between us.

Jumping in front of the patio door, Dalcour postures himself squarely in my view. "Damina, look before we tackle whatever it is awaiting us outside that door," Dalcour starts, his voice surprisingly calm. "We need to talk. About last night—"

"It doesn't matter, Dal. Really. The only thing I'm interested in now is finding Dacari." I try to peer around Dalcour's broad frame to see outside, but it is of no use.

"I know that but—"

"But what, Dal? Not only have I learned she is Decaux's

daughter, but we now know he has plans to use her in some supernatural song of enchantment and take over the world! Nothing else matters to me but finding her!"

I want to tell him that he matters. But not now. I have sculpted an impenetrable icy fortress around my heart. I can only hope its coldness is enough to ward off any further overtures from him or Jackson. With what we just learned about Decaux; I can no longer afford to linger in the lure of either man.

"I understand that, Damina. I do. Still, I need to apologize. I should not have treated you the way I did."

"You're right. Throwing me in my room was a pretty crutty thing to do."

"Crutty is right. My actions were brash, I admit. I guess I was simply scared. Seeing you in the CC with all those blood thirsty Scourge and Altrinion vampires everywhere, I just wanted to keep you safe!" Dalcour explains.

"Okay, I understand that Dalcour, but what does that have to do with blocking me out?" I question.

"*Blocking you out*? Are you kidding me? You are mad because you could not read my mind? You can't be serious!"

"Yes, I am, Dalcour Marchand! Why are you blocking me out? What do you have to hide from me?"

"Wow, Damina! Well let me ask you a question," Dalcour says, his face mixed with both awe and annoyance.

"What?" I snap, trying feverishly not to gawk at the way his dew-kissed skin glistens or inhale too much of his aromatic scent.

"Can you read Jackson's mind?" Dalcour's question hits below the belt just as he intended. I don't know whether he can read my mind, but it seems he also wants to push my lustful thoughts aside.

"What? He is a wolf, Dalcour! You know I can't read his mind!"

"Well, then I guess the playing field is finally fair!" Dalcour smirks with folded arms and a raised brow.

"Fair? How is that fair, Dal? Is what you're keeping from me that bad?" I insist. His stubbornness is annoying but slightly charming. *Oh no! He is sucking me back in!*

"It's fair, Damina, and you know it. I expect you to trust me the same way you trust Jackson. You can't read his mind, so why should I just be an encyclopedia. I need you to trust that short of me tossing you in a room for your safety, I'd never willingly put you in harm's way or do anything to deliberately hurt you." The warmth and sincerity of Dalcour's words melt the remaining iciness of my heart.

I am a dripping puddle before him.

"Well, Dal, I know that already. I don't need telepathic powers to tell me that about you," I say softly as I consider that even Jackson suggested the same of Dalcour last night. "I guess these new powers are throwing me for a loop. I just wish I knew how to control it all. I need to get a handle on it."

"Okay, well, that I can help you with. That is something we can do—together," Dalcour says as he takes my hand, pulling me closer to him. "Besides, if we're going to have any success in finding your cousin, I'll need you to understand how to use your powers fully."

"Well... together sounds good. I—I mean you training me is all," I reply weakly, fearful of looking at him in the eye. I cannot allow him to pull me back in any more than he has already.

"I know what you mean, Beautiful," Dalcour continues softly, lifting my chin to meet his hauntingly beautiful crimson eyes. "We'll focus on your cousin for now—but we will get back to the matter of us. Soon."

"Ah-hem," Jackson bellows a loud faux cough at the patio entrance. With a clinched jaw, his face is hard, but his bright, golden eyes glow wildly at the sight of me and Dalcour so close. Dalcour issues a small snarl, lowering his hand, and I step away from him and turn my attention to Jackson.

Awkward.

"Damina, Dalcour, there's someone here you need to see," Jackson says as he and Mark open both sides of the French patio doors. Shifting his eyes away from us, he blows out a loud sigh before calling out to Gregory. "Bring them in now!"

The uneasiness of the moment quickly dissipates when I see Cal and Lorien drag an injured Perry through the kitchen and prop him against a small dinette table.

"Perry!" I scream, shocked to see Allyson's boyfriend in such a state. "What happened to you?"

"Hey there, my lady!" Perry says with a quaint smile through bloodied, cracked lips. "It seems you never see me at my best."

"They got over on him pretty bad, ma'am," Cal says, patting Perry's head with an ice pack. "It's a good thing some poor soul took pity on you, boy!"

"Perry, how did this happen? Is Allyson okay?" I question.

Pushing back to steady himself against the wall, he winces, grabbing his waist and I see bruises along his ribcage with dried blood staining his shirt.

"I told Lord Nashoba they put a pretty bad beating on him. Put a beating on him and left him for dead. All because he got involved with that girl!" Cal exclaims as he tries to keep Perry stable in his seat.

"I tried, my lady. I tried. If I had known she had gotten herself mixed up with them, I would have never let it get this far!" Perry replies.

"Just tell her what happened, big bro," Lorien adds, lightly pushing Perry's shoulder.

"The Jadeites. She got mixed up with them, but I swear I didn't know," Perry says.

"Someone, please get him some water and a cold towel and bandages!" I shout over my shoulder. Both Dilano and Alana spring into action, aiding Cal with tending Perry's wounds, and helping him chug down a few gulps of water.

Perry pushes himself upright after helping himself to a few more rounds of water, mustering enough strength to continue. "It seems my alley cat got involved with the Jadeites before we even met. As a matter of fact, I now think that is why we met in the first place, but I can't prove it. Anyway, one night we were walking back to my place, and we got grabbed and tossed in a van. I was gagged, blindfolded, and woke up days later in a cellar just before the apex of the full moon. They put her in there with me! Waiting for me to shift and wolf out. I fought tooth and nail, begging my wolf to stay dormant while they tortured her—probing her back and forth, question upon question."

"What did they want to know from her?" Aunt Delia asks as she comes to my side.

"They asked questions about Damina mostly—but a few about Lord Nashoba and your daughter," Perry responds.

"My daughter?" Aunt Delia exclaims.

"Yep, and that is what got her in trouble. Look, I tell you, she just got in over her head! If I knew then what I do now, I would've never—"

"How did Allyson get in over her head?" I question.

"Well, I think originally they only knew about you, my lady. That you existed. They never knew about your cousin. That is until she started spending more time with Allyson after you left. When her dog died, she came looking for you and Allyson was there for her. Afterward, they were inseparable. Allyson and Dacari talked every day and a few times each day from that point. I suppose the Jadeite spies got wind of your cousin and wanted to know more. All Allyson had ever said was that you were an orphan."

"But that's not all, is it?" Mark says, grabbing a counter stool and hanging his leg over one side.

"Well, no sir. They knew Lady Damina was an Altrinion," Perry answers with his eyes lowered in shame. "But it was when they found out about Dacari they became incessant. Once they discovered she was one half of the LeClaire-Peyroux lineage, they were obsessed. You see, both Allyson and Dacari bonded over their apparent daddy issues—or the lack thereof. So, Allyson being Allyson, started looking deep into your family tree. I don't know how she figured it out, but she came across an Altrinion Vampire named Cade DeLuca who claimed to know of a supernatural child born of all three earthbound bloods."

"Impossible!" Aunt Delia cries. "When I left Decaux, no one, and I mean no one, knew I was with child. There's no way Cade DeLuca could have known!"

"Cade has always been a crafty one. If you left even a trace of your truth behind, I do not doubt he knew of her birth," Dalcour responds in a dry and low tone.

"What happened next, Perry?" Jackson asks.

"Somehow they found out Allyson had been in talks with Cade to get Dacari to him. That was her big mistake! At first, they only wanted Ally to get them Damina. But I guess Allyson had no plans to comply."

"Explain, Perry. What do you mean they wanted Damina?" Aunt Delia questions, concern filling her face.

"Well, she was supposed to get Damina to them somehow. Instead, Allyson sent Damina here—to my cousin Bessie's place. The Jadeites were pretty pissed about it too! But you see, they didn't really know about Dacari. However, they must've tapped her phone or something, because when they found out Allyson had sent the child of Decaux Marchand to New Orleans, they were enraged. She betrayed them!"

"Are you saying Allyson isn't a Jadeite, Perry?" I say, hopefully my friend is not the traitor I fear she's become.

"Oh she's a Jadeite all right! You should've seen the beating those buffoons gave to some of our pack. As a matter of fact, we didn't even think you were still alive!" Gregory counters. "The

Jadeites might be upset she sent Dacari away, but the fact that she and this lying mongrel were working with them tells us all we need to know!"

"Hey, now! Perry may be a lot of things, but he said he had no idea Allyson had any dealings with these Jadeites. She tricked him! He's as much a victim here as anyone else—I mean, look at him!" Cal shouts back at Gregory over his shoulder while still tending Perry's wounds.

Walking closer to Perry, I kneel near Lorien so that Perry and I have eye contact. Although I know I cannot read his mind, I need to look him in the eye to tell truth from a lie on my own.

"Is that true, Perry? Did you know anything about this?" I ask.

Gazing up at me, Perry cracks a weak smile and a small twinkle shimmers in his eyes. "I promise you, my lady, I did not. I honestly thought she cared about me. Truly, I did. Truth is, I think the Jadeites sent her to the lair I'd been a part of just so she could get close to a lone Dunes like me. I guess that's what I get for not keeping with den rules, huh?" Perry looks over to Jackson and Mark before lowering his head as shame further mars his countenance.

"None of that matters now, Perry. I'm only glad you're okay," I reply quietly with a light hold of his knee.

"I'm afraid it does matter, Damina. We can't just let this slide! He's a traitor!" Gregory exclaims.

"What?" I snap back. I am growing tired of Gregory's self-righteous stance.

"Didn't you just hear this man? He got beaten down and somehow the first thing he managed to do is to come and tell us the truth! You Prime Alphas are all the same—always on your moral high horse, yet you do nothing when it comes down to it!" Brian yells at Gregory.

The room erupts in an uproar of snarls and rumbling shouts between Gregory, Brian, and Cal.

"Stop it!" Jackson roars, pushing a stool across the kitchen floor, halting their clamoring. "Listen, none of this matters now! Mark Perry is of your parish. You deal with him as you please. For now, we must focus all our efforts on finding Dacari. She alone is our priority. Now, Perry, do you have any idea where they may have taken Allyson?"

"No, my lord. I was knocked out cold and dumped along the river. Thankfully, some late-night gator enthusiast found me along the River Bayou when I came to. The last thing I recall is seeing the Jadeites striking Allyson in the face before telling her she'd pay severely for not turning Damina in and for keeping Dacari a secret," Perry answers in a low and solemn tone.

"Dranoel," Dalcour begins, "Please take Perry down to the CC and so that he can get his wounds fully healed. Allow him to help himself to anything that would speed his healing. We'll need his help when the time comes."

Dranoel nods his head in courtesy but defers his glance to both Jackson and Mark. "My lords?" He questions.

"Oh for mercy, Dranoel!" Dalcour protests. "Am I not still the keeper of my own vineyard? Does the consent of Lord Nashoba now outweigh my own—in my house?"

"He does what is right," Jackson counters with a husky growl. "Mark is his alpha as am I his Prime. I know you vampires know nothing of order or etiquette, so let this be an education!"

Dalcour rushes toward Jackson, but I step in between both men, placing my hands on their chests. A tingling jolt of energy springs through me, halting their motion. While a part of me is in awe of having both men at a standstill by nothing but the touch of my fingertips, a bigger part of me is more amazed at how the pacing of their hearts slows with the light tap of my hand.

Jackson rumbles a low snarl as he works to restrain himself while Dalcour grinds his teeth with his narrowed eyes set sharply on my once betrothed, daring him to flinch.

"Stop it, you two!" Aunt Delia shouts. "Can either of you stop behaving like cavemen for a moment? Or at least long enough to find my Dacari. After you both can return to your brute behavior!"

"She's right," I say softly, gazing back and forth at both men.

Jackson pulls back slowly, casting a longing stare at me while softening his stance. Dalcour, on the other hand, remains in place as he observes Jackson's retreat. His posture is still stiff as he keeps his chest pressed into my palm, but it is the familiar cadence of his heartbeat that lets me know he is working to restrain his inner beast; and for that I am thankful.

Turning to Mark, Jackson blows out a lengthy sigh as he leans against the kitchen island, extending his hand toward Mark.

Mark stares awkwardly between Dalcour and Jackson before walking closer to Perry and Cal. "Jackson is right," Mark begins. "Your actions and connection with this Allyson character could have caused even more calamity. However, it is evident you are both remorseful and had no direct part to play in the plan of the Jadeites. For that you are pardoned."

"Thank you, my lord," Perry answers, dipping his head in submission.

"Still," Mark continues, looking over his shoulder at both Jackson and Brian. "You did cross state lines without permission and removed an Altrinion from the protection of the Primes. For that you will be subject to a tribunal hearing."

Gasps echo throughout the kitchen, and Cal and Lorien stand in front of Perry in both defense and protest.

"A tribunal!" Lorien shouts. "There has not been one in this parish in decades! The last one didn't end well—you Beta Primes—your father Abraham had our father killed because of your tribunal!"

"What? Wait? I don't understand," I cry, rushing to Mark's side. "Mark, please this isn't necessary. Perry was only helping me leave because Allyson told Perry and Bessie that I had been abused," I plead, pulling his arm.

"Hold on," Jackson says, jumping between me and Mark. "Damina, is this true?"

"Yes, Jack. I—I am sorry. I didn't tell Allyson that, but that is what she told Bessie to get her and Melvina's help." I reply. I knew this would come to back to bite me at some point.

Jackson's eyes fall at my admission and the room grows eerily quiet. "Damina, I know I hurt you that night, but we both know I would never lay a finger on you," Jackson whispers as he runs his thumb like a feather across my face.

"I know, Jack. I know," I say softly, leaning into his palm as a lone tear falls past my cheeks. Watching the hurt in Jackson's eyes is painful.

"She is right, my lords," Cal interjects. "When Ms. Allyson called my wife to seek accommodations for Ms. Nicaud, this was what we were all lead to believe."

"Lord Nashoba," Dalcour says gently, his tone returning to the more respectful manner the two shared at my awakening. "Calvin speaks the truth. Bessie's Tavern has long been a shelter for battered women. That is well known in the Quarter. Even I thought the same of Damina when we first met."

Jackson's thumb presses firmly into my cheeks as he stares at me with a tender gaze. His nose twitches as Dalcour speaks and I know that while this information is helpful, there isn't much Dalcour can do to rein in Jackson's growing antipathy for him.

Pulling his hand slowly from my face, he turns back to Mark and Perry. "Mark, if it was by Allyson's pretense that Perry committed these actions—if he only did so to protect her— protect an Altrinion—I will forgive this action."

"Thank you! Thank you, my lord!" Both Lorien and Cal profess with bowed heads as Perry nods in agreement.

"However," Jackson continues. "As part of your valuation, you may still conduct a tribunal."

"What! I thought you pardoned Perry, my lord?" Dranoel asks, as he places a hand at Brian's chest who growls deeply in protest.

"I did, Sir Dranoel. Perry is pardoned. I wasn't referring to him," Jackson answers.

"Then for who, my lord?" Mark questions, puzzled.

"For my brother. Keiron. It is time he meets his judgement," Jackson replies, and the entire mansion stands quiet.

Chapter 15

Quietly, everyone exits the kitchen only moments after Jackson's announcement. Sheer expressions of both shock and wonder filled the faces of those congregated, but no one dared said a word.

Not even Dalcour.

The wolves held their stances of awe the longest as Brae, Khalil, Vonnie and Dalcour all stood a distance from the encircling parade of the packs as they surrounded Jackson, nodding their heads in submission as the weight of his words stirred each to their core.

I even overheard Dilano tell Alana never before has a brother offered his own sibling for tribunal review. Brian, on the other hand, seemed more concerned that such a weight had now been placed on Mark's shoulders. While I could tell Brae wanted to comfort Mark and offer him some solace, Dalcour kept her back, citing that she shouldn't involve herself in wolf business. Aunt Delia and Dranoel escorted Perry, Cal, and Lorien to the Civility Center as Gregory remained dutifully at Jackson's side.

Like Brae, I wanted to provide some consolation to Jackson,

but I heeded Dalcour's warning as well and let him leave the kitchen without disturbance. Although it was evident Mark now had a heaviness upon his shoulders, Jackson seemed as though the weight of the world now rested on his entire being. I've never seen him so disconsolate in all our five years together. Coupled with the limbo state of our relationship, leading the wolves, and now the judgement of his brother's machinations, I am certain everything is taking an adverse toll on Jackson.

Oh, how I wish there were something I could do to make life easier for him. The only thing in my power I can offer him is my heart, but I am uncertain to whose hands it belongs.

I am still torn between the two.

Dalcour gets a call on his phone and he exits the kitchen from my view and Khalil begins cleaning up as the others scurry into various parts of the mansion. Brian announces he is going to freshen up, promising to be quick and return to Mark, leaving just Brae, Mark, and me in the kitchen.

Mark's face remains etched in shock, but as he paces between the kitchen and Great Room, I sense he wants and needs a distraction.

"So, do you like what we've done with the place?" Brae begins, likely sensing the need to change the subject.

"Oh, yeah. I noticed the changes you've made. Everything looks great!" I reply, attempting to sound as chipper as possible while both Brae and I cast worried glances with one another as we observe Mark's somber state.

"Well, we did have to make a few revisions—you know after the big battle," Brae adds softly.

"Yeah, the place was a wreck. Busted glass, torn drywall—and don't get me started on the décor!" Mark chimes in, his eyes lifting from the floor with a half-grin. "I mean basically we wrecked the place that night."

"I can only imagine," I answer.

"Oh believe me, Damina, you don't want to imagine it!" Mark continues. "Those vile Scourge husks smelled like all to be damned and the Skull carcasses were just as bad. Not to mention the slime, blood, and filth they all left behind. It was horrid! Be glad you missed it!"

"Sounds pretty bad. Still, it looks like you guys worked around it," I say.

"And all the credit goes to my guy for that, Damina. You would've been proud of him! He was so take charge! It was actually pretty hot to see him in action!" Brae brags while looping her arm with his and nuzzling the nape of his neck. Mark's tense posture relaxes with Brae now at his side and he kisses the top of her head with a broad smile spreading his face from ear to ear.

"Way to go, Mark! See, I told you guys that you didn't need me!" I reply.

"Please, Lady D! We needed you all right, but we had to make do. With Dorine and Padma gone and Ms. Jeffers ill, it was only the four of us left to get things done," Mark states.

"Only the four of you?" I question, surprised by this revelation. "Okay, I get Dorine and Padma, but what about Vonnie and Claudia?"

"Well between being on guard for you and Bulwark training, Vonnie didn't have much time to assist us," Brae answers. "And well, Claudia knew after her actions there was no need for her to return."

"*Her actions?* You mean because she started hitting on Mark? I recall Dauphine telling me that Claudia would try to fast track herself to get with him if—"

"Mark?" Brae exclaims, surprised. She and Mark share puzzled expressions as Mark buries his hands in his pockets and walks slowly toward me.

"No, Damina, this has nothing to do with me. Claudia is the one who stabbed Jerrica that night," Mark says in a low tone as he keeps eyes set on me.

Both shock and rage kindle within me at his revelation. I know Dauphine said Claudia wasn't to be trusted, but this is beyond my belief.

"No!" I breathe out a whisper, fearful that perhaps I am not up to speed on all there is to know of my new nightmarish life.

"I'm sorry, Damina, I thought you knew. I just assumed Dalcour or Jackson told you," Brae adds softly, coming to my side.

"No one told me anything," I answer, looking into Brae's bright and watchful gaze.

"Well, I'm not surprised. Although Jackson said the Skull was responsible for her father, Colin's death, I still suspect she was working with Mikkel and the others somehow. I just can't prove it," Brae continues.

"You're still going down that road, baby? I highly doubt it. Colin wasn't a Jadeite and Vitreous like Mikkel have no use for humans otherwise. My money is still on Grenoble. How else would she get such a blade? Besides, Vonnie said Claudia ran off once the knife fell out of her pocket when they reached the back. No doubt Grenoble gave it to her. And you know just how much she hates Jerrica! Who else would want Jerrica out of the way?" Mark counters.

"No one better than good 'ole Chartreuse Grenoble!" Brae's proclamation is loud, but her expression remains vacant as she stares at me.

"Wait!" Suddenly, more fragmented puzzles form a clearer picture in my mind. "You mean Jerrica's rival?"

"Yep the one and only!" Brae responds.

"Hold on—I met her last night—in the Civility Center!" I shout back as the revelation becomes apparent. More memories of Jerrica admitting her dislike of Chartreuse flicker through my mind. Thoughts of the slithering and sinister way Chartreuse spoke with me when we met last night makes my blood boil.

"You met her last night?" Brae questions as her gaze darkens. "Hold on, Damina! Are you saying you went to the CC?"

"Well, yes, but I only went to see Dal and then she was there, so—"

"I'm sorry, Lady D, but it's not good for you to be around Chartreuse for any reason! I mean, let's forget the fact that she's the most venomous Scourge to ever exist—I mean, she makes those vermin at Saint Roch's seem like the get-along-gang! There's no universe where you two should ever breathe the same air!" Mark admonishes me as if he were my eldest brother.

"Yeah, Damina, Marky is right! Big D hardly lets me within five hundred feet of the old dame and I'm a Scourge just like her!" Brae exclaims.

"You are nothing like her, baby!" Mark sternly counters, looking over his shoulder at Brae. "I've heard rumors that she isn't even a Scourge like we know it. She's something much worse." Mark's tone is heavy, and he regards me with almost the same expression as Dalcour did last night before he threw me in my suite. If he could, I have no doubt he'd resort to similar tactics. After searching my face for a few moments, the hardness of his jawline softens, and he bites his lip into a crumpled smile, reminding me of the youthful guy I know him to be. "Look, she's more than Jerrica's rival, Damina. She's bad news!"

"Even more reason to keep you locked up in the bell tower!" I hear Dalcour's deep, lush voice call from behind me just as his lavender and jasmine scent waft pass my nose. While his enticing scent helps to lessen my angst, a looming and grim mood at the name of Chartreuse Grenoble rings through the atmosphere.

Turning to meet the depth of his crimson eyes, Dalcour lifts his supple raspberry colored lips to a crooked smile and I feel my remaining gloomy state dissipate. His eyes look upon me tenderly and I know without telepathy he still regrets his actions from last night.

"So, Dal, is Chartreuse Grenoble the reason you—um—sentenced me to my suite last night?" I ask, my voice soft and low as I feel his lure sweeping over me. Dalcour stares back at me, still smiling as he walks toward us, coming into the kitchen.

"You did what?" Jackson's voice shouts over Dalcour's shoulder from the hallway. I'm not sure how long Jackson has been in the vicinity, but the scornful scowl etched over his face lets me know the truce the two once had is all but faded.

Dalcour's countenance immediately sours at Jackson's overture, but he manages one last smile toward me before turning his attention to Jackson.

"You've got some explaining to do, Marchand!" Jackson lashes as Gregory rounds the corner with him.

"I owe no one an explanation for how I choose to keep Damina safe!" Dalcour snaps back.

"So, you had Vonnie lock her in her room?" Jackson protests and I now see Vonnie standing sheepishly just beyond Jackson. By the way she's holding her head down, I know she likely told him of the events of last night. Her eyes cut up toward me and I smile, I don't want her thinking I am upset with her. I'm not.

"Yes, I did! Do I wish I could've done it differently, sure—but I did what I had to do. And I'd do it all over again if it meant choosing her safety!" Dalcour growls back.

"I see," Jackson begins as he rushes to square off in Dalcour's face. "Well, can you explain how lying about the fact you two never slept together protects Damina?" A deep snarl ripples through Jackson as he gnashes his teeth while his eyes glow bright.

Although Jackson does his best to whisper his words, low gasps echo throughout the kitchen as he belts out his accusation.

"Stop it, Jack!" I yell, placing myself between both Jackson and Dalcour. "We don't need to talk about this now!"

"*You should listen to her, Jack,*" Dalcour seethes, his skin shimmering in a fiery hue and I know his inner beast is raging to be free.

"Hey, Big D, Damina is right, you both should stop it we've got bigger fish to fry," Brae adds, coming to my side.

"Yeah, besides, I thought you were taking Damina to the CC to train with Trieu," Mark says, tugging on Dalcour's arm, attempting to avert his darkening gaze.

Both Dalcour and Jackson back away from one another, but it remains clear their antipathy for one another has grown. Vonnie and Gregory walk into the kitchen and Jackson turns, placing his hand on Gregory's shoulder.

"You're right, Braelyn," Dalcour begins, dousing his rage before it sets in. "We need to get Damina to the Civility Center to begin her training. That's all that matters now."

"My training?" I ask, turning toward Dalcour.

"Yes, Lady Damina, it is time for you to train. You must learn to control your powers. Trieu has agreed to start your training," Vonnie replies, raising her voice just as Dalcour parts his lips to speak. I am surprised by the new tone Vonnie has taken with Dalcour. I guess even she is upset by his behavior last night.

Dalcour presses his lips tight and sighs with a dismissive laugh and continues walking toward me. "Your Protector is right, Beautiful. But Trieu isn't the only one training you."

"She isn't?" I question, puzzled by the mysterious grin gleaming across Dalcour's face.

"Nope. We'll be there too!" Brae announces with a bubbly bounce, clapping her hands as she comes to Dalcour's side.

"That's right, Lady D! You gotta learn to fend off wolves and vamps. You think you can handle that?" Mark says with a small smirk.

"Do you think I'm ready, Dal?"

"Well, there's no better time than now to find out," he answers.

"And I'll trust that you'll do everything possible to keep her safe, young alpha," Jackson says, pushing his way back to my side.

Although he is speaking to Mark, he keeps his eyes fixed on Dalcour, and Dalcour refuses to blink, returning the gesture.

"Yes, Lord Nashoba," Mark quickly replies in an almost militant fashion.

"We will both keep her safe," Vonnie concurs as she brushes past Mark's side. Brae's eyes trail Vonnie's movements with annoyance, but she loses none of her zeal. Brae is certainly more excited about my training than I am.

"Okay, I understand the need for training, I do—but what about finding my cousin? When will we get back to that?" I ask.

"That's where I come in," Gregory states, his chest seemingly swells with his typical haughty posture. "I have some of the best trackers on their way here now. Lothian den wolves! They are the best of the best. If anyone can find Dacari, they can. Only the best for my—um—your cousin." Gregory's face betrays him as Jackson jabs Gregory's ribs.

Crap!

Is Gregory interested in my cousin now, too? Really? I wonder if Brian knows. If it wasn't bad enough that I'm stuck between two stallions, now it looks my cousin might have her own tug-of-war to contend.

I force the thought aside and swallow the thick air in my throat as Gregory's uneasy glare searches my face, likely trying to discern my mood.

I do not have the energy for him or his feelings for my cousin right now.

"Well, I hope your trackers are as good as you claim!" Dalcour adds, breaking the forming awkwardness. "If we're to go hunting for Little Miss Peyroux tonight, we'll need nothing but the best."

"And they are the best," Gregory answers. "We are leaving to meet up with them now. No worries, Damina, we'll have your cousin back with you in no time."

"I hope so," I quietly respond, fretful of what Decaux is up to with my cousin. His daughter.

"Okay, well we should get going, Damina," Brae says, tugging my arms and pulling me from my thoughts.

As Brae and Mark begin walking me toward the door leading to the CC, Jackson places his hand on my shoulder, halting our motion. "Damina, before you go, I think there's something you should know about the trackers," Jackson begins.

"We really don't have a lot of time. I've only booked the CC for a few hours and Trieu cannot be out for long," Dalcour interjects, now coming to my side as Brae and Mark continue down the stairs.

"One minute, Dal," I add. "Look Jackson, I appreciate everything you and Gregory have done. Thanks for getting the trackers. There's no way I could do any of this without you. No way," I say before throwing my arms around his waist and planting a soft kiss on his cheek. His posture relaxes as his face warms as my mouth lingers at the edging of his beard. He only smiles in response, but I know he wants to say more.

"Damina, let's get going." Dalcour's husky voice alone pulls me from Jackson's embrace, and he takes my hand in his and leads us down the stairs.

Chapter 16

"**A**gain!" Trieu shouts back at Mark and Brian who charge at me in wolf form.

Rising from the floor, a golden light surrounds me, and a powerful wind emits from within me, pushing both Mark and Brian away with a hurricane-like force. Stretching my hand toward Brae, small fireballs shoot from my palms, sending tiny flames at her shoulders. She winces with each contact, grinding her razor-sharp fangs, but still manages a small smile, encouraging me to continue my assault.

"Remember, Damina, wolves are mortal so you must attack them with elemental and natural sources. Scourge are only weakened by the sun or tearing them in two," Trieu instructs. "If needed, you can pull the very oxygen from a wolf's mortal soul."

"I don't want to do that! I'll hurt them." I protest as I work hard to keep all three away from me. Marking a boundary line with my light is not as easy as either Trieu or Vonnie made it look. My energy escapes me, and I slowly drift to the ground as I try desperately to hold on to the remaining surge pulsating through me.

Brian is the first to take advantage of the opportunity as he rushes toward me, but I have just enough strength in me to force one final blow of wind in his direction, crippling him on all fours to the ground. As I do, the strength of the flames I once hurled at Brae douses to smoke. She heals before my eyes, wiping away the smoldering dust on her arms and shoulders while scaling the walls and yelping an ear-splitting shriek that nearly deafens me.

"Pull the oxygen from the room, Damina! Do it now! No air. No sound!" I hear Trieu command me through the glass wall.

Annoyed, I turn my head at her to protest, but Mark uses my distraction to pounce on me, gripping me by the arm. Although his hold is tight, he keeps my forearm behind his canines, lessening my pain. Brae screeches once more, and I fear I'll lose my hearing if I don't do as Trieu instructed and halt her screams. Keeping my free hand aimed at Brian, I know I must get Mark off me if I am to summon enough strength to draw out the oxygen as Trieu instructed.

Spinning to my side, I twirl my arm as fast as inhumanly possible until I am able to toss Mark from my arm, flinging him across the room. Mark's wolf is shot like a cannon from my arm straight to the ceiling where Brae is perched. As he plunges into her, they both fall on top of Brian and I tighten the force of wind around the three of them, holding them captive to the floor beneath me. I manage a modicum of power to once more hover over them while encasing them with my light.

Looking over my shoulder, I smile at Trieu, pleased at my obvious feat. More so, I'm thankful I am able to hold everyone off without having to actually suffocate my friends. Still, Trieu doesn't appear to share my enthusiasm. Her eyes fall as I gaze at her and a small frown etches the creases of her thin pink lips.

Irritation fills me as I look on at Trieu and back again at Mark, Brian, and Brae. Why can't Trieu be happy for me? Brae's eyes grow wide as she stares at me. Her sharp teeth retract and her blackened eyes constrict to her normal opulence and I see her mouthing something to me, but I am unable to hear her as my eardrums are still muted from her deafening pitch. Both Mark and Brian paw at me, but in their wolf form I cannot understand them.

As I turn back to Trieu, she lowers her head, closing her eyes tight. She seems disappointed with me.

Just then, I am lifted from behind and thrown across the room into the wall. Before I have a moment to get my bearings or see who threw me, I am flung once more, by my ankles into the air, hitting the ceiling. My barrier surrounding Brae and the others fade, and both Mark and Brian lunge at me.

Anger pools inside me as the room spins around me. And I am thankful for it. The kindling of rage is just the provocation necessary for another resurgence of strength to bellow through me. A loud scream like that of shock waves rivets from the deepest parts of my core and I send a barreling gale force toward Mark and Brian, knocking them back to the ground.

Regaining my levitation, I recall Trieu's earlier teaching today on vibing my energy, my chi. Trieu taught me how Altrinions can harness a power from our solar-like center with enough strength to channel the four winds from the far corners of the earth. As much as I hated the notion of hurting my friends, I knew I needed to do what was necessary to protect myself. Except this time, using my own control. I take in a deep breath and exhale the remaining toxicity of fear and self-doubt.

Exhaling, I blow a strong wind of air toward Brian, Mark, and Brae, holding them in place. As I do, I feel strong hands grip my sides, but sidestep my assailant, turning counterclockwise, until I become my own tornado-like force.

Without a thought, I take the hands of my aggressor, only to find Dalcour staring back at me. In shock, I release his hands and my funnel slows its pace.

"Well done, Mina!" Brae cheers from the floor below us.

"Bravo!" Both Mark and Brian applaud on with whistling and a series of hand clapping.

"Yes, Beautiful, well done, indeed," Dalcour adds. "I hope I didn't hurt you," he continues as he grazes his hands through my hair, searching my face.

"That was you?" I question, still in awe of our tussle.

"Would you have rather it been me? I mean, I told him I was all in helping you train, but he thought it best for it to be him," Titan says, standing at the doorway with Trieu who now wears a more gleeful disposition.

"And I told Titan—there is no world where him laying a hand on you is remotely tolerable," Dalcour states in a throaty tone as he pulls my hand in his and lowers us to the ground.

"Well, there's no better way for her to learn. Besides, I've trained hundreds—no thousands down here in the CC. My training methods are renowned!" Titan brags with a broad smile.

"The only thing legendary about your trainings is the hollowed walls of this former underground railroad hideaway!" Brae scoffs while tossing clothes to Brian and Mark, who are now behind a large curtain in the corner of the room.

"If I recall, you rather enjoyed my trainings, Young One," Titan smirks as a devious crease folds along his brow.

"Really, leech? Can you not just take a hint? The woman isn't interested in you!" Mark snaps as he rushes from behind the curtain wearing only his boxer briefs and socks.

"Please come closer. I dare you," Titan snarls at Mark. Brae jumps in between the two men as Trieu pulls Titan at his wrists, pleading with him to stop picking fights.

"Pay them no attention, Beautiful. Again, I'm sorry I had to toss you around a bit," Dalcour says, with a soft, sly smile.

"You had to?" I ask, puzzled.

"Well, yeah, I did. You must understand, Damina, you do not

practice combat in neutral. You must train as if it's D-day. You must train as if you expect the fight to begin—right now, in this moment."

"Basically, what Lord Marchand is saying is if you train soft—you fight soft," Brian states mildly. His voice is a bit wispy and I can see Brian is still trying to catch his breath.

"Yes, Lady Damina. We would never willingly put your friends here at risk," Trieu says with whispered words, as she pushes her way past Mark and Titan's standoff. "But I am glad you found your center."

"Yes! Thank you, Trieu. Dalcour, Mark, Brae—everyone, just thank you for your help!" I state as I gaze around the room.

"Beautiful, again I only pushed you to react because if you're going to go around with my brother Decaux you're going to have to come prepared," Dalcour says in a soft, yet eerily dark tone.

"So are you saying fighting you is like fighting your brother?" I ask.

"Not at all. Decaux is his own brand of Altrinion. He has no rules. Remember that, Beautiful." Dalcour's eyes narrow as he speaks. He searches my face for a moment, ensuring I take his advisement seriously. "But you did good for today. Not bad, my lady. Not bad at all." Dalcour laughs, softening the mood as he walks toward me and kisses my forehead before turning back to talk with the others.

"Good. I am glad you're doing so well. But there is still much more to learn," Trieu continues with a motherly gaze that's almost hard to see through her translucent hue.

"Well, there's certainly more I'd like to work on. All of this is still so new to me."

"Is there anything in particular you'd want to try next?" Trieu asks with a small, but curious smile. She stares around the room, looking at Brae and Dalcour as they talk with Mark and Brian. I notice Titan has disappeared, but I see Dranoel now standing at the door.

"Whenever you are ready, Lady Trieu," Dranoel says from across the threshold. He looks at me with a tender smile, I nod in response, but I cannot help returning a smile when I detect a light scent of my aunt's perfume pouring from his pores.

I suppose they really are spending a lot of time together. Good for them.

Looking over my shoulder, I see Dalcour and the others talking, and Trieu takes me by my arm and begins leading us to the hallway of the CC.

"So would you like to learn how to control your telepathy?" Trieu questions with a knowing smile.

"Why, yes," I answer, knowing she's likely read my mind. "How can I stop people from reading me? Other Altrinions, I mean."

"Of course, well since you are not an Altrinion-Vampire like Lord Marchand you still need the cloaking powers of a wolf to keep your thoughts hidden," Trieu says in a cottony quiet tone.

"What makes us so different? I mean, he's still an Altrinion." I reply, confused.

"Well, yes, but the vampiric strain douses the Altrinion light that is covered by the wolves. In that way, Altrinion Vampires can control a good deal of their mental range and power. Blood drinkers who have never killed or those to whom the curse is lifted, like Jerrica, require the assistance of wolves."

"So that's why Dal can block me out?" I mutter to myself.

"Precisely," Trieu answers. "Thankfully, I have Dranoel and a few others who have cloaked me and my family for centuries as Jerrica has Brian and Charlotte."

"Dal once said Jackson and my Peyroux family cloaked me. I wonder what happened?"

"I suppose the minute you became more accepting of the Altrinion nature within you, it lessened their ability to shield you."

"Do I have to accept their cloaking? Is that how it works?"

"Something like that, I suppose. As your guardian, I am sure your aunt took that charge for you in your formative years. Later, as you fell in love with Lord Nashoba, you naturally submitted to his protection out of your love for him. I'm sure it didn't take much coaxing. Besides, with your father's permission, it was quite an easy task for him. But as your heart waned from him—"

"It lessened his protection," I say, finishing Trieu's thoughts.

Trieu smiles down at me and takes my palm in her hand. "Look, Damina, I know this is all still very new territory for you. Don't try to trouble yourself with all the ins and outs too fast. Most of it will come in time."

"Excuse me ladies," Dranoel says, walking with Brian toward me and Trieu. "Brian and I just got texts from Gregory and Delia that the Lothian Den trackers have arrived."

Excitement bubbles through me at Dranoel's words. As much as I have enjoyed training, none of it matters if I don't find my cousin. "That's awesome! Hey, let's get going everyone! The trackers are here, and we need to finally find my cousin!" I shout over my shoulder to Mark, Brae and Dalcour.

Dalcour, Mark and Brae are at my side in an instant and we begin making our way down the hall after I thank Trieu for her training.

Brian shouts my name from behind us and I turn to see he, Dranoel, and Trieu standing stiffly at the end of the corridor, all giving one another awkward glances.

"What is it, Brian?" Dalcour calls back over his shoulders with his hand cupped tight with my own.

"Perhaps Mark and I should go with the Lothian Den and do the first series of tracking. You know, make sure we survey the land before letting Lady Nicaud trek along with us. You know— just in case." Brian's unusually shifty posture doesn't go unnoticed by me or the others, and Dalcour's expression seems as irritated as I've become.

"If nothing more, I want to meet them." I exclaim as I watch Mark's face also grow with worry. "I mean, are they dangerous or something?"

"Or something," Mark mutters with his head down.

"Brian, is there something more?" Dalcour demands, his voice pitchy. I can only assume he is as eager as I am to find his brother and end this once and for all.

"Oh this is ridiculous, B!" Brae quips. "You're just standing there like a frigging statue and saying nothing. Damina, come on, let's get upstairs and find your cousin!"

"Yes, you're right, Braelyn. You can take Damina back to the mansion. Mark and I are right behind you," Dalcour says, kissing my hand before placing it in Brae's cold and gloved palm.

Although I am curious as to Brian's strange behavior, I don't have time to speculate before Brae whips me through the long dark corridor.

As the doors open both Delia and Jackson are the first to greet us. While I can understand Jackson's diffidence with his growing ire toward all things Dalcour, I would have thought both he and my aunt would be pleased to have the Lothian Den Wolves here to use their keen tracking skills to find my cousin. Instead, both look at me with such a grim countenance I almost wonder if the Reaper himself is at my back.

"Where's Dalcour?" Jackson asks as I lift to the top of the landing. His tone is stiff, and I can't help wondering why he's asking for him.

"He and Mark are coming right behind us," Brae replies as I watch Jackson's pensive posture shift back and forth. Jackson has never been an easily unnerved person, so I wonder what has gotten into him.

"What's wrong, Aunt Delia?" I question cautiously as I notice glassy pools of water form behind her eyes. "Did something happen with Dacari?" I sputter my words so quick I am not even sure if I rehearsed the thought before speaking the words.

"No, Damina, there's been no change in Dacari's status that we are aware of," Jackson softly responds as my aunt looks away nervously. Her nose twitches and I now see a more angered tint behind her eyes. Jackson's stance also stiffens as his eyes dart to a shadowy form coming from the adjacent hall. I indistinctly hear Gregory's mumbling from afar and I suspect he's done something to upset Jackson.

"Okay, so where are these super wolf trackers?" Brae blurts, breaking through the gloomy gazes of both my aunt and ex-fiancé.

"Um, Damina—" Jackson starts, but it's Brae's loud gasp and flurry of expletives that turns my attention to the approaching company.

My mouth drops open with both shock and fury, rising my boiling blood in a split second. Rage swathes my sight and darkness cloud my view beyond my mania. Heat seeps out my pores like steam and my body warms like a fire. Dripping sweat beads at my brow and I dig my feet deep into the marble floor beneath me, cracking the hairlines with a tremorous stomp.

Flashing images of the eve of my wedding score through my memory and a haunting chill I have not felt since *that night* erupts a volcanic madness within me like I have never felt before.

Everything in me wants to maintain my composure. But I am struggling.

I want to be released from the infuriating sight before me. But I cannot. Instead, I am now captive to a resurging ire I can no longer escape.

A foe I had never hoped to see is now the face staring back at me.

Kyra!

What is she doing here?

Why would Jackson bring her here?

How dare she!

How could he?

This time, sadness holds no sway to my soul. Only vexing vibrations course through me, enticing me to flirt with a deep darkness within me I never knew existed.

"Hello, Damina." Kyra's whispered words meet my ears like nails on a chalkboard, and I can barely fathom her insolence.

Who does she think she is?

Who gave her permission to speak?

Not once have I extended an olive branch! It is nothing but her own hubris to think I would offer such consent.

I do not.

Once more, she parts her lips to speak, but this time I will not hear it. None of it.

Again, a looming darkness encapsulates my being at the mere sight of her. A malign essence swelters like heat along my body and a reddening sheen hue emanates through my skin. My feet rise just a few inches from the floor as I grant my fury permission to release.

Stretching my arms toward Kyra, I inhale deeply and tug my arms back to my chest, and Kyra is drawn to me as though I had an invisible ripcord. Without touching her, my two fists mound near her collarbone and I dig my nails into my palm, yanking the invisible ripcord tighter, suffocating her.

Kyra's weakened hazel eyes bulge and she struggles to breathe. The sight of her struggle casts a shadow of joy over me and my mal intent becomes clear.

Perhaps I can pull the oxygen out of the room after all? If not, I can surely pull it out of her!

A sinister lilting chortle escapes the corners of my mouth and a malicious grin mars my face.

"Damina, stop it!" I hear Jackson plead from my left. Still, I don't take my eyes from Kyra as my pleasure increases as she squirms, suspended in the air at nothing but my will.

Both Brae and Aunt Delia call my name as well, begging me not to do anything I'd regret. But I have no remorse. Just as she had none for the part she played in the demise of my would-be-nuptials.

Two men I suspect to be with her company growl at my right side and I pay them no other attention than guiding my hand toward them, crippling them to the floor with the wind I emit as I'd just done to Mark and Brian. Gregory also petitions me from afar, but I refuse to let her go.

Why should I?

This woman has earned my retribution. She willfully deceived Jackson. She aligned herself to Keiron. And is to her I owe our break-up, my current state and perhaps even Dacari's departure. Every horrid detail of my life as of late could rightfully be laid at her feet.

Every. Single. Thing.

"No, Beautiful!" Dalcour's voice alone breaks through the dissonance of my dismay. "You're better than this, Beautiful. Let her go."

With Dalcour's hands now rested on my shoulders, the sweet effervescence of his scent permeates my being, cajoling me to a much calmer state.

Slowly, I exhale, releasing small currents of rage as I lower her back to the ground.

"That's it, Beautiful," Dalcour whispers softly at my ear. "Keep going, baby. You can do it."

With his final words of reassurance, I fully release my hold on Kyra, and I exhale again as Dalcour wraps his arms around me, pinning me to his chest. The cadence of his heartbeat strums like a lullaby in my hearing, dousing the kindling rage burning within me.

It is in this moment I find myself thankful for one thing, and one thing alone.

Dalcour Marchand.

Chapter 17

"**W**ow! Nashoba you are a piece of work!" The tremble of Dalcour's shout toward Jackson sends tremors through his chest as he keeps my face pressed against him. "I can't believe you'd bring her here!"

"Please, Damina, Jackson had no idea *she* was coming," Aunt Delia replies. "Gregory should have taken better care of knowing who Merle had in his company before he asked for their aid!"

"She's right, Damina. It's all my fault. Jackson is just as troubled as you are," Gregory adds.

"*Oh, is he?*" I snap back, pulling myself from Dalcour's embrace.

"Come on, Nashoba! Damina deserves better than this!" Dalcour contends, with his hands rested on my shoulders.

"I know what Damina deserves!" Jackson huffs in a grumbling low growl.

"*Really?* Because this right here—this isn't it!" Dalcour exclaims.

"Don't you begin touting your self-righteous indignation with me, Marchand. You claim to care for Damina. *Love her*. But you don't. *You can't*. How can you even comprehend what love truly is?" Jackson growls as he takes cautious steps toward us.

"I can tell you what it's not, mutt. It's not bringing your ex—no, excuse me, the one woman who you cheated on your fiancé with—to parade her in front of the woman you claim to love!" Dalcour yells.

"Perhaps you think it's more acceptable to allege an intimacy between you and Damina for no other reason than to control her narrative."

"To the contrary, Nashoba. I have no need to feign any intimacy between Damina and me. You see, what we share is real. What we've shared in five days was more real than you ever experienced in five years. So real, in fact, we've bypassed all myth and legend! So real that our connection alone revealed an intimacy so powerful we didn't have to even take our clothes off. But that's what scares you the most. Isn't it, Nashoba?"

Jackson snarls as he rushes toward Dalcour, reaching over me to grab his collar. Dalcour roars back at him and the sound from him reverberates from my back through my chest.

Caught between the two, both anger and frustration sweep over me and a strong tidal force blows from me with a glaring white light, forcing both men away from one another. Now standing in the center of the foyer, I turn and observe the worried and watchful glare of everyone and my heart falters.

I don't know how much more of this I can take.

"Why don't we all leave Damina and Kyra to talk?" Aunt Delia says in the strong, dominant manner I've always known. The scowl now etched on her face tells me she's grown tired of the back and forth between Jackson and Dalcour. More important, she wants to find her daughter and we all need to move past these petty matters. "Lothians, please exit to the parlor with Brian and Gregory. The rest of you—make yourself useful. I'm sure Braclyn and Mark could use your assistance in some manner."

"She's right," Brae adds. "Shows over folks! You heard the lady.

Come on and follow me!"

My heart lightens as I see Brae and Aunt Delia exchange smiles. Perhaps my aunt is warming to Brae after all? Still, I can tell she is not pleased with either Jackson or Dalcour. As the two remain stewing in their shared animosity, Aunt Delia walks to the center where only I stand, and she reaches down to help Kyra from the ground.

"Gentlemen, the time is long overdue for these two women to speak. And they need to do so without your interference or chest-beating, cavemen-like antics. I am sure you can find some way of busying yourselves and allow them some time to talk." Aunt Delia's tone is brash and matter of fact. While both men maintain their face-off for a brief moment, Jackson is the first to retract his stance and Dalcour slowly follows suit as each turn to go their separate ways. "Will you be okay, Damina?" My aunt questions.

Nodding with my eyes only, I carefully watch Kyra's hands as she dusts off her dusty rose trousers and cream blouse. Aunt Delia narrows her eyes, searching my face before she exits to the kitchen after a brief squeeze on my shoulder.

Kyra's posture varies from the strong, overly confident woman whose eyes once regarded me with contempt at Sonfries. Her eyes alone tell me of her destitute state. This is not the same haughty diva who exchanged daggered-eyed glances with me on the eve of my wedding.

She is different. *Broken.*

Even still, a part of me refuses to give in to my normal bouts of empathy.

She has not yet earned such an emotion.

As much as I want to rest in my anger, I feel my legs wobble like noodles beneath me. Keeping my sights on her, I walk to the steps and sit on the fourth step from the floor. I want to say something, but I even feel the darn frog stuck in my throat, so I extend my hand to Kyra, gesturing her to talk.

"I owe you an apology, Lady Damina," Kyra begins. "For so many things, but mainly for my part in breaking up your marriage—for my interference."

"Interference? It was quite more than that!" I choke out my words.

"Yes, you are right. I know I should not have aligned myself with Keiron. I knew better than that, but I was desperate."

"Because you were broke? Are you serious, Kyra? Jackson told me because you and your mother swindled your inheritance, you were exiled."

"Well, yes, it is true we haven't quite maintained the status quo necessary for an alpha, but truthfully that is not the real reason behind my actions," Kyra quietly admits.

As she does, my heart melts. Could it be that she actually loves Jackson? Crap!

"The truth is, I am sterile. I cannot have children."

"What? What does that have to do with anything?" I mutter as I watch diamond-like tears drop past her cheeks.

"All alphas must be capable of procreation. There must be an heir. This rule is absolute. Non-negotiable. Far beyond wealth. Even far beyond any other capabilities. An alpha must be able to propagate the bloodline. Secure the continuation of the entire den. I did what I did because I am infertile."

Silence sits between us and despite my restraint, my empathy for her breaks through the remaining hardness of my heart. She stares back at me, cautiously observing my responsiveness. I work hard to remain stoic. I refuse to let her know my heart aches for her.

She is still the woman responsible for my reckoning.

"So what does that have to do with Jackson? Why align with Keiron to break us up?" I sharply belt out. Her eyes fall at my words and a stinging ache pains through me. How can I be so callous?

"Well it is the reason I needed a Changeling. While Keiron knew I would get a Changeling to serve as your imposter, he did not know I had bartered a deal with a Changeling to aid in my impregnation. You see, although Changelings are without form, they can still procreate. In order to break their shadowed curse of formlessness, they must pledge their life for a life. Women throughout the ages have consulted Changelings to aid in fertility."

"Really? I've never heard of such," I quietly reply.

"Oh, I am sure you have but you didn't know it. Oshun, Eshu, Demeter, Dionysus and even Isis. All Changelings. Until they were released from their shadowed curse, they too lived in voided form, roaming the earth, hopeful to one day make themselves whole again. The Changelings were once powerful beings—that is, until the Order of Altrinion began. But that is a history lesson for another day," Kyra states in a demure and gentle tone.

Still watching me carefully, she sits with her back to me on the bottom step. Exhaling, her stiff posture relaxes, and she flips her long, wavy brunette waves over her shoulder as she presses her back to the wall and turns toward me.

"Okay, so you used a Changeling to get pregnant. Are you saying you were trying to get pregnant with Jackson's child?" Although anger teases my emotions, I don't have the energy to give in to its temptation.

Kyra stares at me, obviously surprised by my monotoned response. "Well, yes. Having an alpha's child would most assuredly keep my status as alpha intact. But I would have settled for Keiron—I mean, he is still a Prime. Heck, Merle even! I just needed a child." The desperation in Kyra's voice as she speaks makes my inaction palatable.

"And let me guess, Jackson doesn't know this."

"No one. Except for my mother. And Merle."

"Who is Merle?"

"He is the newly appointed alpha. When he took over, I told him.

But no one else. Being infertile is a fate worse than death to an alpha. Many Skull herd were birthed out of impotent and infertile wolves." Kyra's voice fades as she speaks, and a haunting and chilling memory of my encounter with the Skull wolves plagues my mind.

Despite my gnawing antipathy for Kyra, her story tugs my heart's strings. I don't want to care about her. But I do. To be ousted for infertility is heartbreaking—even if it is my foe.

"What happened to the Changeling?" I quickly ask, pushing past the empathetic overture taunting its release as I jump from the steps and brush by Kyra.

Once more, her eyes fall, making her bare before me. "The Changeling—um—well, it got sent to a Jinn's jar. And there it must remain until it fulfills the pledge."

"A Jinn jar? You don't mean a genie's lamp, do you?" This is getting ridiculous! I heave a laugh as I saunter in circles in the foyer.

This new world is becoming unbelievable! Vampires, wolves, Bulwarks, Altrinions, and now Jinn? What's next? Dragons?

Don't even think it, Damina!

"I know it all sounds ridiculous. I assure you; it's sounds even worse as a bedtime story as a kid," Kyra replies.

"So now what? You just open the Jinn jar and find some unsuspecting fool to get you pregnant. I mean, I hope you know that's not happening with Jackson—now or ever!" I snap in a low snarl that rumbles through my chest. No matter where I stand between Jackson and Dalcour, I will never budge on this.

"Of course, I know, Lady Damina. Besides, I missed my opportunity. You only get one chance with a Changeling. If you back out, that's it. Thankfully, I am a wolf so I could take the expulsion. But humans or others aren't always so fortunate." Again, Kyra's voice drifts as she speaks, and I can sense both disappointment and regret leak from her pores. "Look, I know that despite how dire my situation, what I did to you and Jackson is unforgiveable. For that, I am sorry. My actions were selfish and there is truly no excuse. But if it is any consolation, please know the Lothian Den had no part in my actions. I also know you have no reason to trust me. Please believe me when I say, there are no better trackers more capable of locating your cousin that the Lothian. If you would still permit their search, I promise you will not be disappointed. And if you prefer, I will stay away from the search, but please allow them an opportunity to assist you in finding Dacari." Kyra's eyes are earnest as she stares up into my own.

For the first time, I see in her something I did not expect to find. An ally.

"You are right, I have no reason to trust you. But despite everything, I still trust Jackson. I know if nothing else, he would never involve anyone unless he thought it necessary. So whatever there is between you and me, Kyra, *you are necessary.*" Large droplets of tears drip from Kyra's eyes at my words. Sincerity graces her smile as she bows her head graciously toward me. Far be it from me to ever allow another woman to feel less than in my presence. No matter what she's done. Even more, Dalcour was right, I am better than the manner in which I reacted. Much better.

"Thank you, my lady," Kyra cries in gratitude.

"Very well, darling! I am happy to see you have made amends," Aunt Delia says as she rounds the corner from beyond the kitchen.

"You were listening?" I ask, shaking my head, hardly surprised by my aunt's actions.

"Of course, my dear! You know me well!" Aunt Delia replies, wholly unashamed. Both Kyra and I share a small chuckle at my aunt's unapologetic stance.

"I am glad to hear it too!" I hear Jackson call from behind us.

Turning to meet his face almost melts my heart in two. While we are far from reuniting, I am more comforted now in knowing

Jackson never meant to hurt me than at my awakening. In fact, for the first time, I believe Jackson was as much a victim of Keiron and Kyra's treachery as me.

A small smile forms beneath his goatee and his eyes dance with a glint of hopefulness as he continues toward me. Although I wonder if Jackson now knows the motivations behind Kyra's deceit, I know we've spent too long on the matter. We must get back to Dacari!

"Well, now we can focus our attentions on finding your cousin!" Jackson says with a broad smile as he wraps his arms around my shoulders, planting a light kiss at my forehead. A surprisingly sincere smile grazes Kyra's face as Jackson holds me, and I feel the remaining weightiness of my disdain toward her fall aside.

The two men from Kyra's company come out of the parlor with Mark and Brian, gathering themselves with Kyra.

"Baby," Jackson says softly, turning my chin up to meet his eyes. "Please know I am sorry. I didn't know she would be here. You know I'd never do anything to hurt you."

"I know, Jack," I answer, nuzzling my chin in his palm. Deeply inhaling his sweet and spicy aroma, a flickering image of my dreamscape flashes through my mind and I am comforted by my recollections of the White Wolf. My Jackson.

"Ah-hem," Mark begins, forcing a faux cough. "We've gathered enough of Dacari's things to trace her scent. We can probably get going, Lord Nashoba."

"Good work, Mark!" Jackson calls over his shoulder, gently pulling himself from our locked-in gaze. Smiling at me once more, he steps aside but takes my hand in his. "Gregory, is everything else secure?"

"Yes, sir," Gregory responds. "We now have everything we need for Mark's valuation. The minute we procure Ms. Peyroux, we can proceed with assuring Mark's alpha status."

"What?" Mark gulps in surprise. "But it's so soon! How did you—"

"You are more than deserving!" Gregory shouts.

"I couldn't agree more!" Dalcour says from the top of the staircase landing as he and Brae stare over the railing. Brae's smile beams from ear to ear as she looks at Mark, and pride fills Dalcour's chest as he speaks.

"And it is the only area where Lord Marchand and I are in agreement." Jackson's clipped tone slice through the merriment of the moment, but Dalcour ignores his sentiment as he trots down the staircase, wearing his fondness for Mark in full stride.

Once more, Mark seems torn between his loyalties for Dalcour and Jackson, but his excitement for the news of his valuation pushes through. Everyone congratulates Mark and even Dilano and Alana make their way into the foyer and share in the cheerfulness of the news.

"Oh I can think of still another area of agreement. The Lady Damina Nicaud!" Dalcour says in a bright and jovial tone, despite Jackson's daggered-eyed glare pinned on Dalcour.

"Me?" I question, surprised.

"Yes, you Beautiful! This is the first time in ages where a full blood Altrinion will give a blessing of valuation for a rising alpha—even more so, Dunes. You, my lady, are once again making history!" Dalcour reveals.

Dalcour's words send flurries of shock through me! Slowly, I recall Brae telling me that it was important for me to choose Mark for the mansion project from the beginning. "Has this been your plan all along?" I ask as the puzzle pieces form a clearer picture in my mind.

"I wish I could take all the credit, Beautiful, but that all goes to Jerrica. Although she is no longer cursed, she could have sat in your stead, but having a pure blood such as yourself on the valuation panel helps to make Mark's status assured."

Heaving small gasps of air, I am once again shocked that I find myself at the epicenter of Jerrica's grand plan. The frog invades my throat, leaving me standing speechless.

"Thank you, Lord Nashoba!" Mark yelps, hardly containing his excitement. His outburst is just what I need to break from the searing stand-off and tug-of-war holding me between both Dalcour and Jackson. "And thank you, Lord Marchand! You, Brian, and Ms. Jeffers believed in me when no one else did. I only wish my father—" Mark's eyes glass as he chokes on his words at the memory of his father.

I can relate.

Brae squeezes herself beneath Mark's arm as Brian and Dilano swarm his side and Mark smiles, mouthing a quiet *thank you* to me as I nod in reply. Refusing to linger in his own celebration, Mark catches my eye and regains his about-face posture.

"But the time for rejoicing is not now." Mark begins, wearing his leadership like a badge of honor. "Our first priority is to find Dacari. And Lady D and Ms. Peyroux, that is exactly what we're going to do!" Mark exclaims, and the foyer erupts in echoes of agreement. "However, Lady Damina, I do agree with Brian, it is probably best if you stay behind for now. We need to survey the area first."

While a part of me wants to protest, deep down I know Mark is right. I still need more training.

"Our resident alpha-elect is correct," Jackson adds. "Damina, do you mind?" Jackson asks with a tender gaze. I know he expects me to object.

Just as I part my lips, Dalcour walks near my side and throws his arm around my shoulder, pulling me close to his side. "It's quite all right, Lord Nashoba. You all go. Survey the area. Damina still has more training to complete. And tonight she'll get a chance to try out what she's learned so far."

"I will?" I ask, surprised.

Jackson's lips curl at the sight of Dalcour's palm squeezing my shoulder, but he keeps his eyes fixed on me. "What are you talking about, Marchand?"

"Scourge sighting," Brae interjects, now leaning into my side. She takes a huge gulp through her straw and turns to me and smiles while using her knuckles to wipe away small drops of blood from her mouth.

"Nothing to worry about, Beautiful. Cedric, Lux, and Abigail will join the three of us. The Guard got word of a sighting near a school just outside of the city limits," Dalcour says.

"Yes, my Lord, and we have every reason to believe the Vitreous is behind it!" Lux says, announcing his entry from the doors leading to the Civility Center. He smiles at both Dalcour and me, but casts a cautious glance to the remaining wolves in the foyer. I see his brother Cedric and a lovely woman; I assume to be Abigail.

"There's so many of them," she whispers over Cedric's shoulders as her long, wavy, brunette curls hang against his biceps. Her features are strong and while she has a no-nonsense presence, I detect a softness behind her eyes that is likely reserved for Cedric. Both she and Cedric gaze on the large group of wolves in the foyer, and I realize there may be a natural animosity between the two.

Interesting.

"Well, then, I suppose we all have our marching orders," Jackson announces, breaking through the forming awkwardness of the Lothian wolves and the arrival of Lux and his family. Turning to me, Jackson shoots a quick darted glance to Dalcour, but gives me a small smile before planting a kiss on my forehead. "Be careful out there, baby."

"I will, Jack," I answer softly. "You do the same. Please."

"Yes, do be careful, Nashoba. All things aside, my brother is more cunning than you can imagine. Whatever bedtime stories you've heard of him barely scratch the surface of his depravity," Dalcour says in a dark and low tone.

Jackson stares at Dalcour, affirming with his eyes only. Mark and the company of wolves gather at the door waiting for Jackson, but I can tell he remains hesitant to leave me.

"I will be fine, Jackson. Go—find my cousin," I mutter, pointing to the wolves who await him on the mansion porch. Keeping his eyes on me, Jackson grants me his most dashing smile before joining the others.

Even with Dalcour beside me, it's still hard to resist the pull of Jackson Nash.

Dalcour nudges my shoulder and smiles down at me with a wide-eyed, boyish grin. Then it hits me.

I am officially screwed.

Chapter 18

"**S**o are you ready to go all Bonnie and Clyde with me?" Dalcour says with a broad smile as his almond-shaped crimson eyes beam with hopefulness.

"Bonnie and Clyde?" I reply, taking a step back so as not to linger in his luring scent. "More like Queen and Slim or Jay and Bey, don't you think—yeah, let's go with Jay and Bey! The others don't end too well," I tease.

"You're right!" Dalcour laughs as he stuffs his hands in his pockets and leans down toward me. "Damina," he whispers. "I've got a little secret."

"What is it?" I question, curious.

"I've kind of envied Cedric and his wife Abigail from afar," Dalcour reveals as I watch the pair look over weapons with Lux and Brae.

"Really? Why?" I'm surprised. Dalcour doesn't strike me as one to envy anyone.

"Well, they've always had that power couple type of vibe. You don't see it much in our world, but their love is the stuff of legend.

It's the kind everyone wants."

"Everyone?"

"That is, only if I can have it with you," Dalcour answers sweetly. "Look, I know you still feel stuck between me and Jackson, but I am not going to stop campaigning for what we have. Because I think what we have is more than a legend—I think it's so much more. Don't you?"

"Dal, I—I don't—"

"It's okay, Beautiful," Dalcour says softly, placing his finger on my lips. "You don't have to make a choice right now. But I am not going to stop reminding you how I feel. Besides, it's obvious Jackson isn't shying away from his affection. Though, I can't say I blame him. I'm just hoping tonight you'll finally see what is possible for us—the type of life we can have. *Together.*"

"Lord Marchand," I hear Abigail's voice call from behind Dalcour.

My, am I glad for her interruption. Had she delayed a second longer, I have no doubt Dalcour's lips would be locked with mine. I am already torn between Jackson and Dalcour. I don't think my heart could take him kissing me right now.

Dalcour maintains his posture, leaning over me. If I could read his mind, I know he's likely contemplating whether to crush his mouth to mine. A small smirk lingers at the corners of his supple raspberry-coated lips and my eyes dance with desire as I gawk at the sexy curling of his mustache against his glistening pecan skin.

Get a hold of yourself, Damina.

"Lord Marchand," Abigail says once more.

Winking at me, Dalcour quickly turns to face Abigail but reaches back to grab my arm, pulling me to his side. "Yes, I'm sorry, Abigail. How can I help you?"

"My apologies for the interruption, my lord. I was wondering if I could go see Jerrica before we set off. Lux is going to talk to his contact. I'll just be a minute," Abigail says with a warm smile that meets her eyes.

"Yes, but first I'd like you to formally meet the Lady Damina Nicaud."

"Of course, where are my manners!" She exclaims. "It is a pleasure to meet you, Lady Damina. I have heard nothing but good things," Abigail says, extending her gloved leather hand to me.

"No apologies needed, Abigail. It's a pleasure to meet you as well."

"You two get to know one another. Let me check with Charlotte and Zamora to see if she's up for visitors," Dalcour says and quickly exits down the hall.

Abigail and I stare at one another for a few awkward moments until her eyes flutter as a tender smile graces her lightly painted lips. "I hope this doesn't sound rude, but I guess I pictured you differently. You know the way everyone talks about you, I thought you'd be more deity-like. You know, standoffish."

"Oh, really? Me?"

Abigail laughs and the strong lines in her face softens. "Don't get me wrong, I'm glad. I suppose I only thought that because I assumed it would take a cavewoman of sorts to tame Lord Marchand."

"No cavewoman here," I laugh in response.

"Well, whatever you are doing to him—thank you. It's good to see him smile. You make him happy."

"How long have you and Cedric been married," I respond, pushing past Abigail's sentiment.

Her eyes fall slightly, but she smiles when Cedric comes to her side.

"Almost two hundred years," Cedric answers with a broad smile. "And forever left to go!"

"Wow! I think that is the longest marriage I've ever heard of!"

"It's more common than you think. Divorce stats are quite low among our kind. Once we pledge our fidelity it kind of sticks from there," Cedric states.

"I'm sorry, Abigail," Dalcour calls from behind us. "Charlotte says now isn't a good time. She's trying to get her to eat a little. Maybe when we get back."

"Of course, no problem. We can certainly check back later, Lord Marchand. Thank you," Abigail replies. She offers me a smile as she and Cedric head to the front door as Lux waits on the other side of the threshold.

"Damina, darling," Aunt Delia calls from the doors of the parlor. "I've asked Vonnie to stay behind with me and Dranoel. Since Charlotte is tending to Jerrica and everyone else is out."

Vonnie stands near my aunt, but her eyes tell me if I only said the word, she'd be right on our heels.

"It's not a problem, Aunt Delia. Vonnie, please keep watch on things here. Thanks!"

Vonnie nods her head in reply and turns to go into the parlor with my aunt and Dranoel, leaving Dalcour and I in the foyer. Before we leave, I tug his arm, turning his attention back to me.

"Yes, Beautiful," Dalcour answers with a sly smile. While he likely thinks I want to pick up where we almost left off, he's wrong.

"Um, did you go see Jerrica?"

Dalcour's eyes quickly fall at my words and his posture instantly stiffens.

"No. I called Charlotte. Why?" He replies in a flat and grubby tone.

"Well, when was the last time you've seen her? Dal, she's not doing well, but I'm sure she'd appreciate a visit from you."

"Look, Damina, we don't need to get into this now," Dalcour says, spinning on his heel toward the door.

Speeding past him, I am in front of the door in an instant, blocking his exit. "Dalcour Marchand, can you answer me, please? What are you afraid of? Why haven't you seen your friend?"

"Damina, we really don't have time for this right now!"

"Then just tell me! Jerrica is your friend, Dalcour."

"I know exactly who she is, Damina."

"Look, I didn't want to do this. I—I'm probably not the one who should do this, but here it goes. Dalcour, Jerrica is more than your friend. She cares for you—deeply. More than that she's in lo—"

"I know, Damina. I know." Dalcour's head dips low as he speaks and his shoulders hunch inward.

"You do?" I ask, puzzled. "How? I thought Jerrica said she never told you."

"No, you're right. She never told me—but—" Dalcour taps on his forehead and purses his lips tight.

"You heard her thoughts?"

"It wasn't intentional, but yes. Anyway, Damina one thing you'll find is Altrinions aren't too keen on death. We don't embrace it like humans. In my long lifetime, I've seen too many die. It is not a pretty picture. And in instances where it doesn't have to be, it's even harder," Dalcour's words fade as he speaks, and I can see the hurt in his face and the glassy waterfall forming behind his crimson eyes.

"What do you mean—it doesn't have to be?"

"Jerrica hasn't had human blood in over a century. It's bad enough she was stabbed by Claudia with an Obsidian blade—a Mercy—but without human blood her body cannot regenerate. I went in to see her on the first day and she refused to drink. Zamora's only feeding her goat and pig blood. She'll never survive on that crap. At this point, it's only delaying the inevitable. And I have no desire to see my best friend be captive to a slow and agonizing death."

"Dal, I understand—well at least I get what you're saying, but she's your friend. Even more, if it weren't for Jerrica, I know the two of us would have never met. We owe her! I'll go with you if you need, but just please promise me you'll see her."

"Look, we really need to get going but I promise I'll think about it. That is, if you go with me," Dalcour answers, forcing a small smile.

"Of course, I'll go with you, Dal."

"Good," Dalcour replies, widening his smile and taking my hand in his. "That's why after all this crap is over, we'll get you started on human blood right away. I refuse to let her fate be yours," Dalcour huffs as he gently yanks me through the doors of the mansion.

He doesn't leave room for my response, but I can't help thinking about his assertion. Since my awakening, I have given little thought to how things actually work in this world—his world. But I know one thing.

I have no intention of drinking blood.

Human or otherwise.

Chapter 19

Once we arrive at the school, I notice people running through the courtyard. Panicky screams and mentions of the word gun permeate throughout. Dalcour gives me an awkward glance, but he takes in a large gulp of air and then turns to Lux.

"Do you smell it, my lord?" Lux questions as Dalcour nods in agreement.

"Yes, I can smell it. Can you, Damina?" Dalcour questions in a hurried tone.

"No, I don't smell anything."

"Try, my lady," Abigail whispers behind me. "It should smell of raw chicken and dried blood."

"It's the stench of the slimy trail they leave behind," Cedric adds.

Inhaling once more, I detect a faint scent of the raw chicken smell Abigail mentioned. My nose crinkles at the odor I detect and Dalcour pats my shoulders, offering a covered grin. "Yep, she smells it all right. Okay, Lux, so where is your contact?"

"He's inside," Lux replies.

"Who is this contact?" I ask. With my mind clouded with Dalcour's goals of turning me into a blood drinker and the churn just the thought of it gave to my insides, I didn't really know much about what I was getting myself into.

"His name is Rashad Robinson. He and his wife care for children of the supernatural variety if you will. Both he and his wife were orphaned Bulwarks. They are not of the Order, but they do their best to protect halflings and other orphaned supernatural children. The girl they have is exhibiting some Breaker-like abilities. He has kept me apprised of her progress, which to date hasn't been much. But when the Guard informed us of the Scourge sighting and Rashad contacted me stating they were in trouble, I thought it best for us to lend a hand."

"You did the right thing, Lux. Damina, you'll need to go in with Lux first. Use your light. They are Scourge so your light should vanquish them almost immediately. Cedric will let us know when it's safe for the rest of us to enter. You got this, Beautiful," Dalcour says, drifting his fingers along my chin.

I nod as Lux takes my hand, leading us into the school. Briefly looking over my shoulder, I notice other members of the Guard have arrived, but Dalcour keeps his eyes fixed on me. He nods his head, giving me one final boost of confidence before I am fully out of his eyesight.

While I've had several opportunities to fight Scourge and protect myself since I've entered this new world, I have very little experience marching into it headfirst. Still, I push through my fears because I realize even helping the Guard tonight at the school is the training I need to help rescue my cousin.

Once we're inside Lux points out his contact Rashad with his wife and child nestled in his arms on the floor by the door. Rashad turns to see us, but Lux covers his mouth, motioning for him to remain quiet. Rashad's wife directs our attention to the other side of the basketball court where we see a large, menacing Scourge toss a young girl across the floor. She lands headfirst into a large table, toppling books and a computer on top of her head.

More Scourge enter from opposite sides of the arena and Lux looks at me with his wolfen eyes glowing a bright gold. "Are you ready, Lady Nicaud? You light the way and I'll be right at your side," Lux whispers.

Looking up, I see a glint of the moon's light shining through the gymnasium and it gives me the assurance I need to take my flight above the bleachers. Lux quickly scales the bleachers behind me, mounting four or more rows at a time. His movements are rapid as we keep a stealthy flow to the top of the bleachers, and I am hovering at its center.

"Now, Lady Nicaud," Lux directs as I summon the Altrinion force within me.

Bright rays of sunlight exude from my pores and a bright, golden white shines throughout my entire being. Loud screeching cries bellow from the Scourge as they burn in agony.

"Okay, my lady. Pull back, Lord Marchand is here," Lux shouts and I look down and see Dalcour and the remaining Guard at the door. Dalcour gazes up at me, but I can hardly see him through the iridescent rays of light encapsulating me.

Just as the brightness fades, Dalcour and the Guard swarm the gymnasium, putting a swift end to the Scourge with an almost effortless assault. As the vampires vanquish to mounds of Sulphur and dust, my eyes scan the floor and I see the young girl still laying on the ground. I also spot another family huddled at the base of the bleachers.

"Damina!" I hear Brae shout from below. "He's hurt pretty bad. You better get to him first!"

At my descent I find a handsome young teen wearing a basketball uniform bleeding from his shoulder. He's laying against the chest of an equally handsome man I assume to be his father. The man looks up at me as I land, and a gripping familiarity lingers between the two of us. His honey-coated hue slightly mirrors my own, and his eyes carry the reminiscent gentleness of my Grandma Roux. A lovely woman with thick goddess blonde tendrils and a teen girl who is her mirror image is also kneeling at his side. It doesn't take long for their scrambled thoughts to invade my mind, giving me just enough information to know they are a blended family.

"I can help," I say softly to the man and woman as the two lock their hands together. The young teen looks up at me, his eyes filled with both tears and pain.

"Please help my brother!" The young girl calls out to me as a waterfall of tears flood her face.

Placing my hand at his injury, a soft warm light permeates through me. He grimaces at first contact, tensing up as the healing rays seep through his flesh, cauterizing his wound. As the warming light dims, his muscles relax under the weight of my hand and his feverish sweat subsides.

"He's going to be just fine," I state, leaning the teen back into his father's lap.

"Thank you! Thank you!" The woman exclaims, gripping her son's hand to her mouth as she kisses his knuckles.

"Whoever you are, thank you. We are in your debt," The father replies in a still small voice. His eyes remain locked on mine and I can't shake the vibe I get from him as though we were familiar.

Strange.

"Who are you, people? Are you related to Theadra?" The young girl asks. "Are you here for Grant?" She says pointing toward a young man on the floor—an obvious Scourge victim. "He came in here like a lunatic! Said he was trying to protect me from something. But then he pulled out that gun—and then those things came—and then Theadra she—"

Unable to finish her rant, the young girl breaks out into a series of sobs and falls into her mother's arms. Brae looks at me as she examines the slain boy's fatal wounds. She opens his duffle bag, pulling out a stash of pictures, weapons, and cash. Hunching her shoulders. Both Brae and I wonder what part the boy played in the events of tonight.

"Damina!" Dalcour calls from across the court. "The girl! Come help!"

"Theadra!" The young blonde screams. "Oh, my gosh! Please, can you do something?"

"Theadra!" The teen boy erupts in a series of shouts as he stretches his arm toward her still body on the other end of the court.

"Travis, son, calm down!" His father commands, gripping him tightly.

"Damina!" Dalcour shouts once more.

"Travis, your father is right. Stay calm. I'll go see to Theadra," I reply, running my hand along his forehead, hoping to douse his erratic energy. Once more, I feel him calm beneath my palm.

"*Please, I love her.*" Only his thoughts echo his sentiment as it pierces through my mind. Although he seems too young to express such a commitment, his eyes alone tell me his declaration is sincere.

Making my way toward Dalcour, I watch the synchronicity of Cedric and Abigail's movements. Even as they fend off Scourge, they move as one. Now, I can see Dalcour's fascination with the pair firsthand. A small smile dances across my face despite the onslaught being carried out before me. Inside, a giddy, girlish joy bubbles to the epicenter of my heart knowing this is possibly the life Dalcour wishes for us two.

We shall see.

Arriving near Dalcour, I see the young girl try to push herself from the floor, but her strength is all but spent. Reaching down, I grab her before she hits her head on the wooden deck. "It's okay, you're safe. I've got you," I say, nestling her into my arms. There is a small bruise on her forehead and a trail of blood leaks down her cheeks. Cupping my hands along her face, I allow the warming light to heal her wound. A look of relief crosses her face and she exhales. "Now, that's better," I add.

Slowly, her blurry vision dissipates, and her eyes open wide before Dalcour and me. A wide smile blankets her face and she is oddly happy to see us.

"Heaven," she whispers. Images of her standing alone at the funeral of her parents and brother, along with happier moments of them together, flood my mind. A deep longing for her loss pains through me at the realization of her grief. Looking up at Dalcour, my eyes water with thoughts of losing my own parents.

"Not quite, I'm afraid," Dalcour replies, taking a firm hold of Theadra's hand.

Squinting as she comes to, she looks at Dalcour and me in awe. Both worry and intrigue cross her brow line as she looks at us and around the auditorium. One last shrieking cry from one of the creatures as its wretched body is torn from its limb and she jumps to her feet.

"Please don't be frightened. We're here to help you, Theadra," I say, raising my hand in caution as I notice how wobbly she is.

"How do you know my name?" Theadra asks, wary.

"Your friends told us," Dalcour answers, pointing behind us.

Theadra turns around, looking at her friends, and she blows out an air of relief as she spots Travis. Her eyes continue scanning the gymnasium as she watches as Cedric piles the Scourge husks aside.

Batting her eyes, she places her hand along her brow, staring off confused. *Was I dreaming?* Theadra inwardly wonders.

"No, you weren't dreaming, Theadra," I answer her thoughts. Although I do not detect a trace of the Altrinion force within her, I am strangely curious as to what I should make of her.

"How did you—" she begins with a more guarded stance.

"Because I'm special—like you," I quietly reply.

"What do you mean, *like me*?" Theadra's stubbornness is ringing true and I cannot help admiring her doggedness. For someone who's been through so much, she wears her grittiness like a badge of honor.

Good for her. She'll need it in this world.

"She's certainly a tough one like you," Dalcour laughs, plunging his hands in his pockets as he paces between us.

"Why don't you give us girls a chance to talk, Dalcour?" I say, not wanting to crowd her too much.

"Okay, Beautiful, I'll just check in on the basketball star. He should be fully healed by now," he answers with a broad smile while kissing my forehead before heading across the court.

"Dalcour? Some name," Theadra replies.

"*Yes, he's some man,*" I proudly reply.

Cute couple. I hear her mutter secretly.

"Why, thank you," I answer, revealing her hidden thoughts

"How do you do that? You can read my mind? What are you?"

"Firstly, it would be rude of me to say *what* I am, without first introducing myself. My name is Damina."

"Got it. Damina and Dalcour. Now, what are you people? And what were those things earlier?"

"Dalcour and I are Altrinions. We are a supernatural species if you will."

"Supernatural?"

"Yes. And those things were what we call Scourges—but most commonly known as vampires."

"You're telling me vampires are real!" Theadra shouts and the gym goes quiet. Dalcour and the others stare back at us and he walks back toward us with his posture more stiff and his face stern.

"Shh," I begin, placing my finger at her lip as she gazes around the gym. "It's probably not a good idea to blurt such things out."

"I'm sorry, but I mean they've already seen it."

"Yes, but they are mortal and it's best to keep them separate from such things. You understand, don't you Theadra?"

Looking over my shoulder at Travis, Theadra smiles when she spots his sister patting the top of his head.

Theadra's eyes fall slightly as if a thousand-pound weight now rests on her shoulders. "Yes, I understand. "So am I like you? Am I Altri—whatever you called it?"

"No, I'm afraid you are something different entirely," Dalcour announces, once more at my side.

"What does that mean?"

"Well, you're the first I've known in quite a long time, but long ago we called those like you *caesor* or breakers."

"Breakers? Am I supposed to know what that means?"

"Well, isn't she feisty?" He laughs over his shoulder. "You see, Theadra long ago when Altrinions or other supernaturals wanted to hide their existence from the world they would intermarry with mortals—humans. As time went on, their supernatural DNA would wane. That is, until such a time a caesor or Breaker was needed."

"Needed?"

"Yes, needed. If we pure line supernaturals abandoned our post or at any moment of heightened emotion, a Breaker could have hewn their supernaturality from within—much as you've done tonight," Dalcour answers.

"And with Grant's actions tonight, you must've felt forced to allow your power to break out," I add.

"But that doesn't explain why those creatures were here tonight. Were they after me?"

As I part my lips, Dalcour places his hand on my shoulder and shoves a heap of information to my mind. My mouth gapes open at the telepathic revelation Dalcour shares. Once more it is evident the Vitreous are at work. Even more, it's obvious had it not been for Theadra's intervention, these people may not be alive.

"What?" Theadra demands. Her patience with us is waning.

"To tell you the truth, Theadra, we were tracking a herd of Scourge heading near the school. We had no idea you were here. But now it's evident who they were tracking here and why," Dalcour says turning toward Travis and his family.

"Your boyfriend Travis and his family—well, they are LeClaires—like me," I confess, still in shock. I always knew there were more LeClaires in Louisiana I'd never met, but to know my bloodline is being hunted to extinction is maddening. Still, I do my best to maintain my composure for Theadra's sake. "He and his father are pure line Altrinion. They are my distant kin. An evil group of Altrinions called the Vitreous want to end the LeClaire bloodline, and they sent the Scourge here to do so. I'm afraid if you weren't here tonight, Theadra, they might have succeeded."

"How can you be sure?" Theadra asks, her eyes growing wide in both concern and fear.

"We found Grant's bag," Dalcour says while handing her four photos. "There are pictures of Krista, Travis and their entire family. In almost every shot a Scourge is seen following them."

Scanning the photos, Theadra now sees the dark shadows of the Scourge in each.

Oh no, Grant was trying to protect Krista! Theadra's thoughts sear through both Dalcour and me as the gravity of it all pulls on her already weighted shoulders.

"Only Grant went about it the wrong way. Frankly, he never stood a chance. You were meant to be here," Dalcour answers her thoughts gently, placing his hand on her shoulders. A proud smile crosses my face as I watch his genuine care for her. This is a side of him I'd never thought to see, but I like it. "Listen, Theadra, we need to get you and the LeClaire family far from here. It's not safe."

Once more, Theadra's emotions spring into a frenzy. Thoughts of her family's death leading her to this very moment fills her with both purpose and grief.

"Theadra," I quietly say, cupping her hands in mine. "I know this is all surreal right now, but Dalcour is right, we need to get you and your friends to safety. Believe me when I say I know what it is like to lose your family to tragedy only to be put in such a position. I was where you are—just the other day. But I promise, I will help you. We both will. Not only will I vow to keep you safe, but I'll help you understand how to manage what you're becoming. After all, us orphans have to stick together."

Theadra looks up at me and pools of water flood her cocoa-covered cheeks. For the first time, this otherwise spunky and strong sixteen-year-old resembles a child. She's spent the last six weeks since her family's death being strong. For six weeks, she has held it all in. *Her breath, that is.* She even managed to maintain her composure long enough to save her friends. From the fight she put up, it is clear she has no plans to lose anyone close to her ever again.

In this I can relate.

My heart aches for her and I share with her a kinship that can only be felt among orphans.

Pulling Theadra in for a tight hug, she finally allows her grief to have its way as she cries in my arms.

"It's okay, Theadra. Breathe, sweetie, just breathe."

Chapter 20

Today the mansion is buzzing with energy. With the Theadra and the LeClaires now taking refuge here until Dranoel and Lux take them to a safe house and the return of the Lothian wolves, the otherwise enormous estate feels small. Members of the Guard have also arrived, all awaiting instructions on plans to rescue Dacari.

In fact, everything is coming up Dacari.

My cousin has always craved attention, and now she's getting more than she bargained for.

A small part of me is happy to see so many gathered for a singular purpose. For as frail as a union it may be to see the wolves and vampires coming together to stand against Decaux, I am more than thankful everyone can set aside their animosities for a larger goal. Still, even I am aware more than my cousin's life is at stake. The very balance of the supernatural world depends on the allegiances of both the wolves and vampires.

While many of the Guard are accustomed to some shared dealings with one another, it has always been under Dalcour's influence.

Now, Mark, their new leader emerges. And with Jackson taking the helm as the Prime Alpha he was always meant to become, there is an anticipatory hope building in the atmosphere that is unfamiliar territory among those in the supernatural world. Gone are the siloed stances of primes against betas, Dunes wolves or otherwise. Even Altrinion-Vampires and rehabilitated Scourge—vampires like Brae now stand shoulder to shoulder, united under one banner.

Civility.

Dalcour wears a proud smile as he strolls through the mansion, and it is clear he is eager to see what he has worked so hard for to finally come to pass.

I even spy Titan slowly coming to the fold as he and Mark seem to have put away their differences as they survey maps together, marking areas to place the once estranged factions for battle. Even if their allegiance is temporary for this one purpose, it is good to see. Perhaps Titan has conceded that nothing will ever come of him and Brae. I hope so.

"This will work," Aunt Delia says in a low voice as she comes to my side as I stand atop the double staircase landing, looking down into the foyer of the mansion. "It has to." Aunt Delia's tone quivers a bit as she speaks, and I see the worry in her eyes.

Squeezing her hand with mine, I smile, and she looks back at me and strains a smile through.

"Yes, auntie it will," I answer her softly. "Besides, only Dacari could gather everyone together for such an event."

Aunt Delia chuckles in response, wrapping her arms around my shoulders. "You are quite right about that, darling. My Dacari always knew how to work a crowd!"

"And even without being present, it appears," I tease.

"So why am I still scared?" Aunt Delia states, her eyes welling with tears.

I wish I had the right words to comfort her. But I don't.

This time I can't blame the darn frog. I simply have no words of consolation or answers to give. I have none. Instead, I pull her into my arms and hold her tight.

My aunt has never been one to wear her heart on her sleeve, but now it's exposed like a nerve. Still, she manages to grip her composure to some semblance of control as she pulls away from me, flattening the imaginary wrinkles from her black suit.

"So, you and Dranoel?" I say, bumping her shoulder, giving her a knowing smile.

"He's a good friend," Aunt Delia replies over her shoulder, refusing to look me in the eye.

"A good friend, eh?" Bumping her once more. She looks at me out of her periphery, never changing her stance.

"Yes, a good friend," my aunt answers lightly bumping me back. We both laugh and I resign to let it go for now. Knowing my aunt has perhaps found someone to put a smile on her face makes me happy. She's never been one to date or dangle a parade of suitors in front of my cousin and me. I suppose the time she spent with Decaux was enough.

"Damina," I hear Brae call from below. "Have you seen Big D?"

"No, it's been a while since I have seen him. Why, what's up?" I question.

"We just got a big shipment of—um—smoothie juice here for all of us. He needs to sign for it since it's being delivered here and not the Civility Center," she answers.

"Okay, I'll go check to see if he's in his room," I reply and head down the hall toward Dalcour's suite.

Dalcour is standing at his terrace door as I arrive, looking out into the courtyard. He stands just shy of the curtains as he watches the sun preparing for its descent.

"It's going down," Dalcour says as I cross the threshold into his room. The tenor of his voice has an unexpected haunting chill to it. "Soon the sun will set, and the night will awaken. Are you prepared for that, Beautiful?"

"Dal, what's wrong?" I question. Worry fills me as I wonder what could be bothering him.

"I just want to make sure you know what you're getting yourself into is all. While I know the Lothians and Jackson think my brother didn't notice them surveying the land—it just sounds too easy. My brother has never been known to make anything easy for me. I'm racking my brain. What did I miscalculate? What am I missing?"

"Dalcour, don't do that to yourself. All these people are here now, working together—almost harmoniously because of you!"

"And it's the almost part that troubles me most."

"Do you think going tonight is too soon? Do we need more time?" I ask.

"It wouldn't matter, I'm afraid. Whatever my brother has been plotting, he's done to smallest degree. In just forty days after the death of Calida, my brother planned and carried out the Great New Orleans Fire of 1788, killing countless innocents. He's had over two hundred years to orchestrate whatever is coming next. And for the first time, Beautiful, I'm afraid."

"Dal, no! Don't say that!" I cry, coming to his side near the terrace.

"But I am, Damina. I am. Most of all, I'm afraid we won't come out of this. Together."

"Dal, I—I"

"No words, right now Beautiful. Just give me a minute—just me and you," Dalcour says softly, pulling me into his embrace.

Resting on his chest, I hear the strumming cadence of his heartbeat and I can't help but smile. Knowing I had something to do with the return of rhythm to his heart swells me with joy. Never did I ever think I could care so deeply for anyone other than Jackson. Still, the thought of it breaks my heart. I know once this is all said and done, I'll have a choice to make.

Even more, I am fearful that fate will once again intervene.

Holding my face in his palm, Dalcour looks down at me and smiles. Like my aunt, I can sense Dalcour's smile conceals a deep sadness within him. Once more, I try to read his mind, but he's still keeping me at bay. I wish I knew how to help him, but I press myself deeper into his chest, squeezing him tighter, hopeful it gives him some comfort.

He exhales in my arms and the strong scent of his lavender and jasmine aroma permeates the entirety of his suite, calling me deeper into his enchantment. Taking my chin in his hand, his fiery crimson eyes lock into mine with such a desperate fervor I almost wish no one was in the mansion except us two.

Fond memories of our first encounter, our dance at Razors nightclub, our first kiss at the Hall of Isis and the night we spent together replay sweetly in my mind. If I didn't know better, I'd guess Dalcour was pushing a playlist of our happier times through my mind in a single score. And from the way he's looking at me, my guess might be right.

Just as he pulls my mouth closer to his, we are both jolted from our longing stare when we hear the loud shouts of Brae from afar.

I guess I took too long.

"Oh, Dal," I begin. "I forgot to tell you there was a delivery here for you."

"Yeah, why don't you come down and sign for your delivery, Marchand!" I hear Jackson shout. While I'm surprised to find him now at Dalcour's door, it's the anger marred across his face that gives me worry.

Before I have a moment to intervene Jackson tosses a large bag of blood across the room. It lands at Dalcour's feet and he reaches down to pick it up. As he does, a deep grumble rumbles through his chest when he examines it.

"Jack, what's wrong?" I question.

Jackson stares at me, his lips curl with disgust as he shoots glances between Dalcour and me. I'm sure he's not happy finding me in Dalcour's arms, but it doesn't appear to be the cause of his ire.

"What's wrong, you ask? Why don't we let Lord Marchand tell us?"

Dalcour looks at the bag of blood and grimaces. He lets out another low grumble and looks over at Brae, who pushes her way past Jackson into the suite.

"I tried to stop him, Big D, but he's just being nosy!" Brae contends.

"Indeed," Dalcour gnashes through his teeth.

"Will someone tell me what's wrong?" I plead.

"I'll tell you what's wrong, Damina! It's this fraud right here!"

"*Fraud!* How dare you?" Brae snaps back, jumping to Jackson's face, but he doesn't flinch.

"I didn't stutter," Jackson states with his eyes looking past Brae to Dalcour. "So why don't you tell, Damina? Tell her where your blood supply comes from!"

"What is he talking about, Dal?" I reply. Turning to face Dalcour, the skies darken behind him and I know he is at the epicenter of the storm brewing from afar.

"We get the blood from various donors. Some are facilities we have an arrangement with, if you will," Dalcour answers in a softer tone than his scowl suggests. He keeps his eyes fixed on Jackson, but darts a quick glance to me as he speaks.

"And by facilities you mean prisons, Marchand! Private prisons!" Jackson lashes back.

"Is that true, Dalcour?"

"Yes." His answer is stoic and flat. There is no shade of remorse or regret. Still, he keeps his sights on Jackson.

"Are the donors living?"

"Some. But not all," Dalcour responds.

"But Dal, you know that private prisons are responsible for

the over and abundant incarceration of minorities, right? Even more than that—are these people willing donors? Do they even have a choice?" I shout, demanding answers and stepping away from Dalcour.

"I highly doubt it!" Jackson adds, coming to my side. "What's worse is that he doesn't care. Do you?"

"It doesn't matter if I care," Dalcour replies and the skies rumble, echoing his sentiment. "Why should it?"

"Because it should," I answer back, my voice pleading with him for understanding. But Dalcour's eyes tell me the opposite. His posture is unmoved, and his position remains unchanged. "I thought you said you only fed on willing donors?"

"Sure at the Civility Center, Damina," Brae starts coming to Dalcour's side. "With the prisons, well, it's kind of a don't ask—don't tell type of arrangement. But I can tell you we're not instructing them to kill anyone to meet quotas or anything." Brae's wide eyes are sincere as she talks, but's it is the unyielding stance of Dalcour Marchand that gives me pause.

"No, but you'll just turn a blind eye if they do! You're herding people like cattle and do so as if there should be no consequence! You march around this mansion like you should be applauded for your deeds, but you're no better than your brother—no better than the devil himself!" Jackson barks, pushing himself closer to Dalcour, but I keep a steady hand at his chest.

"I've never claimed to be the contrary," Dalcour admits, his position more resolute than before. "Not once have I ever stood under the guise of who and what I am, Nashoba. Not once. Unlike you."

"Dalcour, when we first spoke out on the porch you spoke to me of high ideals. A world of civility. A world of balance. A world where both human and supernatural could coexist. Was that all a lie?" I ask.

"No, there was no lie, Beautiful," Dalcour replies, his voice now slightly softer than before. "But this world is not as black and white as your fiancé would make it out to be. There is a world of gray, Damina. And that is where I sit between a rainbow of gray. That is where the supernatural world fits in the order of it all. There are no easy answers. No easy fixes. I do what needs to be done. Not because it is the easiest or more amenable way—but because it is the only way!" Dalcour protests, throwing his hands up in the air and forcing the terrace doors open.

Mark, Titan, Gregory, Brian, my aunt and Dranoel now appear at the clearing of Dalcour's suite. Mark and my aunt force their way past the others, both demanding an explanation for our raised voices. Dalcour ambles to the center of his bedroom, and gazes back and forth at our newly formed audience. The darkening skies lessen to a murky gray as he sighs and turns back to Jackson and me.

"How do you think we got to a place of civility, Damina? Do you think we just have humans lined up willing and ready to give us their blood? No, I am afraid not. The small faction of humans knowledgeable of our world are hardly enough to keep reformed vampires like Braelyn sufficiently fed. So yes! We've bartered agreements with private prisons, hospitals, blood banks, and whoever we can to ensure not only knowledge of our existence at bay but the large population of humans safe! Rehabilitated Scourge and vampires can now drink from the fountains we provide, sating their thirsts—but doing so off the streets! Because whether Scourge or Altrinion Vampires there is one thing and one thing alone we will always crave, and that is human blood! That is the truth, Damina. Anyone who tells you different is peddling horse dung!"

Dalcour's words sit between us and for the first time, despite our attraction, I see our differences. Innately, I step back and away from Dalcour, closer to Jackson.

Who is this man? I ponder.

I am not sure if this is something I can willfully push aside.

"But what about Jerrica, Dal?" I say as though inspiration strikes. "You told me yourself she has lived on animal blood for over a century. So that means *it is* possible, right?"

"Possible and doable are two very different things, Lady Nicaud," Brian replies, breaking through Dalcour's silence. "I have watched Lady Jeffers suffer for years as she tried to subsist on animal blood. Charlotte even told me how you once punctured yourself in front of Jerrica and it took everything within her not to kill you. Now imagine going through that every day. It hasn't been an easy road."

"And look at her now, Damina," Brae begins, in a low and gentle tone. "She's dying. Maybe if she had human blood—"

"Are you all listening to yourselves!" Aunt Delia interjects. "At least Jerrica has been fortunate to survive this long. Perhaps it's worth consideration."

"Well, that didn't work out to well for Damina's parents, so—" Titan says coolly.

"Titan! Quiet!" Dalcour roars.

"Wait—what? What does this have to do with my parents?" I ask, walking closer to Dalcour. "Tell me!"

"Now isn't the time, Damina," Brae begs.

"No, it's the perfect time, Marchand! What exactly do you know about Damina's parents?"

"Beautiful, there's no easy way to say this, but please know this is not how I intended to tell you." Dalcour gazes back at my aunt and then back at me. "I don't know if Delia told you, but your mother gave up her supernaturality to the Sacred Waters. But your father. While he was a blood drinker, he was like Jerrica—he lived on animal blood only. Now, it was probably easier for him than Jerrica because he was not subject to the curse of the sun. But had he been on human blood, the likelihood of his survival would have been higher. Instead, like Jerrica, his wound was fatal.

His death eminent."

"Is that what you've been keeping from me all this time? That's what you're holding back from me? Not only is your brother responsible for the death of my parents, but you have kept this truth from me too! How could you?"

"Because it should have been a conversation just between us two and not the entirety of the mansion!"

"That's why you want me on blood?" I say as the realization of it sweeps over me.

"What!" Both Jackson and Delia scream, protesting in unison.

"Damina, I only want what I've always wanted—to keep you safe! And if it means you drinking human blood—then yes, I will do whatever in my power to get you comfortable with the idea."

"But what if that's not what I wanted?"

"I can't risk losing you, Damina," Dalcour replies in a whisper. His eyes are desperate as he stares into my own. I know it is taking everything in him not to pull me into his embrace and whisk me away. But even he knows better.

Tears pool in my eyes and disbelief shakes my core. My aunt tried to warn me, but I didn't listen. *They are monsters*, she said. What did I expect? Still, if others have to die for me to live, that is not a life I want.

My eyes are now fully open to the truth. Can I accept it? Blinking, I allow my tears their release as they flutter against my lashes. Swallowing the dry, thick air in my throat, I look back up into Dalcour's eyes. Everything in me wishes the frog once again serves his purpose, instead he evades me, leaving me left alone with words I am almost too fearful to utter.

"No, Dalcour, you've already risked everything."

Chapter 21

The once bustling mansion is now eerily quiet.

It took all my might to refrain from taking my flight straight out of Dalcour's terrace to escape the agony of my heart. But I fought through my frustration and slowly walked past the suite filled with onlookers and took solace in my room.

Not until Dranoel came to inform me that he and Lux were taking Theadra and the LeClaire's to the safe house did I come out of my room. Thankfully, our resident Breaker and my distant kin didn't get wind of my upset. Dilano and Alana did well to keep them occupied while Khalil kept them full of all types of decadence from the kitchen.

The plan is to get back with them as soon as we get Dacari back and things settled with Decaux. Dranoel said Trieu has always wanted children of her own, so she is actually pretty tickled about having kids other than Ketu and Keitai with her.

"Damina," I hear Jackson call to me from the parlor as I wave farewell from the door to Theadra and the others. "We need to talk."

Four words I really don't care to hear right now.

"It's about Mark's valuation," Jackson hurriedly responds, likely anticipating my pushback.

Good.

I am happy to discuss anything other than me and Dalcour—or me and Jackson. Or even me—for that matter.

Walking into the room, I find Mark, Gregory, Brian and surprisingly Dalcour. His eyes meet mine as soon I cross the glass threshold and I almost feel air escape my body as our eyes lock as one. Jackson notices our exchange, but walks in front of Dalcour, blocking my view. He is intent on keeping my attention.

"We called you in here because we feel it necessary to perform Mark's valuation before we face Decaux."

"What? Look, I don't want to put this off any longer. I know how important this is but I'm going to get my cousin—with or without any of you!" I snap.

"That won't be necessary. Actually, that's why we want to do the valuation right here. Right now," Jackson answers.

"Since it was one of the requirements of my brother's plan, we need to have the Dunes back in position before we see him. I have to be able to account for every detail. I can't risk leaving any stone unturned."

"Every detail?" I question, knowing Dalcour was also tasked to find true love.

"My heart beats. That is all my brother needs to know," Dalcour answers flatly. Almost annoyed. He plops down on the ottoman adjacent to the long corridor leading to his office. His posture is still as pensive as before, but he's working hard to stay focused.

"That's why we need you, Damina. With Trieu keeping watch of Theadra and the LeClaires, we need you to stand in for the Altrinion line and conduct Mark's pronouncement. As a Duacin Altrinion you can establish a decree for Mark and his pack just as Saint Roch did for the Peyroux family. Lifting the Dunes curse,"

Jackson says.

An overwhelming heaviness cascades over me, but I resolve not to let it overtake me. If this is what it takes to get my cousin back, then so be it. Actually, I don't want to waste another minute discussing it.

"Don't worry, Damina, we'll be there with you every step of the way," Dalcour begins.

"I'm not worried." My response is short and less polished than I intended. "What do I need to do?"

"Well, first we'll let you and Mark have a chance to talk. Together you can come to some arrangement and conditions for his decree. The good thing is, Altrinions usually gets something out of it. By all accounts, Roch himself wasn't a Saint, per se, until he issued the pronouncement for the Peyroux line. After that he became deified," Jackson responds.

"I don't want to be a deity. I just want to help however I can," I answer gazing at Mark.

"Actually, I already know what I want to stake as my claim," Mark says, rising from his seat.

"Mark, you're not going to actually consider asking for what I think—are you?" Brian says, with his hand on Mark's shoulder.

"What else would I ask for?" Mark grits through his teeth, annoyed and pulling his shoulder from Brian's grip.

"What is it?" Jackson asks, curious.

"Um, really isn't an *it* as much as it is a *who*," Mark shyly answers with his head lowered.

"Spit it out," Dalcour says dryly.

"It's Braelyn, my lord. I want her as my wife." Mark states.

"Well, that's easy! Done!" Dalcour says with a thunderous clap, standing from his chair.

"Unfortunately, it isn't that simple," Jackson replies, his tone somber.

"Why not?" I question.

"Because Braelyn is a vampire and vampires can't procreate," Jackson mutters in a throaty tone. Cupping his jaw, his eyes remain fixed on Mark and I know his request seems undoable.

As my mind quickly recalls my conversation with Kyra, inspiration strikes. I just hope it will work.

"What about the Jinn Jar?" I swiftly interject.

Both Dalcour and Jackson gaze at me in shock.

"It will never work! She's a vampire, Damina!" Gregory shouts through the contention building in the parlor.

"He's right, baby," Jackson begins. "The Changeling only worked on Kyra because she's still a living being. Braelyn isn't technically *alive*. A Changeling's pledge of fertility can only be bound with a living being. A wolf. An Altrinion-Vampire even, but a vampire? A Scourge?"

"Then what about an Altrinion? The Changeling can bind its pledge to me but fulfill it through Brae."

"Beautiful, the only way to do that is to ensure you remain the same as you are today!" Dalcour exclaims. "You can never succumb to the curse or the Changeling will depart from Braelyn. If it departs before its pledge is fulfilled, Braelyn will die."

"Damina, I'm sorry I asked," Mark states. "I can't let you do this!"

"Wait—it's okay. Look, the whole purpose is to procreate, right? So how about the pledge only lasts through the gestation period. All Mark has to do is get her pregnant and in nine months— voila! I'm sure I can avoid drinking blood or killing a human until then!" I reply, darting my eyes at Dalcour.

"Lady Nicaud, are you certain?" Brian asks, his face full of worry. "It may not be that easy."

"Yes, Damina, are you certain?" I hear a small, shaky voice call from the dark corridor adjacent to the parlor. Brae ambles from the darkness with a weak smile as she plucks her fingers nervously through her laced gloves and walks toward us.

"More than anything, Brae! You and Mark deserve your chance at happiness. If that is still what you two want, I'll be more than happy to serve as surrogate pledge to the Changeling. Besides, nine months isn't that long."

"Well, you actually need less time. Most pups are born in about sixty or so days—" Jackson states. The hardlines of his face softens and I see he is coming around to the idea. "It's certainly unorthodox, but it could work."

"This is absurd!" Dalcour shouts. "Do you all realize what you're suggesting? If Damina fails in any way, Braelyn's life will be forfeit. She will die. Even if she makes it through the gestation period, there is no telling what will happen to her when the Changeling expels itself. Most supernaturals barely survive the transformation. But Braelyn is not a supernatural as we are—she is a vampire—for all intents and purposes she's—"

"*Dead.*" Brae's words are cold and quick. "Look Big D, I've been dead for some time now. But if I have even a remote chance of having this life with Mark, I've got to try!"

"Braelyn, do you understand what you're saying? Are you willing to risk your very existence for him? Are you willing to—"

"Accept my fate? Yes, Dalcour. I'd face the doors of death itself if need be. *I love him.*"

Dalcour holds Brae's arms, locking his eyes with hers. A tender smile crosses his face as he looks at her, and for the first time, I can see his paternal relationship with Brae.

"And I love her," Mark chimes in, his chest puffed like a flume of helium.

"Well, I guess it's a good thing Damina has chosen to abstain from bloodletting after all," Dalcour says softly while looking over his shoulder at me. A small smile curls the corners of his mouth and in his eyes, it almost appears he relents of his earlier stance.

But I know better.

"I guess I'll go see Kyra about a Jinn jar," Gregory says, taking his exit from the parlor.

"Agreed. We've got a lot to do before the valuation. All the neighboring dens and packs have been alerted. Many are coming from hundreds of miles away to take part in the ceremonies. It's the first reestablishment of an alpha of the Beta Prime line in centuries. Mark Brae, you two will need to decide on the plans for your nuptials. But I suggest once that Jinn jar is opened you allow the Changeling to take the reins. There are a lot of very traditional wolves out there. Most won't be as accepting of Mark as their alpha if they see him in covenant with a Scourge. I'm sorry, Braelyn, I don't make the rules." Jackson states.

Both Mark and Brae twine their hands with one another, sharing doe-eyed glances before Mark kisses Brae's forehead. She looks over her shoulder at me and smiles a sweet, girlish grin, I never thought her capable. More than ever, it's obvious just how head-over-heels in love she is with Mark. As much as the two played hard to get when I first met them, seeing them today is a complete change of course.

At least they will get their happy ending. I am just thankful to play a small part in the makings of their new life together.

"Lady Damina," Brian says, breaking me from my abandoned thoughts. "Have you given any thought as to what you'll ask for in return?"

"Oh, well, I thought me serving as Brae's surrogate pledge was sufficient. I can't think of anything I need or what. It certainly isn't sainthood," I laugh.

"Brian's right, Beautiful," Dalcour starts with his arms folded, narrowing his gaze on me. "There must be something you want. It's not often you get to name your price. I'm not saying the Elders will see it done, but at least you can try. The thought you're willing to serve as a surrogate pledge on their behalf should earn you some points with the Elders of the Order."

"Well you have less than an hour to decide," Jackson states

with a forced interjection. "We can't put off the valuation much longer."

"Is there anything else I need to do? How does it work?"

"Mainly, you just have to show up. I'll link the orb from the Elders—your father; and you'll present yourself. They will ask if you approve of Mark. After you answer, they will ask if you have a request for weighing in on the pronouncement, and if you do, you'll use your telepathy to share it with them. From there, it's back in my hands. You know, wolf business," Jackson answers.

"Do you think you can do this, Beautiful?" Dalcour questions as his brows cross with worry.

"Doesn't seem like rocket science to me," I say, hunching my shoulders. I'm scared as crap, but I refuse to let on in front of either Jackson or Dalcour. Too much is at stake.

"Well, there's one thing your Prime Alpha here didn't mention. You'll have to use the ancient tongue. But no worries. It will come naturally to you," Dalcour replies.

"How can that be since I've never spoken it before?"

"Oh you have, Beautiful. That night when you saw my face— my true face." Dalcour stares at me as he speaks, and memories of that night flash through my mind. I recall the strange fusion of force that encapsulated me as I laid my hands on his glistening red chest. As fearful as I was, I never felt more complete or powerful than in that moment. "When you said my name, you were actually speaking the language of the ancients. And tonight, the power of the Altrinion force will allow you to do the same."

Dalcour's words hang between us as the memory of our night together thickens the air in the room. Everything in me wants to linger in the remembrance's sweetness of Dalcour's kiss, the way he held me, and the moment I wanted to surrender myself to him in every way imaginable. As much as I want to hold on to my anger with Dalcour, I feel my defenses once again slipping away.

My, what Dalcour Marchand does to me!

Jackson forces a faux cough, breaking both Dalcour and me from our shared enchantment. Dalcour is the first to break from the magnetism building between us as he abruptly walks out of the parlor, calling for Brian to follow him over his shoulder.

Biting my lip, I work hard to push my abandoned thoughts of Dalcour aside. Jackson saunters to the parlor door and closes it behind Dalcour, leaving just us two.

"Look, Damina, I need you to know something," Jackson begins with a strained voice.

"Sure, what is it, Jackson?" I ask.

"I know I've spent the last five years being less than honest with you and I don't want there to be anymore secrets between us."

"O-oh-okay—what is this about, Jack?"

"It's about the real reason and my motivations behind me pushing for this valuation."

"I thought you just wanted to see the Dunes restored. I thought you were only doing right by the pack? By Mark?"

"Well, of course! That goes without saying," Jackson says, pushing his hands aside. "No, what I'm trying to say is that my brother was right about one thing. I have put my relationship with you above my duty to the pack. That is why he was able to get a foothold and turn some others like Tye against me."

"I'm sorry, Jackson. I never wanted our relationship to be a distraction."

"That's just it, baby, you weren't a distraction. You were my life. You are my life. Keiron knew I'd choose you over the packs any day and he's right."

"What are you saying, Jack?"

"I guess what I'm trying to say is that I want and need a Beta Prime to be in place because nothing has changed for me. You are my life, Damina. Fated curse or not. Even if you choose to stay with Dalcour, I'll do whatever I can to protect you—even love you from afar if I must. I'd make it my mission to not see your life forfeit—fated curse or not. Because I can't live in a world where there is no you."

"Jackson, please don't worry about me. Just lead your people! No matter what happens with us, promise me you'll be there for your people!"

"Look Damina, I've never wanted any of this! I don't wish to be an Alpha Lord or ascend to the Omegas. Sure, I love being a wolf, but I can do without all the alpha business. I'd give it all up for you. For us. For the life we always wanted. Get married. Build a home—a family—a future. *Together.*"

With the deep, yet tender focus Jackson now has on me as he speaks, my heart flutters in my chest. I did not expect this.

"Jackson, I can't ask you to give up who you are for me," I protest.

"Well you should. You deserve that and so much more. And so do I. Damina, you weren't the only one living a life that others planned for you. While I may have known *what* I was—I never truly knew *who* I was until I met you. You brought out things in me I didn't know possible. So yes, if you'd have me, I'd be willing to walk away from it all—with you by my side."

"You would do that for me?"

"No, baby. For us."

My heart sinks to the pit of my gut then rises back to my throat, choking the very air from me. Once more, I see something new in Jackson Nash I never thought to find. There is a desperation in his voice as he speaks that is unfamiliar to me.

Who is this man?

"Jack, I—I don't know what to say," I confess, my eyes welling with tears.

"It's okay, baby. I don't expect you to say anything now. I just wanted to make my intentions clear. For five years I thought the best way to protect you was to do everything by the book and do what I was told. But where did that get me? It took you away from me. I will abandon it all for you—for us—for the life we always wanted to have. Sure, I'll always be a wolf and you an Altrinion. But we can still live a relatively normal life. While some may think your parent's decision to live a normal life showed weakness, I see it as strength. They had the fortitude enough to live their life on their own terms. So, I know life may hold some challenges for us, it's worth it if I can have you with me. Always."

"But what about the packs? Your people? Mark?" I ask, turning away from him.

Jackson quickly circles me and gently takes me by my wrists. "I will give him all the guidance he needs, but only so that he can one day lead. He is a rising beta prime. His very DNA has the makings of all that is required. And more important, having him as alpha is better than me—"

"You mean if I succumb to my fate? You don't think you could take my life?"

"How could I? Your life, baby, is my life. For now and for always."

Chapter 22

I am still breathless.

Here I stand under the pergola in the backyard of the mansion, at the entrance of the maze garden with my repose as stone and still as the statues Mark and I placed here in the labyrinth.

The sentiment of Jackson's heart and his declaration to me lovingly haunts my thoughts as I stand here before a large body of supernaturals. Both the weight of his words and the intentions of his heart hold me captive to the memories of our life together and the possibility of our future.

Looking out at the crowd of wolves, vampires, Altrinions and otherwise, the truth by which Jackson spoke is plain to see. Had he not kept his supernaturality, and all that comes with it hidden from me, I have no doubt I would not stand here as I do now. I am still well aware I am only here as a result of his, albeit noble, deception; and the trickery of Keiron.

I would have never come to New Orleans.

I would have never met Jerrica at Saint Roch's.

Ultimately, I would have never met Dalcour. Or any of these

who surround me in the mansion backyard.

Now, to know Jackson is more than willing to give it all up for the life we had planned pins me in place.

What do I say to that? How do I respond?

Thankfully, my aunt's interruption gave me no time to ponder his proclamation or give any response. Once news of Mark's valuation spread throughout the estate, Aunt Delia snatched me from Jackson's longing stare. With Vonnie's help, my aunt sprung into her usual recourse; fussing over me as if I were a doll in preparation of Mark's valuation. This time, however, my heart was so entwined with thoughts of both Jackson and Dalcour, I did not have it in me to protest.

In no time I found myself arrayed in a glittering golden Georgette gown with Grandma Roux's emerald clamp tucking my hair to one side. I had no idea an alpha valuation was a formal affair. However, when I spied Jackson's Aunt Sophie coming into the mansion as my aunt rushed me to my suite, I should have known better.

Every movie or folklore I've ever known about wolves was wrong. Always described as the rugged, scruffy, nature bound, tree-huggers of the supernatural world, I now see just how wrong those assertions are. Mark may have been the more relaxed of his kin, at least when we first met. But now, even he is more demure and polished. So much so that he's rubbing off on Brae.

I hardly recognize the goth vamp girl I came to know and love.

As she stands proudly at Mark's side with her lovely auburn curls upswept, adorned in a shimmering lilac gown, she seamlessly mirrors her gallant betrothed. With her arms looped through Mark's, I spot her black laced gloves and I smile, thankful some remnant of the real Braelyn Agatha Dortches remains.

Yet, unlike Brae, I have to wonder where are my laced gloves? Have I so quickly given everything to the Altrinion force within me and the supernatural world around me that no trace of Damina

Careese Nicaud remains? Withstanding my grandmother's hairpin. What here belongs to the girl I once knew?

"We call forth Damina Duacin," a thunderous voice from a misty veiled fog calls to me, breaking me from my contemplative state. It's the first time the surname Duacin has been uttered in reference to me. Strangely, it is both unfamiliar and familiar all at once.

Before I can respond, I feel both Dalcour and Jackson loop their arms through mine, leading me closer to the iridescence filling the courtyard. As they do, I find myself exhaling. Finally. While I am surprised by the unison of their march, I am thankful for both of them.

Having both men at my side feels complete. Whole.

Inhaling the intoxicating fragrances of cinnamon, jasmine and lavender still the frenzied feelings bubbling within me as I rest my anxiousness in the depths of their aromatic scent. Surprisingly, Dalcour is the first to release his hold as we near the misty film, leaving just Jackson and me.

"Jackson Lee Nashoba," the same thunderous voice shouts. "As Prime Alpha, do you now present the Lady Damina as resident Altrinion to pronounce the alpha status of the Beta Prime, Markus Avram Helsing?"

"I duly submit the Lady Damina to lay charge to earth, moon, and sky for the rising alpha, Markus Avram Helsing. The rising alpha has met my criterions and is hereby given for your valuation," Jackson addresses the smoking fog before us with a deep bow at his waist and his eyes lowered. Lifting my hand toward the cloud and smoke, a strong arm reaches out from beyond my view, taking hold of my forearm.

"My daughter." This time the voice is recognizable. It is my father.

"Daddy!" I squeal, surprised to see his face. There are others with him as well. Each of them is seated on what appears to be golden branches of a tree. Shimmering diamond-like fog hovers around them like sparkling rays of light. My father smiles at me, keeping my hand steady in his, and I realize I am now standing inside the cloud and away from Jackson and the crowd of supernaturals in the courtyard.

"Did you not expect to see me?" My father replies with a tender smile.

"Well, Jackson said you'd be here, but seeing you now. It seems like it was just the other day, Daddy," I answer.

"I see," he says as he tightly purses his lips from laughter. "Are you ready to begin?"

"Yes, I suppose so," I answer as my thoughts drift away from the moment. Although I want to make this happen for Mark, I'd rather just take this time to spend with my father. Who knows if I'll ever have the opportunity again?

"It's quite all right, Damina. This will not be our last chance together. But we both have responsibilities tonight." Squeezing my hand, my father smiles once more, bringing me back to the moment.

"Yes, father," I respond, forcing myself out of my sulking state.

"As an Elder of the Duacin Altrinion Order do you hereby agree to the pronouncement of the rising alpha?"

"Yes, I agree to the pronouncement."

"As such how shall you pronounce?"

"I hold this pronouncement assured as I bind myself to a surrogates pledge, ensuring the rising alpha's bloodline continues." The words slip from my mouth as though I were trained to speak them.

"Do you understand the full measure of such a pledge?" My father's face is laced with worry, but he restrains himself. Looking over his shoulder, the stone cut expressions of the other elders send chills up my spine, but I work hard to keep my wits about me.

"I do," I mutter.

"That you seek such a pledge in the pronouncement demonstrates the depth and sincerity of your heart for not only the rising alpha but the supernatural order as well." Slowly, I see my father's fretful frown lines retract as a smile frames the corners of his mouth and pride swells his chest. His posture shifts upright from his deep fatherly gaze and he squeezes my palm in his hand. "What pardon or request have you?"

At his questioning, my throat chokes up and I fail to form words. I notice some elders shift behind my father, and I know I must say something soon. As I open my mouth, a mystical and lyrical language escapes my tongue that is strangely familiar. I have no idea how I know to speak such a dialect, but it is as though English were my second language and this my first.

Standing in the misty cloud, it is unclear whether the crowd of supernaturals behind us can discern our exchange. I hope not. The pardon I now request is the most private of utterances ever to leave my lips. While it was not until now I knew the full measure of my request, I am certain as the words roll over my tongue this is exactly what I want.

It is what I need.

My father's posture resumes a pensive stance as he turns from me to deliberate my request with the elders. As the elders confer with my father, the loud sound of rushing waterfalls echo through the cloudy encasement and my heart races as I try hard to make out their reply. Once more, my heart races and I wonder whether my request was too much to consider.

Turning back to me, my father places his hand on my shoulder and smiles. "Your request has been weighed and your pardon considered. It shall be as you have asked, my daughter," he says with his eyes beaming brightly, as though my request gave him joy. "Now we charge you, Damina Duacin, to commence with the pronouncement of the rising alpha, Markus Avram Helsing as the new Beta Prime. At your word, the stain of the Dunes curse will be lifted from him and all that swears fealty to his regency."

Taking my hand in his, we walk to the edging of the cloud, looking out at the supernatural congregants before us. Kissing my forehead, my father pulls his hand from mine, and whispers, "I love you," as the cloud retracts. The emptiness I now feel at the release of my father's hand sends a shooting ache through me and a lone tear falls to my cheekbone. Although I am not completely certain, I find great comfort in my suspicion that I will see him again.

Before I have too long to ponder the loss I feel at my father's exit, Jackson's sturdy hand entwines with mine once more and he leads us back to the center of the garden. Gregory walks toward us with the Jinn jar in hand and Mark and Brae follow behind him and stand adjacent to the cobble firepit.

"Rising alpha," Jackson begins as he rests his hand on Mark's shoulder.

"Yes, my lord," Mark replies, slowly kneeling to the ground.

"You have chosen this woman, Braelyn Agatha Dortches, to be your mate?"

"Yes, my lord."

"By the Altrinion Order of Duacin elders, you hereby pledge your fidelity to your mate for the sacredness and propagation of the Helsing bloodline. As such, as your Prime Alpha I grant you rights to take an outsider as your mate for the sole purpose of procreation. Should either of you diverge from your oaths to the Duacin elder or should the Changeling rescind its duty, you must fulfill your pledge to find a worthy mate within three lunar cycles. Failure to do so will result in a reissuance of your Dunes curse for you and all you yield to your leadership."

"Yes, my lord."

"Rise to your feet, young alpha," Gregory commands.

Dalcour walks closer to us, fixing himself by Brae's side.

Brae gives a wide smile to Dalcour as he wraps his arm around her. Nervousness grieves Brae's face and I see her anxiously pick her fingers through the lacing on her gloves.

"Are you ready?" Dalcour whispers in Brae's ear and she nods in affirmation.

Gregory opens the Jinn jar and a dark misty form rises to our view. Green-yellowish eyes flare open as the Changeling takes its shape, mirroring Brae. Brae gasps, ambling back toward Dalcour, but he keeps her steady. Mark moves to assist her, but Gregory keeps his hand on Mark, preventing him from getting closer to Brae.

Everything in me wants to help Brae as I see the fusion of the black foggy matter attach itself to her. Though, as I look around, I notice no one else seems as bothered by the sight of the Changeling as I am. Brae continues to struggle, writhing in apparent pain as the Changeling takes one last plunge into her being. Brae's eyes flash a bright green and I now see she is fully overcome by the creature.

"Brae, baby, is that you?" Mark questions.

Blinking rapidly, Brae forces her eyes open, revealing her normal hue. Mark smiles, thankful for her transformation. Running her fingers along her incisors, she winces when she notices her fangs are now gone.

"You're the closest you've been to human in a long time, kiddo," Dalcour teases, still holding Brae steady from behind.

Brae looks up at Mark and a weak smile forms at the corners of her mouth. Alana pushes a black chivari chair to Brae's side and helps her to her seat. Dalcour extends his hand to me and I take it after looking to Jackson who only nods and acquiesces our motion. Brae lifts her palms toward me and once more her eyes flash a bright green and I take her hands in mine. A warm force of wind whips through both Brae and me, and I know we are now both bound to the Changeling.

"The binding is complete," Gregory announces, and a loud chorus of claps erupts through the atmosphere.

"You have witnessed the officiating of your new alpha's mating and now we shall set forth his charge," Jackson declares. "Den leaders come forth."

Several wolves approach the landing of the patio steps, each ceremoniously kneeling with a fist over their chest as they bow before Jackson and Mark.

Once more my mind drifts as Jackson bellows his charge to Mark before the crowd. His litany is just as muting as the words of Charlie Brown's teacher to my ears. Instead, my eyes gaze around the mansion courtyard in sheer awe of the supernaturals gathered around me.

When did this become my world?

What happened to the once mundane existence I came to know and perhaps love?

How did I get here?

And while Jackson's declaration to me was sincere, I can hardly fathom him apart from this world. It seems to fit him like a glove. Even Dalcour folds into the tapestry of this new-to-me world which such an elegance it is hard to imagine him without it.

As usual for all things me, even surrounded by so many, I yet feel all alone.

And for the first time it becomes evident, I was not meant for this world.

This is not me.

"Lady Damina," Jackson says loudly, breaking me from my reflection. His gaze softens as he grabs my hand when I jump at his call. He smiles at me and the beating pace of my heart slows its rhythm. "You may now declare your pronouncement."

Looking back at Jackson, a part of me is unsure what to say in reply. My eyes drifts to Dalcour and I recall his earlier advisement of the ancient language. Once more, my throat seems to clog, but I open my mouth and allow the lyrical ancient words to effortlessly flow through me.

The den leaders gathered before us howl in response, baying up at the moonlit sky. Mark lifts his face to the moon and yelps loudly as his body transforms into his wolf, breaking out of his black suit. Another line of wolves' echo in a chorus of howls and their eyes glow bright yellow and orange, like flickering flames. Even Gregory, Dilano and Alana wail in unison with the others with their faces lifted to the moon.

A bright golden light shines through me as Mark falls under the weight of my pronouncement and the rumbling roar of Jackson as he submits to his Prime Alpha. Jackson's canines lengthen, and a thick white furry coat cascades down Jackson's sideburns, but he doesn't shift. Tonight is Mark alone.

"Rise!" Jackson roars and Mark shifts back to his human form, naked and bare before us. This time, however, he is much larger and muscular than before. I even notice Brae's eyes pop open at his new revelation and her once hidden thoughts are now exposed to me, crowding my mind. I work hard to push her abandoned thoughts aside, but I know with all certainty the two will have an enjoyable time mating tonight.

Must be nice.

Dilano slowly approaches Mark, draping a black linen cloth around his waist, covering his nakedness. Steam fumes through Mark's body as his muscles continue to contract and constrict as he turns about to face Jackson once more.

Jackson places his hand on Mark's chest and growls, and I watch in awe as the Dunes marking slowly vanishes from Mark's skin. The wolves in the yard yelp and howl in reply, and a stammering chorus of claps and shouts once more erupt through the crowd.

Mark grimaces at the burning sensation and removal of the Dunes marking, but he remains steady. Jackson turns Mark back around to the crowd and they all shout and cheer in response.

"I present to you, your Beta Prime and resident alpha, Markus Avram Helsing!"

Chapter 23

A harmonious howl rings through the courtyard maze of the mansion as all the supernaturals celebrate Mark's ascent to alpha status.

It is heartwarming to see the smiles among both vampire and wolf alike. Their shared merriment of this moment is evident throughout the labyrinth. Even Titan seems uplifted as he watches his sisters, Ketu and Keitai, playfully run about the grounds.

While I am happy for the part I've played in Mark's ascendancy, the pendulum that is my heart instantly swings to Dacari. Now more than ever I want to find my cousin, safe and well. Though, as I look out to the crowd of vampires, wolves, and Altrinions before me, I am thankful to have such a grouping ready to aid in the quest.

Dalcour hasn't wasted much time enlisting factions of both vampires and Altrinion-vamps to our cause. He is just as eager as I am to find my cousin and his brother—her father.

"Don't worry, Damina," I hear Brae's soft voice behind me whisper. "Mark already said he won't rest tonight until he reunites you with Dacari."

"Can you read my mind now?" I quietly ask, smiling at the softer features now rounding Brae's apricot blushed cheeks. It's odd not seeing her with her typical pale, white skin. The flush of red glowing beneath her skin reminds me that she more resembles a human, despite the undercurrent of supernaturality brewing beneath the surface.

"No, ma'am. I have no parlor tricks left in my bag, I'm afraid," she laughs.

"Well, you're certainly not a vampire or Scourge anymore, my dear! I had quite the cracked door to your—um—very vivid thoughts on your beau's new physique!"

"Oh my gosh, Damina! You could hear my thoughts?" Brae questions in shock.

"I heard enough, but don't worry, I turned it off when you started moving away from the PG-13 version."

"Well, there you have it! I'm really not living on the dark side anymore. It's been more than two-hundred years since I've felt remotely mortal—and now—look at me!" Brae says, twirling in laughter. While her bubbly persona has always been a key quality in my once favorite gothic vampire, she is now more giddy than I could imagine.

"And what a sight you are!" Mark's smile is wide as he lifts Brae up from behind and continues twirling her in his embrace. The two share in a sweet kiss as she holds her small hands against his jawline, twining her tiny fingers through his clean-cut beard. "I can't wait to make you all mine! We'll have a league of pups after tonight, baby doll. I hope you're ready," Mark whispers, nipping Brae at her neck. She squirms between his broad biceps and laughs, pounding his chest.

Looking at the two, I am so happy for them. Seeing their love makes my heart leap. Even more, I'm thankful Mark found some clothes. It was hard enough eavesdropping on Brae's impassioned thoughts, and I don't want a repeat.

"Just the other day that was us," Jackson breathes his words softly in my ear from behind me. Despite the muggy evening air, his breath is cool against my skin, sending tingling sensations throughout my entire body. Gently placing his hand at my waist, Jackson's sweet and spicy scent invades the space around me as he lingers at my neckline. My pores prickle as he leans himself against me, and I hear his breath hitch as a low rumble churns through his chest. Pointing to the crowd of supernaturals, Jackson places his lips at my earlobe and whispers, "All of this, baby, I'll gladly give it all up for us."

"Jackson," I plea in protest.

Placing his forefinger at my mouth, he lifts my chin so that our eyes meet. "Maybe not tonight, but soon, baby soon. It *will be* us again," he says as he looks over my shoulder, admiring Mark and Brae's affection.

Quickly pulling himself away from me, he turns to Mark and forces out a faux cough, interrupting Mark and Brae in mid-swoon.

"Yes, my lord," Mark answers dutifully, slowly dropping Brae to his side, keeping her hand locked in his.

"So, Mark is ready to issue your first orders?" Jackson asks, with his arms folded at his waist.

"Yes, my lord. First orders?"

"Well, somebody has to get this bunch out of my yard and out looking for Dacari," Dalcour adds, now coming to Brae's side. He gives her a warm smile, and she wraps her arms around his waist, and he plants a light peck on her forehead.

"But my lords," Mark counters. "This is your home, Lord Marchand. And Lord Nashoba, you are our Prime Alpha. If anyone has the right to address the assembly gathered here, it's the two of you."

"Ha! At least the mutt has kept a sense of propriety about him!" Titan scoffs as he saunters up the patio stairs and leans on the iron railing.

"That's enough, Titan! The newly appointed alpha, Lord Helsing, has much a right to speak as either Lord Nashoba or I." Dalcour says in a stern rebuke.

Titan blows through his mouth and laughs, forcing his hands in his pockets. He shakes his head in annoyance but keeps reins in his frustrations.

"I like the way that sounds. Lord Helsing!" Brae merrily snickers and we all laugh.

"Well, then Lord Helsing, it's time for you to address your people," Jackson adds.

"My people?" Mark answers as the reality of it all takes over.

"Yes, young lord. Your people. The wolves of Louisiana are now of your regency and den. And with the removal of your Dunes curse, you have also taken rank as Beta Prime."

"But you are our Alpha, Lord Nashoba," Mark replies graciously, bowing his head toward Jackson.

"You are their Beta Prime, young lord. You are their alpha," Jackson continues. "Besides, it is good for them to get used to hearing your voice." Jackson lifts his eyes toward me as he speaks, and I know he's referring to shifting the entirety of prime wolf responsibilities to Mark.

"Not only are you their alpha and Beta Prime, Mark, but you now also control the Guard," Dalcour says as he pats Mark's hulking shoulders.

"As it should be," Brian says in agreement, now coming to our side. His smile is bright from ear to ear and a brotherly pride swells his chest as he looks on at Mark.

"Well, baby, are you ready?" Brae questions.

Mark gives a quick glance to the circle around him and I watch as he exhales his remaining trepidation while stepping to the edge of the patio and begins to pull the attention of those amassed in the backyard.

"Wolves of Louisiana!" Mark roars to the thunderous sound of cheers. "I thank you for standing with me to reclaim our rightful ranking. I will not soon forget each of you who stood by me. But our time for celebration has not yet come. Our first singular charge as those of the lupine strain are to protect the Order of Altrinion. We are first and foremost the protectors of their sacred lineage. Now, just as the Lady Damina pledged herself to aid in the rebuilding of our packs, from her work with the mansion to her pledge to my bloodline, it is time we did the one thing we were created for. We protect what we love—"

"Because we love to protect!" The crowd chants in response.

As many times as Jackson has spoken that very phrase to me, tonight is the first time I've heard it come from others. It must be a wolf thing.

The assembly of supernaturals continues their sprawling shouts, and Mark lifts his hand to quiet them.

"Now, you all have your orders so let us—" Mark begins but is interrupted by a lightning bolt of light cracking the night sky, sending a bright blue current straight to the center of the labyrinth.

Loud gasps and hissing sounds echo through the courtyard as a raucous outcry is heard from the place of the lightning strike. At the sound, both Dalcour and Jackson sandwich me between the two of them as Brian, Titan, and Gregory group together to shield the corners of the patio, leaving Mark standing front and center. Brae remains at Mark's side, but I quickly pull her back with me to keep her from harm. Her initial reflexes worked to push me away, but her newly given human-like state keeps her in my grip.

"Well, well, well," A smooth and lush voice calls from the center place of the maze. "Look at all these supernaturals gathered here together! I don't suppose my invite got left in the mail, eh little brother?"

"Decaux!" Dalcour shouts.

The entirety of the compound grows pin-drop silent at the calling of Decaux's name, and I push my way from between my two protectors so that I can finally set my eyes to his face.

As I do, I am in awe of what I find.

The face of a man who looks like Dalcour but doesn't.

Decaux's features are just as captivating as Dalcour's but there lies a sinister ring of fire outlining his irises that instantly lets me know *he is not his brother.*

Even his wicked smile is enchanting. Pearly white teeth, with half-protruding fangs showcase a haunting allure that is hard to miss. I can see why my aunt fell for him.

He stands just a few inches taller than Dalcour, but his muscular frame is leaner. Wearing all black, a dark fedora with a gray feather and the same dagger necklace at his jugular as Dalcour, their similarities are jarring. And much like Dalcour, just his looks alone make even the surrounding female wolves coo in response.

Pulling myself away from his wickedly enchanting grin, I gaze over at my aunt and see her face pale before me. Looking back at Decaux, I hope to see what is troubling her.

And now I do.

Dacari.

Seeing my cousin now at Decaux's side prickles pins and needles like acupuncture from head to toe. I don't know if it is the red staining her lips or the leather jacket and fishnet tights she's wearing, but everything about her seems off.

"Dacari!" I scream in response. She ambles slowly from his side, still remaining in his shadow. Smiling weakly, my cousin looks at me and my heart warms knowing *she is happy to see me.*

But why is she with him?

"Stay near me, Damina!" Dalcour snaps, gripping my wrist. I'm sure he fears I'll run to my cousin, but I won't. From what I can see, my cousin is not a hostage. There have been few times in Dacari Peyroux's life where she has ever allowed herself to be bullied.

Now is not that time.

"Hi, Damina," Dacari answers softy, allowing a brighter smile to fold over her face until it reaches her eyes. As I stare at her, I see no pretense. Nothing in this moment makes me believe she is doing anything against her will.

I am also surprised to see Dorine and Padma standing on opposite sides of both Dacari and Decaux. After their disloyalty, their appearance is still shocking. Rippling snarls race through Dalcour and Mark as they stare at both women. Even Brae's lips curl in disgust and I know if there were a moment she wished she was still vampire—this would be it.

"Are you all right, Dacari?" I question, hurriedly. "Has anyone hurt you?"

"I am fine, cousin," Dacari responds with a cool low tone. Her smile slowly fades as her eyes shift to her mother. "No, I am not hurt; at least not how you might think, Damina."

"Dacari!" Aunt Delia cries as both Dilano and Alana press their hands into her shoulder, preventing her from rushing to Dacari.

"No worries, my sweet daughter," Decaux starts as he pulls Dacari closer to his side. "We will get to the heart of that matter at another time indeed."

"Then why are you here, brother?" Dalcour demands.

"Well, I came to see your oaths to me fulfilled, my dear brother. And from the looks of things, you're doing a splendid job!" Decaux claps his hands and the resounding boom of it flashes memories of Keiron's treachery in the same spot replay in my mind.

"Speak the truth, Decaux! Why are you here?" Dalcour shouts back.

"I am speaking the truth, brother," Decaux answers in a more subdued tone as his eyes lock with Dalcour. "I suppose I could have waited for your little battalion of misfits to descend on my compound, but I wish no one here any ill will. Well, most everyone," Decaux says, shooting a dark glare at Aunt Delia. "But I must say I am impressed! You have a horde of Dunes wolves—all with their proper rankings and an alpha to match. And with your worldwide blood collection sites, the Civility Centers are thriving, sating the thirsts of vampire and Altrinion-vampires alike. Some say they never grow thirsty," Decaux finishes with a wicked grin, licking his lips.

Dalcour shoots an uneasy glance at me, and I know a part of him wishes I never knew about his dealings with the private prisons.

Decaux lowers himself and Dacari to the ground and begins walking toward us. Stopping short of the patio, he turns about looking at the crowds of supernaturals gathered in the courtyard. Low snarls and hisses radiate throughout the yard, but he lifts his hand to silence them and points to the hedges along the property line.

"Now, now, I wouldn't make too much ruckus if I were you. My league of Scourge and Skull only awaits my word and they will descend upon this place with a fury with the likes of that of which you have never seen." Decaux's pointed finger rings around the crowd and grumbling growls echo from afar.

Mark walks closer to the edging of the patio and gives a rebuking glare at the wolves and they rein in their ceremonious wail at his command.

"My brother, it looks like you've got a keeper in this young alpha! Good work indeed!" Decaux teases.

"Take one step closer, you murderous leech and I'll—" Brian barks

"And you'll what? Kill me? Please!" Decaux dismisses Brian, tossing his hand over his shoulder, laughing with Dorine and Padma.

"You killed my family! The Abahana's! Women, children—"

Brian cries in an ear-splitting roar. A small uprising of wolves in the back of the garden who Dalcour earlier pointed out were from Brian's hometown begin pushing their way forward. The pain of his cry is almost deafening. Slowly, memories of the second line parade for Abahana, Brian's grief-stricken face, and the night we first met rip through me.

"I killed no one!" Decaux protests and the burgeoning clamor of the crowd instantly grows silent.

"What lies do you now tell, Decaux," Cedric shouts from afar. "We saw the bodies!"

"How easy is it for you to blame me than acknowledging the fact your greatest enemy came from within!" Decaux snaps back.

"What are you saying, brother?" Dalcour questions, curiously.

"I speak of Mikkel, dear brother. It was he and his blood thirsty Vitreous clan. Their little faction is hell bent on destroying any trace of pure-blood Altrinions or their distant kin. Abahana was one such kin of the LeClaire family."

"Are you suggesting you were set up?" Titan asks, coming closer to Dalcour's side.

"I suggest nothing. I have nothing to defend—well, that is, until now" Decaux replies softly, as Dacari loops her arm tight with his, resting her head on his shoulder.

"But Decaux, you called me only moments before they were attacked!" Dalcour counters.

"Coincidence, I suppose. But I had no need or want to kill a pure-blood Altrinion. You well know I have never fallen in league with such thoughts of supremacy, brother. Has not the city of New Orleans witnessed firsthand the flaming fury by which I detest such bigoted barbarism? And from what Dacari has told me, the Vitreous has even come close to threatening the very life of her cousin—also a LeClaire. What would I gain from it?"

"Then tell me brother, what do you hope to gain now?"

"Balance, brother. Simply perfect balance. And with that,

tell me little brother have you settled the third and final matter wherewith such a balance may be measured? Does your heart now beat?" Decaux whispers in a low, sly tone. Lunging forward, he presses his ear to the sky and smiles. "Ah, so my Dacari was right, your heart indeed does beat! May I presume it was the lovely Lady Damina who is responsible for its rhythm?"

Decaux's eyes quickly scan to me and he looks me over, smiling widely.

"Well, brother, that is good to hear. Although not surprising. She is quite fetching! But I suppose that is an oddity coming from me. I mean, she is my daughter's cousin. She could have very well been my niece—isn't that right, Delia darling?" Decaux states.

"Enough, Decaux! I have given you everything you asked for. So end your grandstanding! End your war! Give Dacari back to her family!"

"I am with my family!" Dacari shouts back, gripping her hold on Decaux.

"I do not hold my daughter against her will. In fact, I am just as surprised as you to discover her existence. But it is without regret," Decaux begins, looking over his shoulder at my aunt. "You see, I was in love with Delia Peyroux. In love. After Calida, I never thought I'd find a love to bring my captive heart to rhythm. When Delia came into my life—an unmarked Dunes wolf, I first only thought to help her. I wanted nothing more than to restore the ranking of the true guardians of the Order of Altrinion—the Beta Primes. After the treasonous deeds of the Alpha Primes, who for fear, used Changeling trickery to keep the Betas from ever challenging their rank, I've wanted to aid the Dunes in their reclamation. I thought I could do that through Delia. And then we fell in love—and then poof—she was gone!" Decaux exclaims.

"I left you because you were a monster! A ravenous beast! I saw you feasting off children! How could I have a child with such a monster?" Aunt Delia objects.

"Perhaps the knowledge of our child would be the one thing to put the monster at bay?" Decaux's dissent with my aunt is clear. He blames her for taking Dacari from him. "But alas—I am what I am. For too long we have lurked in the shadows, hiding from humans, or like the Skull—starving to near death all because we are labeled as monsters, meant for nothing than tipping through the shadows of night!"

"So is that why you killed my parents?" I shout through the dissonance of the still assembly. "Were you so hurt at the loss of my aunt that you commissioned their murder?"

"Beautiful, no, not here. Not now," Dalcour says with a disapproving scowl, placing himself between me and Decaux.

"No, Dalcour the time is now! I want to look into his eyes. I want to look into the eyes of the one who killed my family and watch his explanation purge his lips as he speaks!" I yell back, lifting myself above the patio and taking flight closer to both Decaux and Dacari. Jackson and Dalcour rush to my sides, keeping wary gazes on Decaux, Dorine, Padma and even Dacari.

"My brother is right, dear one. Now is not the time." Decaux keeps his eyes lowered as he speaks, but it is the somberness of his tone that distresses me.

"Baby, he's not worth it," Jackson calls to me over his shoulder, never taking his eyes off Decaux. "He's caused you enough pain."

"My father has caused you no pain!" Dacari screams, breaking my one-sided stare off with Decaux.

"You don't know what you're saying, Dacari! I told him I was a Nicaud—he came after Damina's parents thinking it was me!" Aunt Delia cries from behind us.

Dacari's eyes shift to her father, but he shakes his head, disavowing his involvement.

"Damina, my father had nothing to do with it!" Dacari maintains, keeping her position at her father's side.

"Maybe not directly, Dacari but he had his minions carry out his wishes!" I insist.

"Damina, beautiful, not now," Dalcour says once more.

"My darling, Delia," Decaux begins, looking up at my aunt. "Did you really think I fell for your poorly constructed name swap? *Anne Nicaud.* Dear love, I knew you were a Peyroux from the moment we met. While I wasn't entirely clear that your first name was not Anne, I undoubtedly knew you were a Peyroux. Why do you think I agreed to help you meet your valuation criteria? My brother and I knew the good Elias Peyroux quite well! I may not have known you carried my child—but yes, woman, I knew you!" Decaux snaps at my aunt.

"So you admit it? You knew all you needed to kill my family. So what—did you do it to punish her for leaving you?" I cry. I need to know the truth.

"If you do not tell her, dear brother, I will," Decaux seethes through his teeth.

"Father, no! Not here!" Dacari pleads.

"Tell me what, Dalcour?" I question, turning to see his fear-filled eyes.

Chapter 24

What could he possibly have to fear from me? Is it me he fears?

"What is Decaux talking about, Marchand?" Jackson demands, pressing himself closer to my side. A wicked grin maligns Decaux's face as a deep rumbling sound roars through Jackson's words. Mark moves closer to our side and Titan, Gregory, and Brian press forward as well.

"Dal?" I mutter as a familiar foreboding gall wrangles my insides into knots. Looking at him, my instincts drive me to dig deep into Dalcour's mind. Forcing myself through his thick blockade, images of a dagger with a ruby-crowned hilt and the face of his sireling, Chartreuse Grenoble, score through me like a wrecking ball. Although I cannot discern its meaning, I know the truth I have waited for abides in Dalcour's next word.

Calling his name once more, Dalcour looks at me with sweat beading the lining of his brow as thick droplets rush from his temple toward his jaw. "Damina, please, we can talk about this. Just not in front of everyone," he whispers back to me.

"Why, dear brother? You have nothing to hide! You have

committed no ill. Nor have I!" Decaux sneers with a malicious grin. Dacari casts a worried glance at me but still maintains hold of her father.

"Well, spit it out, Marchand! What new lies are you keeping from Damina!" Jackson shouts.

"Dal, please tell me. What are you keeping from me? Did you— *kill them?*" My mind wanders.

"Of course not, Damina! I had nothing to do with the death of your parents! Absolutely nothing!" Dalcour refutes quickly, keeping his gaze locked with mine.

"Then what, Dalcour? You've been keeping something from me. And it has something to do with Chartreuse Grenoble," I dig further as his thoughts become more vivid in my mind.

Dalcour looks around the crowd, biting his bottom lip, restraining himself.

"Oh spit it out, brother!" Decaux quips, tossing his arms up in the air.

"My brother Decaux is right, Damina. He had nothing to do with your parent's death. I know—I know, at first, I thought so too. But then I had Nara, our recordkeeper, pull our annals. The Guardians keep records of any public supernatural deaths. I was able to look into it and found evidence of Chartreuses' involvement," Dalcour reveals in a low mumble.

"You mean to tell me that red-headed banshee killed my sister!" Aunt Delia yelps from behind, breaking free of Dilano and Alana's hold and rushing to my side. I've never seen her move so fast. Ever.

"Is that true, Dalcour?" Mark questions with a darkened glare as he holds my aunt to his side.

"Dal?" I say, questioning him once more. His glassy eyes stare back at me, laden in a well-placed fear. "So that's why you dragged me from the Civility Center? It's also why you've kept your thoughts hidden from me!"

"Damina, please! I was going to tell you! I just needed some time to—"

"To what, Dalcour? Get her out of here?"

"No, baby! I only wanted to keep you safe!"

"By lying to me!"

"No, by keeping you safe! That's all! Damina, the last thing I wanted was for you to find out like this. Believe me."

"How can I believe anything you have to say, Dalcour?"

"Well, what did you want me to do? Tell you that one of the most sadistic and lethal creatures to ever walk this earth killed your parents? And, oh, by the way she's down in the CC if you want to go talk to her! I've seen Chartreuse tear people apart and bring men to their feet!"

"*I am no man*! And do not suppose you know what I would have done, Dalcour Marchand!"

"I know you well enough to know you'd rush off, headfirst and challenge her without a thought for your safety or a plan."

"Wow, Dalcour. It's good to see you have so little confidence in me."

"Please, Beautiful, can we just go somewhere and talk? Please," Dalcour pleads. I detect the coolness of his jasmine and lavender scent fill the space between us, but by some new inner strength, I force it away. The thought of his wildflower fragrance is almost repugnant to me in this moment. His eyes lower to meet mine and he searches my face, looking for any semblance of understanding, but I have none to give.

"Yes, by all means don't mind us," Decaux mocks as he saunters casually between me and Dalcour.

The crowd around us is also eerily quiet. However strange it may be, I almost feel this new piece of information is drawing a line in the sand, rattling the forming alliance of the supernatural community right before our eyes.

With his arms folded behind his back, Decaux paces back and

forth, shooting speculative glances at the onlookers surrounding us and Dacari. My cousin maintains her posture, but her gaze softens as she stares at her father and he relaxes his double-dealing stance.

"Listen, Damina—is it okay if I call you Damina?" Decaux asks with a sly smile as he rubs his hands together and continues pacing. But I refuse to answer, and I keep my attention fixed on Dalcour. "I suppose I am as much to blame in this as is my brother."

"How so, Decaux?" Jackson quickly questions as he keeps a steady stand at my side.

"Well, had I not loved Chartreuses' big sister, Calida, with such an ardent passion perhaps she would not have died at the hands of those bigoted talking monkeys! After I escaped the death, they ultimately meant to be my demise, I set this City on fire. Leaving my brother behind to clean up my mess. And that is what he has done since that day," Decaux says as though his lament was a source of pride as he smiles widely, gazing at Dalcour. Still, Dalcour keeps his sights on me.

Noticing our exchange, Decaux continues ambling back and forth between Dalcour and me. "About twenty or so years after the fires, Dalcour gave me a present. Chartreuse Grenoble. I suppose since she looked so much like her sister, he thought I'd fall in love with her too and perhaps ease my pain. But I did not. All I saw when I looked at Chartreuse was Calida's baby sister and nothing more. As time passed, she begged both Dalcour and me to turn her. He eventually gave in. But I warned my brother that her taming would never fully take—"

"What does this have to do with my parents?" I have no interest in this story.

"Simply put—nothing. Your mother was neither wolf nor a Peyroux by blood. When Chartreuse discovered a member of your family was responsible for exposing our whereabouts, she vowed to make the Peyroux bloodline pay. Unfortunately, she meant to kill your aunt. When she realized Delia got away, she vowed to hunt and find her. Instead, she found your mother and father." Decaux says in a more demure and controlled tone than his cagey expression suggests.

"Did you know what she was planning, Decaux?" Aunt Delia quietly asks, with her hand resting at her chest.

"No I did not, Delia. I kept my distance from Chartreuse over the years for many reasons. If you can believe it, she's more high maintenance than you, my sweet. But recently, when Cade told me the story of the day even he walked away from Chartreuse and how he had now come into connection with my daughter, I was shocked. But the minute I saw her, I knew without question she was *my daughter*." Decaux says as Dacari offers a bashful grin. Looking at the two of them, I am surprised to find remnants of Decaux in Dacari's smile and eyes. The care laced in his eyes as he regards her is also hard to miss.

Still, none of it does much to douse the kindling rage brewing at my thoughts of Dalcour.

"How could you," I grumble, casting a dagger-eyed stare at Dalcour.

"Damina, please, I never meant to keep it from you."

"But you did, Dal. You did. More than anyone you know, everything I've been through is because others continue to decide when it's the best time for me to know something that is mine alone to decide. Yet, none of that pales in knowing you didn't tell me because you didn't think I could handle it. You of all people. If there was anyone to think better of me, I thought it was you. Now I know the truth. You don't believe in me. You never have."

"Ah! This is indeed a sadness!" Decaux adds, walking once more between Dalcour and me. Jackson snarls at his passing, but Decaux continues his stride. There's a new pep in his step as he speaks, and I know nothing good will come of his next words. "Hopefully, you two will get things on the mend. I mean, truly, the fate of all is dependent on your great love story. Although, I get the feeling the Prime Alpha at her side has something to say about it. It's quite a conundrum indeed!" Decaux exclaims.

"Enough, brother! Haven't you done enough damage for one day?" Dalcour shouts back, turning his attention to Decaux.

"Now, little brother, you know I'm capable of more carnage than mere teasing. But you are correct. Too much time has been given to your lover's quarrel with my niece—or my sister-in-law—what is she, exactly? Oh, never mind that. What matters is that your stipulation to find love has yet to be met."

"My heart beats, Decaux. And yes, I have found a love—at least for my part," Dalcour mumbles his last phrase. "That's all you need to know!" He shouts, snapping himself from his forming sulking state.

"To be fair, that is not quite correct. You two are destined for greatness as it were, and we need to witness the foretelling of your great and powerful love fulfilled. Are you two here and now ready to commit your lives to one another and fulfil the prophecies for the good of all?" Decaux's probing is as mocking as it is infuriating.

His timing of bringing up Chartreuse was calculated.

"And I suppose that is why you brought Chartreuse, brother?" Dalcour counters, aware of Decaux's intent.

"Touché!" Decaux does nothing to hide his motives as he lifts his fedora from his head as he bows to his waist.

"Damina, you don't need to choose now," Dacari says in an almost rebuking tone as she nudges her father's shoulder, coming to his side. He hunches dismissively, but extends his hand toward Dalcour and me, gesturing for us to respond. Dacari's tender eyes gaze back at me as she searches my face, watching my falling tears. While everything inside is prompting me to run, I remain steady, but my heart is once again broken. Once more, my cousin is front and center of my heartbreak with a backyard as my stage for all to see. "Father please," Dacari continues, as her eyes pool with tears as she stares at me. "Don't put Damina through this. She's been through enough already. I think it's best if we go with Plan B."

"Plan B?" Jackson prods, taking his place in front of me as a shield. Gregory and Mark flank his sides. Dalcour looks over his shoulder at me, his countenance still grieved, but he turns his gaze back to his brother.

"Ah! My little dewdrop has kind of skipped ahead," Decaux answers, as he nods to both Dorine and Padma who now come closer to his side. Snarling sounds echo from the hedges of the estate and bright red eyes glow back at us in the distance as those who came with Decaux close in around us.

"Decaux what are you up to?" Titan shouts as even he pulls his sisters protectively to his side.

"Well, fine, I'll bite," Decaux exclaims. "Look, as much as my darling daughter told me there's no way Damina is truly over Jackson enough to be with Dalcour, I contested her at every turn. You see, I believed in the prophecies. Knowing that one day my brother would regain his beating heart, love again, and restore the balance was truly all I ever wanted. Still, my dulcet darling insisted that Jackson was Damina's one true love—yada—yada— you know all that sappy love talk. But it appears my Dacari was right after all. I mean, if you Damina are willing to walk away from my brother for this one offense, perhaps your love wasn't of storybook legend after all," Decaux sneers with a slithering smile.

"Decaux, stop it!" Dalcour grits his teeth, with his redness shimmering through his skin and anger filling his face.

Tears freefall past my cheeks as he speaks, and the weighted truth of his words torment me. I do love Dalcour, but I am not in love with this world. And it is to this world he belongs. A world with Chartreuse Grenoble. A world I want no part of. More than anything, I wish I could awaken from the nightmare of it. And I know when the curtain of night unveils my sight it will be Jackson Nash standing there for me to behold. We want the same things, and none of it includes this world. Brae gave up a part of this world just to be with her one true love. I know Dalcour will never give up this world. Not for me. *Perhaps not for anyone.*

"Fine, I'll keep my words short," Decaux answers in a dark and menacing tone. "We no longer need to wait idly for you to restore balance to the land through the grace of true love or your beating heart, brother."

"What are you suggesting?" Titan questions, coming closer, but keeping a tight hold on both Ketu and Keitai.

"It is not what I'd suggest good friend, it is what I now do. With my daughter now at my side, we can finally put an end to the power wielded by the Order of Altrinion. All their rules. Curses. All of it will finally meet its end!"

"Decaux, brother, what have you done?" Dalcour screams.

My heart quivers as I watch a malign grin mar Decaux's otherwise perfect face.

"My father does what you've had the power to do but failed to perform!" Dacari lashes back.

"Dacari, what are you talking about?" I plead, pushing myself through the shield of wolves guarding me.

"You are only partly correct, daughter," Decaux adds. "Your uncle may have had them in his possession, but he hadn't what is necessary to wield such a power!"

"Decaux, brother, tell me you didn't" Dalcour replies as his eyes grow wide in horror.

"No, he didn't" Dacari quickly responds. "I did!" Dacari's face darkens as she reaches over her shoulder and pulls out a glass cylinder encasing the bamboo scrolls I once saw in Dalcour's room. In her other hand she reveals the large katana blades that once hung over Dalcour's bed.

"How did you?" Dalcour gasps, breathless.

"Oh, it was easy enough. I had seen them when Brae took me for the tour when I first arrived. Later, when father told me the story of their power to finally set us free, I knew I had to help him."

"No, Dacari, he's tricking you! He's lying to you!" Aunt Delia cries out.

"No, mother! The only one who has lied to me from the day I was born was you! You led me to believe my father wanted nothing to do with me. But the truth is, he never knew I existed. You took him from me! But now that he is in my life, I will never let him go again!"

"Dacari, please!" I beg. "Aunt Delia is right! He is lying to you. He's using you!"

"No, cousin, he's not. Just because everyone has jerked your chain for years, you toggle back and forth! You don't know who to trust or believe. And I get that, Mina, really, I do. But what I am about to do will not just help you—but all of us. You don't need the pressure of being the savior of the supernatural race. You don't have to be the hero or the chosen one—or anything like that. Instead, we can all finally have freedom!"

"My daughter speaks the truth," Decaux shouts over the murmuring crowd. "For years, my brother has had this tool in his possession, but now we have the power to finally end the tyranny of the Order of Altrinion! We can finally put an end to their curses and ultimately their control over our lives! Dacari is the only supernatural of pure descent from all three supernatural lineages capable of uttering the sacred words. And soon I will have all that is necessary to end the power of the Great Oak—by using this blade to sever its power!"

"Brother don't do this!" Dalcour protests.

"Why not, Dalcour? With Dacari uttering the sacred words, she can finally release us all from the curses by which we are bound. And to test the theory and prove us correct, she will recite the phrase on some of our less fortunate of supernaturals—the Scourge. Bring them forth!" Decaux yells and three frail Scourge come from the shadows, led by both Dorine and Padma. Now with these words we will free them from their Scourge-like state, and they will become vampires in power only; less the brutality and deplorable state."

"Stay close to me," Jackson whispers in my ear, locking his arm in mine.

Dalcour looks over his shoulder at us but returns his focus on Decaux and Dacari.

Pulling the scrolls out of the casing, Decaux holds the rice paper open by the bamboo poles and Dacari begins to recite the words on the page. Everyone stands in awe as golden shimmers of light hover over the three Scourge. As we watch, their more reptilian features fade, leaving them with mortal faces. The sliminess of their skin regresses and in shock I watch as their looks soften, revealing a more attractive version of themselves than their earlier Scourge state. Staring back and forth with one another, they too are surprised that only their fangs remain intact, and their eyes now reflect a radiant blue opulence.

Gasps and whispers permeate the mansion lawn and other vampires rush to the front line begging Decaux to allow Dacari to do the same to them next.

"All in good time," he replies to their pleas. "Is there anyone else who wants to finally end their Scourge status?"

"We do," Dorine and Padma answer in unison.

"Of course, I cannot ask others to do what I will not ask of my sirelings," Decaux answers.

"Brother, you've proven your point!" Dalcour contests.

"All of you who want liberation! Come forth—Skull wolves included!" Decaux declares, and the Skull come from their hiding. Kneeling before Decaux and Dacari, my cousin speaks the ancient language over them as well, and we watch in awe as the same transformation takes place.

"Damina, we need to get out of here," Jackson says, now pulling me to his side. "There's nothing more we can do for your cousin."

Watching Dacari fluently belt dialect I never thought her capable as she stands in agreement with her newly found father, stirs a heartache that pains more than imaginable.

"Lord Nashoba is right, Damina. We need to get you out of here. You're a pureblood Altrinion—the tastiest dish on the grounds." Mark says as he yanks Brae to his side.

"You go, Lord Helsing. I will not leave Dacari alone with her father," Brian declares as he maintains a dutiful watch of Dacari. A part of me is thankful for him, but she doesn't deserve his loyalty or affection.

"Get her out of here!" Dalcour commands. "Braelyn too! She's mortal meat to them now. You all need to leave!"

As Dalcour and I lock eyes with one another, I know his sentiment has more long-term implications than his words suggest.

This is his goodbye.

Grabbing my forearm, Dalcour pulls me close, but it does not feel as it has before. Something has changed. His aromatic lure does not call to me as I am accustomed. It is almost as if his scent faded. Dalcour's eyes are a glassy pool of crimson, and the sweat along his brow and upper lip reveals the trepidation of his heart.

Farewell, Beautiful. Dalcour's words raid my mind in an instant as a final pulse of kinetic energy pulsates through him with his final squeeze on my arm before he lets me go.

Jackson wastes no time pulling me from Dalcour's grip as he lifts me in his arms. Looking over his shoulder, I watch as Dilano and Alana pull my aunt behind us. Cedric and Abigail maintain their post with Dalcour. I am surprised to see Titan hand his sisters to Kyra and Merle as the Lothian den follows us off the premises. Mark, however, works hard to pull Brae from Dalcour as she pleads with him to come along.

As he pushes her into Mark's arms, Brae folds into his muscle-bound embrace, crying on his shoulder. Mark gives one final nod to Dalcour and the remaining wolves follow him out of the yard while my cousin continues chanting, changing the Scourge before our eyes.

Looking over Jackson's shoulder, Dalcour's eyes and mine meet once more. The desolation I now find in the depth of his eyes is unfamiliar to me. One lone tear peddles past his cheekbones as his woeful gaze stares back at me.

A loud crashing sound shatters like glass as my eyes remain on Dalcour and I see him shake as though he quivered for fear. I look around, but I don't see any glass. Then it hits me. The sound I heard was his heart breaking.

Chapter 25

I am surprised to find myself back at Bessie's Tavern.

Melvina greets us, though she was not surprised by our arrival. When I see Cal, Perry and Lorien talking with Mark and Brae, I realize they must have made the arrangement.

"Thank you, Miss Melvina for putting us up for the night and for the barrier," Mark says as we all enter the foyer. "We are not sure what to make of these new vampires yet."

"Well, all thanks go to the Bossier's for giving you a place to rest yourselves," Melvina replies as she points to Bessie and Cal at the top of the staircase. It's the first time I've seen Bessie and although we both share smiles, there is still an awkwardness between us. "You all grab yourselves something to eat and make yourselves comfortable. Ms. Damina, honey, your suite is still there for you when you're ready." Melvina gives us all a big wave while holding one hand to her hips as she makes her way toward the elevators.

"Damina, baby, do you want something to eat?" Jackson asks as he searches my face with worry. "You know what, it's okay.

I'll just have Alana bring something up to your suite when you're ready." Jackson says before giving me an opportunity to respond.

Jackson turns quickly and calls for Alana and gives her instructions as he points to a few things in the pastry bar and other menu items. As the two talk, I gaze around the filled Tavern and notice its swarming with nothing but wolves and a few Altrinions like myself, the twins and Alana who is a hybrid.

Scanning the dining area, I look for my aunt and I find her seated alone in a booth and rush across the room but stop short when I see Dranoel bust into the Tavern, racing to her side. He instantly pulls her into his embrace, and she breaks down, sobbing on his shoulder.

"She's gonna be okay, Damina," I hear Brae's voice softly say as she cups her hands in mine. The new warmth I feel from Brae's touch is both comforting and strange. "And don't worry, we'll figure out some way to get through to your cousin. She's just blinded by daddy-fog. Once Dacari sees him for who he truly is, she'll come running back." Brae pulls me in for a tight hug and I linger in her grip, thankful for her words of comfort.

"Thank you, Brae," I say, smiling at the lovely young woman staring back at me. There is a light radiating through her I've never seen before as she smiles back at me.

"Well, it's not quite the honeymoon suite I had hoped for us, but I think it will suffice for tonight," Mark says coming from behind me. Now I know why her smile was so bright. He taps my shoulder, smiling as he walks past me and pulls Brae to his side.

"Good, I think we all need the rest," Jackson adds as he comes near. "Mark, it looks like you have everyone in place."

"Yes, my lord. Everyone has their orders. Shifts are set. And Miss Melvina has this place so guarded with a barrier no vampire will get through. Oh, and Vonnie came back with Lux and Dranoel from taking the others to Trieu's place, so she's added a barrier of protection as well. We should be safe for tonight. Tomorrow we'll set out on patrol." Mark answers dutifully.

"Very good, then," Jackson says.

"Where is Gregory, my lord? I haven't seen him," Mark questions.

"He decided to keep watch not far from the mansion with Brian. With Brian being divided with keeping an eye on Jerrica with Charlotte, he um—volunteered to keeping Dacari in his sights," Jackson mutters with his hand over his mouth as if I couldn't hear him as he whispers to Mark. He looks over at me and smiles, knowing I'm listening.

"I see," Mark replies with a wink at me. "Why don't you get Damina upstairs, my lord. I'll take one last look around and then we'll retreat for the night."

"You're a good man, Mark—I mean Lord Helsing," Jackson commends as he gives Mark a firm handshake.

In no time, Jackson has me back in my suite. He makes his first priority, checking the latches on the terrace doors and closing the curtains and blinds so tight I can't see the light from the courtyard. He gives a cursory check in the bathroom, closet and even under the bed, laughing over his shoulder as he does.

"No, boogeymen," he chuckles as he sweeps the dust from his knees as he rises from the floor.

"Thanks, Jack," I quietly reply.

"Of course, baby. Melvina said you still had some clothes here so; I'll go so you can get some rest. My room is just on the other side of the wall. Knock on it—say my name and I'll be right here by your side."

"Jackson," I mumble as tears well in the corners of my eyes.

"Yes, baby?" He says with his hand on the doorknob.

"I'm saying your name." Looking up at Jackson, tears rush down my face and he quickly wraps his arms around me, holding me tight.

"I've got you, baby. I've got you."

"How did we get here, Jackson? This wasn't supposed to be our life!"

"I guess I should own my part in it," Jackson answers as he wipes my tears with his hand.

"Jack, none of this is your fault! This is all Decaux. And Dacari. And—"

"And me." Jackson says, stepping back from me. He keeps our hands together as he lowers me to my seat at the end of the bed. "All of this could just as easily be laid at my feet! All of it!"

"Jackson, how could you say that?"

"Because I had five years to tell you the truth, Damina! Five years! Had I told you, I have no doubt things would've worked out differently. You wouldn't be in New Orleans. Without you gone, Dacari would have never filled that void with Allyson, who got her to Cade and Decaux in the first place. So yeah—this is all my fault!"

"Jackson, please don't say that! You were only doing what you thought was right. I know that now."

"But the bottom line is it was me. I lied to you. I co-authored your pain. I broke your heart!"

While there is truth in Jackson's words, the sincerity of his heart speaks louder. He loves me, that I know.

"Then unbreak it!" The phrase rolls off my tongue seemingly without my permission, but they accurately reflect my heart.

"What?" Jackson's eyes are tender yet broken as he stares back into mine.

"Unbreak it, Jackson. I know now you're the only one who can. Only you can replace these tears and bring joy back to my smile. Unbreak it, Jackson! Undo this pain, Jack! Only you can!"

Before I can protest further, Jackson crushes his mouth to mine and electricity rivets through my body like a lightning bolt. Lustful static energy clings to my body as he holds my face to his, keeping our lips locked as one. The sweet and spicy taste of his tongue overpowers my senses as he ravishes my mouth with the sweetness of his kiss.

Slowly, Jackson kisses the ravine of my neck as he inhales my scent wholly, grunting willfully with each touch. Gripping my hand through his long mane, I twirl my fingers through his wavy brunette coils, as I delight in the pleasure of our passion.

Sweet memories of our time on the couch at the eve of our wedding score through my mind and my heart races with delight. The fervor I felt that afternoon dwindles in comparison to the indescribable abandon I feel now.

"Turn around," Jackson whispers softly in my ear.

"What are you doing, baby?" I say over my shoulder as he begins unzipping my gown.

"What I should have done on our wedding eve—unbreaking it, as you say," Jackson moans as he kisses my shoulders while pushing the gown to the floor. Turning me back to him, his face flashes with desire as I stand before him now with nothing but my black thong.

Flexing his muscles and bellowing a loud roar, his clothes combust from his body in the blink of my eye. I suppose its something he's used to doing before he shifts. But that growl was unlike any other I've heard from him. It was the sexiest thing I've ever heard come from him. The primal craving in his gaze as he stares at me knocks my knees together as I buckle under his enchanting influence.

Everything about Jackson Nash as he stands bare before me is—just everything. He is perfect.

He lifts me up, tossing my legs around his waist, holding me just above his arousal, and he locks our mouths together once more. Pulling the covers back while keeping a tight hold on me, Jackson lays me down on the soft duvet.

Lowering his head between my legs, he uses his teeth and swiftly rips the remaining fabric from my hips, tossing it over his shoulders.

"I love you, Damina," Jackson says sweetly after kissing the top of my forehead.

"I love you too," I reply, wrapping my arms around his slender waist, grazing my hand along the muscles outlining his back.

"Are you ready? I've waited forever to make you mine. Completely." Jackson's gaze is full of need as he awaits my reply. Looking at him, desire sweeps over me like I've never felt before. The perfectness of his body calls to me and the way my body fits perfectly under him, I have no doubt we are a perfect fit.

In every way.

Even more than I thought possible, I want him. I want him beside me. Near me. Inside me.

He's the only man capable of unbreaking my heart and breaking through my precious place as only he can.

That other world was never for me. I know that now. As I told Allyson years ago, Jackson was my world and I am his. I want him to explore every part of my galaxy until the stars align and the retrograde of Mercury halts its rotation.

"All I want is you, Jackson. You're all I need," I say, pulling him closer, planting a soft kiss on his delicious lips.

With that kiss, Jackson Nash claims the remaining part of me that was always meant for him. As he does, a light as bright as the sun illumines through me and the entirety of our suite—and perhaps the Tavern. Gazing into his eyes as we become one, I see his wolf staring at me through his eyes. Our connection is now stronger than I thought possible as he transfers the Altrinion orb of light given by my father.

Crying out my name with the cadence of his rhythmic motion, I am overcome with wondrous delight. As the ancient patois of the Order of Altrinion hums around us, Jackson's declaration of love resounds through me with each call of my name.

The brilliance of our lovemaking shines like the brightest

star and the warmth of his embrace comforts me so much I wish I could click my heels three times, because indeed *I am finally home.*

Epilogue

"**G**ood morning, wife," Jackson says with a broad smile as he greets me with a tray of breakfast.

"*Wife*? I guess I don't remember a ceremony or saying those binding two words—I do." I say, pushing myself up to the headboard, fluffing the pillows behind me.

"Well, you said plenty of two-word phrases last night, none of which bear repeating so early in the morning," Jackson softly replies with a light kiss on my cheek as he places the tray down. "But I can assure you, after last night you are my wife in all the ways that matter."

"Fair point, well made, Mr. Nash," I laugh.

"How do you feel?" He asks sweetly, brushing my hair from my face. I wish I knew how looked right now. I hope I don't look a mess. "You look perfect!"

"Wait—how did you know what I was thinking?"

"I know you, wife," he answers as he crawls back to the bed. I am surprised when I notice he's still naked. So am I. More surprising, I am not ashamed.

"There's that word again! Well, husband, did you answer the door naked?"

"No ma'am, I did not. But Melvina had someone bring it up. They left the tray at the door and I just pulled it through. But yes, you haven't looked more beautiful than you do right now. I suppose after a good and proper mating, one could look rather refreshed. And with the way we went at it, I suspect you're already carrying my child—or children. Who knows?"

"Jackson! Really? Trying to get me knocked up so soon!"

"Yep! I'm not even going to deny it. But we can have fun trying until then," he answers with a sly smile.

Nibbling on the fruit and pastries Melvina sent up, and I laugh, teasing Jackson with a cherry.

"Taunt me all you want, but I have had that already!" Jackson coos in a soft and seductive tone before biting it off the stem.

"That you did, Mr. Nash, that you did!"

"Look, baby, I know none of this has played out like we planned, but I want to make sure you're good with it. I wish I could say I don't know what came over me last night, but I do. In that moment, I realized I never want to take what we have for granted ever again."

"Yeah, me too. I guess we kinda took all our vows of chastity and threw them aside," I quietly reply, pulling my hair from my face.

"I don't see it that way, baby. What we have is pure. I almost lost sight of that. In trying to do what everyone else wanted me to do and keeping up with all I thought was right, I almost lost you. Us. Besides, had we done this on the eve of our wedding, perhaps things would have worked out differently?"

"Sure, I suppose," I answer as my mind drifts to thoughts of me being a Fated Altrinion.

"Look, baby, I want you to know I've never stopped thinking of you as my wife. So for me, making love to you was purely an expression of that love. Still, I know you're probably getting over Dal—"

"No, Jack, don't. Besides, I have no regrets. Absolutely none. And more than anything I want that little name you like so much, *wife*, to stick. I want our life together. I want to be your wife."

"Baby, you don't know just how happy you make me!" Jackson says, pushing the tray of food aside and begins kissing me passionately.

The lock and tether of our lips together leads us back to places I ever knew existed until last night. Once more Jackson claims the parts of me, I now know only belong to him, but this time the sun itself reveals the glory of our lovemaking. Throughout each fervent fuse, Jackson confesses his love for me, calling me his wife with every turn. His fervidness explodes in tidal waves of passion over and over, and I have no doubt he's intent on impregnating me before we leave this suite.

Not only have I spoken the ancient language with each bout of delight, but I've screamed his name more times than I can count, and I hear the music outside grow louder, likely trying to drown the sounds coming from the suite.

The depths of my womanhood remain sore long after our encounter, so I am more than happy when Jackson suggests we take a bath together before beginning our day. The intimacy we share is deeper than ever. As he washes me, I feel the weight of the recent events fall aside and I am once again overcome by the love I have for this man.

This time it's me—all me leading the way. I recall our near experience in the pool years ago and decide not to forgo this water love session as I did in the past. I push past the soreness of my preciousness and enjoy the steel strength of my beloved as the warm, milky water nestles us as one.

"Are we ever leaving this suite?" I tease as Jackson puts a robe around me when we get out of the clawfoot tub.

"Well, I certainly hope so," Jackson laughs. He walks around the corner and grabs his phone. "I mean we can't possibly have a wedding ceremony in this suite, now can we? But I'd be more than happy to bring our post-nuptial ceremonies back here," he says with a quick kiss while looping his arm through his robe.

"What are you up to, Mr. Nash?" I say as I watch him texting.

"Who me?" He giggles with a boyish grin, his dancing eyes gazing at me over his shoulder.

"Jack! What are you doing?"

Just then a knock at the door pauses my questioning as Jackson smiles wide as he walks to the door.

"Who is it, Jackson?" I question.

He looks out the peephole and smiles. "Why don't you open it and see?"

As I grab the doorknob, Jackson kisses my cheek and smiles, his face blushing red. Taking a deep breath, I open the door. My aunt is standing at the door holding up my mother's gown.

Stepping back, I am surprised to see my mother's gown looking back at me.

"I am so happy for you, darling!" Aunt Delia exclaims with a bright smile.

"How did you two? When? How? Oh, my gosh!" I scream with excitement.

"When you said you wanted to be my wife again, that was all I needed to know. Delia took care of the rest," Jackson replies.

"Baby! This is amazing! I love you!" I exclaim, kissing Jackson's cheek as he laughs.

"Now I know it will be like pulling magnets apart, but let Jackson go back to his suite and get dressed. I'll take care of you. Mark, Brae and the others have everything prepared for you in the grand foyer of the Tavern."

"Aunt Delia, thank you so much. But what about Dacari?"

"I know, darling, I know. I texted her. I don't know if she'll show. But Gregory and Brian said she was safe when she left the mansion last night. So maybe we can talk. But none of that matters, because today is all about you and—"

As my aunt speaks, I watch in horror as thick red blood oozes from her mouth, spilling out onto my mother's gown, soiling it completely. I scream in shock and Jackson opens the door wide as I step back and see a long thin blade tearing through my aunt's abdomen.

"Delia!" I shriek as I watch her gurgle, choking on her own blood. "No!" I cry.

My aunt slumps to the ground, falling on the blade, and her bloody body toggles between the gown. Jackson tries to pull me back, but when I see Allyson's face round the corner of the suite, my sadness turns to rage.

"I'm sorry, Damina, I can't let this happen. Not with him. Not like this!"

"Allyson! What have you done?" Jackson shouts back.

Fury and rage rut through my being and my insides boil like an inferno inside me. Jackson screams my name, but his call is mute to me. He grips my shoulder, but the heat rising from my skin is unbearable even for him.

Gazing at Allyson, all I see is red and the Spanish bulls within me charge onward. I don't waste time sucking the air out of the room as I had for Kyra, as that would be too kind. I don't send her flailing across the room as I've done to Keiron, because that would show empathy.

Instead, my instinct drives my arm straight through her chest as though an electric current guides my motion. Gripping her heart in my hand, she strains as I squeeze the very life from her body. Her eyes bulge as the oxygen leaves her vital organs, but she allows one last smile.

"That's it, Damina. Do it! I had to do what needed to be done— and now you're finally becoming—" With Allyson's last breath, she falls to the floor and I am left with her heart in my hand.

"Damina, baby! No!" Jackson cries as he kneels down to my aunt.

Darkness veils the sky, and the Tavern rumbles with a threatening quake as blackness shades my vision.

"No!" I hear a wailing cry from the hall. Jackson jumps up from the floor as the cry comes closer. From the distance we see Mark coming down the hall, holding Brae's still and greyish body in his arms. His cries send a shrilling pain through me and I convulse as the power of the Changeling expels from Brae.

A rippling pain breaks out over me and my nails lengthen, and fangs protrude through my gums. My body convulses and contorts, and scaly, thick red skin erupts over my body. Over my shoulder, I see my reflection in the hall mirror, and it resembles the beast I encountered in Dalcour's room.

Pain and grief overtake me, and I am lost in the newfound darkness blanketing my form.

Two people I love dearly are gone. One I thought loved me is now dead by my hand. Life as I planned has evaded me yet again, and I know life itself will never be the same.

Bonus Short Story

With Clipped Wings of Butterflies

Chapter I
Wanting to fly

"DELIA, I'LL MEET YOU THERE IN THE MORNING. Okay? You do not have to do this alone. We can do this together," my sister's syrupy sweet tone comforts and aches my heart all at once. I know she only wants to help but I am not yet sure I want to do this.

Still, everything in me tells me it is the right thing to do.

"Thanks Caressa, I appreciate it." I know she can hear the mild timidity breaking through my otherwise stubborn demeanor, but my big sister remains quiet on the other end of the phone and I know she's waiting for me to affirm my decision, but I still don't know what to say.

I want to call our mother. She would know just what to do. She would know the route I should take. However, this is different. Complicated.

Mother always said this life was ours to choose and our own to live. Never has our mother forced us one way or the other into his world.

Sure, I was disappointed to learn only my sister was a full blood Altrinion, blessed with the *lux aeterna*, or eternal light of the immortals. Me, however, not a full blood Altrinion, but a hybrid. Half-Altrinion. Half Dunes Wolf. Yes, a Dunes Wolf. At least if I were half-Altrinion and human, my Altrinion nature would overtake my human state. I would be a Breaker—as they call it. No, I am half of a treacherous, traitorous, pack of wolves! Alas, I should be thankful I'm from the Peyroux bloodline and not marked with the wretched Dunes curse thanks to our ancestors' great deed with Saint Roch.

But still, I am a wolf.

Not just any wolf. A marked wolf.

Sure, Saint Roch blessed our ancestors' bloodline, so we are no longer bound to the curse of the full moon due to the help the Peyroux's gave them during the plagues. Yet, even having the curse lifted as a result was not enough to douse the kindling rage of our enemies. And I have met one such enemy.

A great and terrible enemy indeed.

Who knew when I ran off to France with the first man who made me feel like a woman, I would meet one who has long despised my family? I suppose the truth is I should have never run in the first place. But I did. I did because I was jealous of Caressa.

Yes, beautifully perfect, full-blood Altrinion Caressa.

For even though she wasn't my father's daughter by blood, he lavished all his affection toward her—at least in my eyes. Mother, well, Mother did her best to show a shared love and interest for us both, but it was evident, at least to me that Caressa was favored. Not only was she the preferred between the two of us, but she was the eldest and by rights all the manner of privilege fell to her.

Thankfully, Caressa never treated me as second class. As a matter of fact, she doted on me. Gave me whatever I wanted or needed. Her perfectly poised affection toward me made it even hard for me not to love her. It is because of her love for me that I did my best to hide my growing antipathy.

I hid it as long as I could—that is, until my eighteenth birthday.

Chapter 2
Fly or Die Trying

THERE WAS ONE THING I LOOKED FORWARD TO. One thing I longed for. My alpha status.

It was the only thing I didn't have to strive for. Something that was mine alone and in need of no competition. Or so I thought.

I wondered why Mother had never prepped me for my valuation. After Papa Roux died, I thought for sure I'd be in succession. But typical for all things Dunes, we were packless. Leaderless. Divided. There was not a cleared Dunes Den Leader or Lead Alpha nor had there been one for some time.

No one within five hundred miles of New Orleans had stepped to the plate in more than one hundred years to claim ranks as Den Leader or Lead. Not even Papa Roux. The last I heard; the only eligible Den Leader was a fourteen-year-old boy named Abraham Helsing that I used to babysit. His father died young—mysteriously too young some say, and Abraham isn't old enough for valuation. He's still a pup.

My father was ineligible to declare himself because the Peyroux's are now considered unmarked. I supposed no longer being cursed puts us into some other category.

So there I was, eighteen and ready for the only thing that could've been mine; should've been mine—the acknowledgement of my alpha status and I was left with absolutely nothing.

Well, not exactly nothing. Mother offered her apologies to me. An apology was not what I wanted.

For me it wasn't just something to best my sister. It was the last part of me that connected me to the person who I loved most. My father. My Papa Roux. Even though Caressa, another man's child, somehow became his favorite, he still remained mine. I suppose it was the one thing I alone shared with him. As much as he loved Mother, not even she could appreciate how it feels to shift beneath the moon's apex or comprehend the tormenting yet exhilarating freedom that comes with broken bones mending to marrow once a month. That alone belonged to us.

And while he was no longer with us, it was the one thing I relished because it made me feel close to him.

So I ran. I ran far and fast into the arms of a man who promised he could help me find what I was looking for. Yes, my actions were deliberate. A part of me wanted to hurt Mother, though she did not warrant my wrath. Perhaps I resented both not being an Altrinion nor an Alpha. Whatever my ire, all I knew is I had to get away.

However, this man was unlike any other. Beautifully dangerous. Seductive. Yet, despite his haunting presence his pull was magnetic, and I was a mere paperclip. Even his words enchanted me. With eyes singed in a fiery hue, bronzed pecan skin, and lips the color of raspberries, everything about this man lured me to a perilous passion I knew would be my reckoning.

But I did not care.

I knew the truth. He was a monster. An Altrinion-Vampire. A progenitor of all Scourge; or what we call mortal-made vampires.

Growing up, nightmarish stories followed by his name were known throughout the community of supernaturals. But still, I did not care. He wanted me.

Me. Not Caressa. He was now the one thing that was all mine. The one thing—and person I needn't share. Or so I thought.

Until I knew better, I let him possess me. Lavish me. Ravish me. Willingly I gave my innocence to him. And he took it. For that I have no regret.

Well, at first, I did. I feared he'd toss me aside once he had his full like the monster I thought him to be. Strangely, I never saw this monstrous beast that I was taught to fear. From him, only kindness was shared between us. Not once did he hurt or threaten me. In fact, he remained a doting gentleman.

While I'd often protest, he had even fought for my honor. If anyone dared treat me with an ounce of discourtesy his retribution would inevitably follow. He was chivalrous. Gallant. That was certainly new territory for me.

For two years we traveled around the world seeking someone who could perform my alpha valuation. I only had until my twenty-first birthday to make my valuation solid. Unfortunately, most were too fearful of his damning reputation that none dared take his request. Still, he tried. He was even working a deal with his brother who he hadn't seen in over a hundred years to meet an Altrinion Elder who could oversee my rights. He told me it was always his plan to restore the rights to the Dunes wolves among the supernatural order. Meeting me was fate he said.

And I believed him.

Until I didn't.

My walls of belief all came crashing down last night. Seeing him gorging himself in the blood of young ones sickened my soul as if the cave of my bower closed within me. Yes, I'd seen him drink from mortals before. More than once had I seen him take life from innocents. Truly, that should have been enough for me. Instead, I swallowed down everything I'd been taught of the sanctity of life and gave him a modicum of freedom. And for a moment, it seemed as though he tried to do better. Be better.

As a gesture to me, he often frequented the local Civility Center where he could obtain rations of his fill or even drink from willing donors. I even believed his promise that when we were married, he'd never drink in the house.

Oh how I believed his lies! Each and every lie. I drank it down like mother's milk.

Until I saw him, indulging in the most depraved way possible! Dozens of lifeless young bodies, none older than twelve, littered like trash and bathed in their own blood across the concrete floor of our flat. There he and his young ward, Cade, and two others indulge with him. But they were not alone.

She was there.

The red head.

The one he said I needn't fear. The one he said for whom he had no affection.

There she was, barely clothed, straddled across his lap as they both tarnish the young soul in their feverish grip.

And for the first time, I see him for who he truly is. I see the monster.

Velvety thick red skin with the mouth of a dragon, his fangs dig far and wide into the child's flesh and he is now before me every bit of the monster I thought him to be.

She is no better.

Although she is unlike any Scourge I've ever seen, just the sight of her viper-like mouth feasting with such savagery sends a sickening grief to my soul.

It took everything within me not to scream but I had to run. Again.

I ran fast. *But not fast enough.*

She caught me.

He had always done a good job of keeping her at a distance. Until now. I'm sure she wondered what made a monster like him give any pause to someone like me. A leaderless wolf. Intrigue marred her otherwise sinfully flawless face as she gazed deep into the burrow of my eyes. It was almost like she was looking for something, but her expression proved she did not find what she sought to see. And for that I am grateful.

Thankfully, she was too overcome with her bloodlust to pursue me, so I ran.

Chapter 3
The Safety of Cocoons

CHARGING OUT OF THE BUILDING, I WAS SURPRISINGLY COMFORTED TO RUN STRAIGHT INTO THE ARMS OF MS. Greenlee. Our family's praesidium—or Bulwark as we call them in the Supernatural world.

"I've got you," she said with fervor as she tugged me tight in her arms. Quickly throwing me in a black sedan, we were at her hotel in no time. She said nothing to me but muttered the ancient words quietly the entire time. Glowing iridescent lights covered the hotel and I knew instantly that she was marking our territory to blanket us from danger. No Altrinion-Vampire would ever be able to see beyond a Bulwark's shield.

"I got here as soon as the Elders told me she was here. As if being with him wasn't bad enough you had to get yourself mixed up with the likes of her? Don't you know who she is? She is Chartreuse Grenoble, child! The sole hunter of the Peyroux-Dunes line! She will never forgive Elias' bloodline for his part in her sister's death. She has issued a swift end to any Peyroux! That includes you, missy!" Ms. Greenlee laid the truth before me in a tongue lashing only spoken by care.

I know it's more than her charge to protect our family—her sentiment is true. Chartreuse has been a known enemy to our family for as long as I could remember. Perhaps being with the boogeyman himself, Decaux Marchand, has numbed me to these facts—I don't know.

I am thankful I never gave my true name. I told him my name was Anne Nicaud. Mixing my middle name with my sister's given name in marriage, I had hoped to throw him off. It's also good Altrinions can't read wolf minds—so he'll never know my true identity.

Most important, neither will Chartreuse.

But I know I can't leave it to chance. I know he'll come looking for me. I know one day he will find me.

That's why I called Caressa.

Now, I must decide if I can do the one thing that will get him off my scent forever.

Caressa has always suggested we live normal lives. Give our supernaturality to the waters of *hominum vita*—life of man. Bathing in the sacred waters will forever erase our supernatural essence, allowing us to live out our lives like humans.

Perhaps I should have waited before calling her. At least until I knew more. Until the test results were sure.

For weeks I had been queasy and with the absence of my period and my frequent passionate bouts with Decaux, I decided to pick up a pregnancy test on my way back to the flat.

I decided to take it before I called Caressa, hoping—no praying a negative result would appear while we spoke, making my choice easier.

I now know my choice will not be easy. Of that I'm *positive*.

Although our Mother gave her supernaturality to the sacred

waters while we were young, she always said she never wanted to make that choice for us. Or as she put it, *"heaven forbid she clip our wings before we knew to fly."*

That is what makes this choice so difficult.

Now, it's not just me. I have cargo. Someone else's choice. If I submerge in the sacred waters, I do not just make a choice for me, but also for him or her.

Would he or she want to remain—whatever he or she will be? Altrinion? Wolf? Vampire? I don't know.

I don't even know how I could give birth or raise a child who is the seed of such a monster! How could I love him or her?

Even more, how could I not?

No matter my choice, one thing is clear—this child is mine. My own. Mine alone to love—and to love me!

I will do for this child what I wished was done for me—or what was done by a monster. Lavishly love them with every ounce of adoration I have within me! For me, this child will always be favored. The only apple of my eye. Now and forever.

"Delia?" Caressa questions once more, bringing me back to the moment.

"Yes, I will meet you there." This time my tone is resolute. I even sense my ardent stubbornness ringing true.

I may not be an alpha, but in this moment, I know what I am—a mother. And I will do what a mother does best: protect her child.

Epilogue
Out of Hibernation

GRIEF GRIPS ITS HOLD ON ME LIKE A COBRA AROUND MY NECK AND I CANNOT BREATHE. Digging my nails deep into the flesh of my hip, I pinch myself, hopeful to awake from this torrid nightmare. Yet, despite the small stream of blood pouring from my newly self-inflicted wound, I am all too aware this is no mere nightmare.

If only it were a nightmarish dream, perhaps I could arise to the beauty of the sun's light while relishing in the grandeur of another glorious wintry Christmas morning. Instead, here I am trying to be strong for my mother and my young, disillusioned niece. How I am able to maintain my stoicism amid the beeping, and buzzing sounds swarming all around is a wonder.

I suppose I am in shock.

Of us two, and I being the more reckless of the Peyroux girls, I always thought if either of us would end on a cold metal slab it would most certainly be me. But once again, I am wrong; and deadly so.

How can I even begin to live this life apart from her? She was my rock. My safety net.

Caressa Peyroux-Nicaud was everything I could ever hope to be. Smart. Beautiful. A heart of gold and a well-spring of kindness issued from her like lava. She had it all. A husband who adored her and a child who loved her more than anything; and loves her still. My admiration of her knew no bounds. From her love for her family to her warm manner toward even the rudest person, I often wondered if she was indeed striving for sainthood.

My big sister has been with me through every joyful and painful moment of my life. No matter how big my mistake, there was never any hesitation in her regard to be at my side. Wrong or right. Still, even her chastisement was with such gentleness I suppose hard lashing was just not in her DNA.

Although it was more than two years ago, I can still remember the day she stood with me at the waters of *hominum vita*. My body shivered for fear, yet she stood resolute as she held my hand. A quivering wreck, I was still in shock that I was pregnant with the child of Decaux Marchand. Tormented by my own thoughts of how I could let myself come to such a pass; it was Caressa's caring assurance that kept me steady.

Dutiful as ever, Caressa went into the water first. She wanted to assure me everything would be fine. Not being as pure as his wife due to his frequent, albeit non-murderous, regular diet of blood consumption, my brother-in-law supportively stood watch as the love of his life entered into the waters. It is known the hominum vita only accepts the purest of the supernatural kind, and while not marked by the vampiric strain and curse, Altrinions who consume blood to extend life are ineligible and are considered tainted.

But of course my perfect big sister is anything but tainted. Caressa is the personification of the word pure.

Still, fear held me hostage. While I'd never tainted myself with the spilled blood of mortals, I feared the waters would not accept me because of my entanglement with Decaux and my otherwise rebellious heart. It is for that reason I took slow steps toward the waters as my timidity lit my path. There Caressa stood, fully abandoned of her supernaturality in the waters, with her hands outstretched, awaiting my arrival.

My stomach churned within me. Although I am not certain whether the churning was due to morning sickness or fear, coiling knots of pain and nausea tormented my every step. Still, Caressa kept her eyes steady.

How could I now abandon the one thing that made me feel closer to my Papa Roux? My lycanthropy. The heart of my wolf pounded like a mad drum in my chest, begging me to forsake this quest. Tears burned like tiny fireballs down my cheeks as I neared the waters and a yelping howl shot through me as my wolf begged once more from within.

As thankful as I was for my sister and brother-in-law's presence and support, even they could not keep my longing for my father away. I missed him more than anything.

But I missed Mother too.

And even though Mother said she'd rather stay home with my young niece; I suspect her pleasure with me had dissipated. She was disappointed and rightfully so. Not only was I now an unwed mother-to-be, but I was the to-be-mother of a monster's child. If I could read her mind, I am sure she pondered where she went wrong with me. Although she never said a discouraging word to me about my pregnancy, her eyes said it all. In fact, it wasn't until my precious Dacari took her first breath into this world that my mother's regard toward me softened.

My Dacari has that kind of effect on even the stoniest of hearts.

Taking one final exhale, my wolf went silent as I reached the waters edge. Releasing both my fear and my grief, I put one toe in the waters and accepted my fate.

But the waters were not as accepting.

A big misty barrier arose from the borders surrounding the waters, preventing my entry. Boiling heat sizzled along its sandy shores, burning my feet, and pushing me back and away from the waters reach. Caressa called to me from afar, but her view was now shielded before me.

The lead Bulwark and caretaker of the waters came down from her perch at the tight edging of the bluff, waving her hand over the waters at her descent. Once more my sister became visible to me and she made her way toward me and her husband.

"Do not fear," the Bulwark began. "For you have done no wrong young Lady Peyroux."

"Then why do the waters not accept me?" I cried. For the first time, I realized I genuinely wanted to give up my supernaturality. I wanted to shed myself of anything Decaux could use to track me down.

"It is not you the waters cannot accept. However, you can only make such a choice for yourself, not for the one you carry. Your unborn child must be allowed to make the choice on their own. It is not a choice you can make. Return after the child's birth. If you are still found worthy, the waters will accept you."

Hearing the Bulwark's counsel, I rested my hand at my abdomen. I couldn't help but to marvel how much the tiny life inside me had once again shifted my course. Despite my apathy toward Mother, a newfound appreciation for her kindled in me that day. Though she's always been private about her past I can only imagine how much Caressa and I reengineered her course.

Now, here I stand with my mother's hand intertwined with mine as both sorrow and anguish flood the deep waters of our hearts. As the coroner pronounced the deaths of both my sister and her husband, an indescribable heartache pained within me.

For two years since the day the waters rejected my pregnant

state, my sister begged me to return with her. And for two years I punkishly ignored her request or defiantly declined. Shortly after Dacari's birth, I even found someone to do my alpha valuation just before my twenty-first birthday, making me ineligible to submit to the waters.

I thought we were safe.

I was wrong.

Throwing myself into all things Dacari and interior design school, I gave little thought of Decaux Marchand or his retribution. I did, however, remain a tad cautious throughout my pregnancy, but once Dacari was born everything changed.

Once we all moved to Washington, D. C. I really assumed the past was behind me.

But now I know that was my biggest mistake.

Upon Ms. Greenlee's inspection of the alleged car accident she found a Mercy blade. The only knife capable of killing a supernatural being. Had it not been for the kind sacrifice of the truck driver, another hybrid Altrinion-Wolf like myself, who rammed the truck into the evil assailants, claiming his own life, my precious niece might also be lost to us.

The Mercy blade had a ruby stone at its hilt. The dark familiarity of the blade told me the truth. I had seen it before, on the hip of Chartreuse Grenoble.

Decaux always sent her on his murderous missions. And this time I was the intended target. If only I had surrendered myself to the waters, maybe they would not know where to find me.

None of it matters now. All that is important now is taking care of my family.

Instead of exhaling as I'd done before the hominum vita, this time I inhale. All of the responsibility and accountability of protecting my family now solely rests on me and I now breathe in my newfound obligation wholly.

I know not whether there will be a second attack. However, I do know this: should they choose to return I will be ready.

Want More?

For more on the darkly enchanting Decaux Marchand, read,
With Hearts Like Fire also available on Amazon and Kindle
Unlimited

About L.C. Son

Known for her Amazon Best Selling Short Story, *With Hearts Like Fire* and the series starter and epic fantasy novel, *Beautiful Nightmare (Book One)*, L.C. Son is the happy wife of more than twenty years to her teenage sweetheart and the loving mom of three.

Growing up, she spent hours reading comic books she "borrowed" from her older brother which inspired her love for heroes and all things fantasy and paranormal. Much like the characters she adored, she lives a duplicitous life. By day she works tirelessly to champion the employment of persons with severe disabilities. By night, she puts on her wife-mom cape, sharing with her husband at their church and juggling their kid's highly active schedules.

Presently, she's working on the next installment in the Beautiful Nightmare series.

For the latest info and to join the member-only newsletter visit: WWW.LCSONBOOKS.COM.

More from L.C. Son

Here are a few more books and short stories in the Beautiful Nightmare Universe:

Books

Beautiful Nightmare (Book One)

Hearts Eclipsed, A Beautiful Nightmare Novella

Awaken: Beautiful Nightmare (Book Two)

Beta Rising: A Beautiful Nightmare Novella- Coming Soon!

Untamed: A Beautiful Nightmare Novella- Planned 2020 release

Breaking Curses: A Beautiful Nightmare Novella-Planned 2021

Origins: A Beautiful Nightmare Anthology- Planned 2021

Short Stories

I AM NO WITCH: A Beautiful Nightmare Short Story

With Hearts Like Fire: A Beautiful Nightmare Short Story